Murder Most Southern

Books by Sarah Osborne

TOO MANY CROOKS SPOIL THE PLOT

INTO THE FRYING PAN

MURDER MOST SOUTHERN

Published by Kensington Publishing Corporation

Murder Most Southern

Sarah Osborne

LYRICAL UNDERGROUND
Kensington Publishing Corp.
www.kensingtonbooks.com

LYRICAL UNDERGROUND BOOKS are published by

Kensington Publishing Corp.
119 West 40th Street
New York, NY 10018

All Kensington titles, imprints, and distributed lines are available at special quantity discounts for bulk purchases for sales promotion, premiums, fund-raising, educational, or institutional use.

Special book excerpts or customized printings can also be created to fit specific needs. For details, write or phone the office of the Kensington Sales Manager: Kensington Publishing Corp., 119 West 40th Street, New York, NY 10018. Attn. Sales Department. Phone: 1-800-221-2647.

Lyrical Underground and Lyrical Underground logo Reg. US Pat. & TM Off.

First Electronic Edition: May 2020
ISBN-13: 978-1-5161-0809-1 (ebook)
ISBN-10: 1-5161-0809-4 (ebook)

First Print Edition: May 2020
ISBN-13: 978-1-5161-0812-1
ISBN-10: 1-5161-0812-4

Printed in the United States of America

To my sister Margo
who came up with the delightful idea
of murder at a cooking contest

Acknowledgments

I'm indebted to my beta readers who tried to catch everything that wasn't quite right in this story: Marjorie Bufkin, Lucy Davidson, Jayne Farley, Linda Newton, Laurie Pocius, Lynne Rozsa, Margo Schmidt, Kate Shands, Donna Shapiro, and Jean Wentzell.

My wonderful writing group—Larry Allen, Mike Fournier, and BettyAnn Lauria—worked hard to catch the rest.

A special thanks to the owners of The Cuthbert House Inn, Connie and Pierre-Edouard (Ed) Binot. I stayed in their bed and breakfast twice while I was doing research for the book. While their inn is located in Beaufort, South Carolina, Savannah's plantation house is in the nearby and completely fictitious town of Veracrue. The Cuthbert House is not an exact replica of Savannah's, but it does offer the same warmth and amenities including a manicured garden, delicious breakfasts along with wine, cheese, and conversation in the afternoons. If you visit Beaufort, which you should, this is a wonderful place to stay.

I also want to thank Mary Rivers LeGree, for providing verbal comments and written information on Robert Smalls and the history and culture of the Gullah people. She is an Information Specialist and recipient of the 2018 Hospitality Employee award for the State of South Carolina. You can talk with her at the Beaufort Visitors Center located in the historic Beaufort Arsenal, "an 18th century structure built in 1798 to protect the town of Beaufort from ever-present caravans looking to conquer colonies in the New World." I hope to use more of her expertise if Ditie, Lurleen, and the kids travel back to Beaufort for another story.

My 241 Fitness buddies and our much-loved teacher, Wendy Bryant, keep me happy, healthy, and sane. That's a lot to ask of one group of people!

I'm also grateful to my tasters, all excellent cooks, who have helped me check the recipes in the book to make sure they work well and taste delicious: Jeanne Lee, Kathy Mosesian, and Lynne Rozsa.

As usual, my thanks to John Scognamiglio, my publisher and editor at Lyrical Underground and Kensington Press. He is unique in the speed with which he responds to emails and sorts out problems. Thanks also to the other professionals at Kensington—Michelle Addo, Lauren Jernigan, Rebecca Cremonese, and Larissa Ackerman who help polish and promote my books.

Finally, thanks to Dan and Alix who continue to provide their love and support for my writing.

Fame is a fickle food

Fame is a fickle food
Upon a shifting plate
Whose table once a
Guest but not
The second time is set.

Whose crumbs the crows inspect
And with ironic caw
Flap past it to the Farmer's Corn–
Men eat of it and die.

—Emily Dickinson, 1830-1886

Chapter One

Finally, I could breathe again after a long stifling summer. October in Atlanta had arrived!

Each day brought a new crispness to the air, and I felt as if I could conquer the world. That was always how I felt in autumn.

Lurleen found me in the kitchen working on a pumpkin pie with Jason and Lucie. Jason was scooping out handfuls of pumpkin glop and dropping them onto the tin foil that covered a good portion of my marble countertop. At five and a half he could now sit comfortably on one of the high stools as he worked. Nine year old Lucie sat beside him. She carefully picked out the seeds, rinsed them in a pan of water, and placed them in a bowl with olive oil and garlic. We'd roast the seeds to have whenever we felt like a snack.

The children's giggling added to my pleasure as I looked online for the best pumpkin pie recipe using fresh pumpkin. They weren't officially *my* children yet, but with luck they soon would be. According to our social worker, the adoption papers could be signed within the year. No close or distant relative had expressed a desire to adopt them in the six months since their mother's murder. And Ellie had left a note that I look after them should anything happen to her.

Lurleen could see I was lost in some reverie. She waved a large envelope in my face.

"Snap out of it, *chérie.* I have big news. An early birthday present!"

She placed the envelope in my hand as if she were giving me a Fabergé egg: something she wanted to give me last Easter—until she found out the cost. Lurleen would have given me the moon if she could figure out a way to get it.

She'd inherited a fortune from an aunt—enough money so she could quit her job as an accountant with Sandler's Sodas. She already had a house near mine in Virginia-Highland with no desire for a grander one in affluent Buckhead, a neighborhood in north Atlanta.

Lurleen remained frugal despite her new wealth. It was only with me and the kids that she splurged. I'm sure Danny, her live-in boyfriend, benefited from her generosity, but I suspect it took forms other than expensive gifts.

"My birthday isn't for months," I said, balancing the heavy envelope in my hand.

"One cannot celebrate an *anniversaire* too early or too often. Enjoy!"

Her French accent was unique, so it took me a moment to register what she was saying.

She stooped to kiss me. Lurleen stood a head taller than me and many pounds lighter. She was gorgeous with her wavy amber hair falling over her shoulders. People often stopped her on the street to ask if she were a model despite the fact she was in her late thirties. It never went to her head—just tickled her. "You are so sweet to say that," she'd respond, either in a slightly exaggerated Southern accent or perhaps her own version of a French one.

"Go on," she urged me, "open it!"

The kids stopped what they were doing to stare at us. Carefully, Lurleen gave them each a kiss on the tops of their heads, making sure to avoid Jason's slimy hands and Lucie's equally sticky ones.

I opened the gilt-edged envelope. Inside was a gold-embossed card, which announced that I, Mabel Aphrodite Brown, had been selected as a contestant on *Savannah Evans's Southern Comfort Cooking Contest*.

"What is this?" I asked.

Lurleen could barely contain herself. "Don't you see, *chérie*? You, the Mighty Ditie, will now achieve the fame you so desperately deserve. Your tea cakes will be famous. Your fried chicken recipe will create a million followers."

"Mighty Ditie?"

"Something Jason suggested when we were giving superhero names to everyone in the family."

"I'm a pediatrician, Lurleen. I don't want a million followers. I have patients to see, commitments." I studied the invitation. "They want me available for a week of shooting. It's impossible, I'm afraid."

Lurleen looked crestfallen. Then she shook back her auburn curls. "One week, just one week, sweet Ditie. And I will be your sous-chef if they let you have one."

"How would they even know I liked to cook?" I asked.

"I had something to do with that," Lurleen admitted. "I happen to know the producer of the show, Chris, and he happens to like me, and I suggested he try your tea cakes, which I happened to have saved from your last batch, and the rest as they say is *histoire*. He said they were the best tea cakes he'd eaten in his entire life, and believe me, that boy has eaten a few tea cakes."

I sighed. "Lurleen, what have you gotten me into this time?"

"Rien du tout," Lurleen said and folded her arms. "If you don't want to go and be on national television and meet Savannah Evans, the person you claim is the best chef in the world, then who am I to care?"

Obviously, I'd hurt her feelings. I studied the dates of the event—early November for the contest, which would be held at Savannah's South Carolina estate. There was also a gathering at Savannah's Atlanta penthouse in one week. A meet-and-greet in which the contestants could size each other up and visit with the illustrious Savannah. Desserts and wine would be served.

"It *would* be wonderful to meet Savannah Evans," I said. "I do have unused vacation time, and I might get a lot of good cooking tips."

Perhaps I could manage it.

First, I checked with the kids to see how they felt about my being away for a week. I promised them that either Grandma Eddie or my brother, Tommy, would look after them. They were both excited.

"Grandma Eddie and I will cook every day," Lucie said.

"I need a stick," Jason said, "so Uncle Tommy can teach me magic tricks."

"A wand," Lucie corrected.

I called my boss, Vic, at the refugee clinic, and she had no problem with my being gone. She scheduled my vacation to coincide with the show's taping.

Lurleen jumped up and down and her luscious curls bounced with her. "I knew you'd do it. Chris Evans, the producer, said I could come along and have a front row seat."

"Does Danny know about Chris?" I asked. Danny wasn't a jealous boyfriend, but he did sometimes have trouble with Lurleen's many conquests.

"Bien sur." Lurleen paused. "It's possible I forgot to mention that Chris was a boy, not a girl. But, he is only a boy—he can't be more than twenty-two."

"Twenty-two and the producer of *Savannah Evans's Southern Cooking Show*?"

Lurleen nodded. "He's Savannah's nephew. I'm sure that helped."

I called Tommy to see if he could look after the kids for a week. I'd never have done that in the past, but my brother had changed. He made room in his life now for me and the kids. His boyfriend, Josh, had a lot to do with his transformation—Josh was as open and loving as Tommy had been secretive and closed off.

Tommy agreed to stay in my house for the entire time I was gone so I wouldn't have to disrupt the kids or Majestic and Hermione. My cat, Majestic, wouldn't care either way—he interacted with humans only on his own terms—but Hermione was a different matter. I swear she was half human, although the vet swore she was a shepherd-collie mix. She needed us around.

Tommy said he had no court cases scheduled for November, but if anything came up he and Eddie would work out the logistics.

My boyfriend, Mason, agreed to help, but even though he'd do anything for me, as an Atlanta police detective, his schedule wasn't his own.

"You know my mom will love this," Mason said. "She's always saying how she doesn't get to see the kids nearly enough."

Eddie was as enthusiastic as Mason thought she'd be. She was also curious about Savannah Evans. "I've always wondered if she was for real," she said. "She's lovely, but on her shows, you never actually see her doing much. She dumps ingredients into a bowl, stirs a little, and the next thing you know someone is commenting on how delicious the food is."

Eddie was a former cop, now retired. She noticed everything.

"I've never thought about that," I said. "I'll let you know the truth when I find out."

Jason was beyond excited at the thought of spending time with his uncle, Tommy. "He'll come stay with us? And Uncle Josh will come too?" Jason loved time with the guys. He'd come to think of Mason as a second dad, and that, of course, pleased Mason no end.

Lucie looked uneasy when she realized I wouldn't be sleeping at home.

"I'm sorry, Luce," Lurleen told her. "I checked. No kids allowed. But, Chris promised that, when Savannah does a cooking show for children, you can be one of the participants."

Everything fell into place.

The evening at Savannah's included an invitation for a second guest—that would be Lurleen, naturally. She was ecstatic.

Mason offered to spend the night with Lucie and Jason. "That'll be a lot more fun than schmoozing with people I don't know and won't see again."

"I'll bring you back a sample of the desserts," I said.

"Deal."

The party was scheduled for the last Friday night in October, several nights before the thirty-first. The actual contest would take place two weeks later. In between, the kids and I could thoroughly enjoy my favorite holiday, Halloween, and I'd be back from South Carolina in plenty of time for Thanksgiving.

The evening with Savannah Evans couldn't come fast enough for Lurleen. "What will you wear to the party, *chérie?* I'll wear my emerald green slinky number. Too much, do you think?"

"Not on you," I said.

I decided on black pants and a shimmery purple jacket. Just enough pizzazz to be suitable for a penthouse gathering. My short curly hair always had a mind of its own. Lurleen offered to use gel to turn it into shiny spikes of dark brown. I declined her offer.

Danny insisted on being our chauffeur, and Mason offered his vintage Jaguar so we could arrive in style.

* * * *

Danny dropped us off at Savannah's midtown condo at eight. He'd be back when we were ready to be picked up.

Savannah's nephew Chris met us in the lobby. He looked like a cherub-faced college student and was obviously delighted to see Lurleen. "You look hot," he said to her and blushed.

Then he turned to me. "You must be Dr. Brown. So glad to meet you." He ushered us into the waiting elevator. "I'll be up in a few minutes."

Lurleen and I joined two other couples in the elevator. We all introduced ourselves as the doors closed. Pepper and Peter Young were in their late twenties, sophisticated Atlantans by the look of them. Pepper had a brittle kind of beauty, shiny blond hair, well-styled and well-colored, straight, dazzling white teeth, and a forehead devoid of wrinkles even when she raised her eyebrows. Everything about her glittered and nothing looked natural. Peter matched her good looks—also tall, well-dressed, black hair stylishly unkempt, with a carefully razored stubble on his face.

The second couple, Izzy and Frank Moran, were older, in their mid-forties I'd guess, well dressed in a more subdued way.

The contrast between the two couples was striking. Pepper and Peter exuded a coldness that made me shiver. Izzy and Frank were more like a warm coat inviting us into their inner circle. It seemed as if the two couples knew each other, but I couldn't tell if they were friends.

The elevator opened into the foyer of the penthouse.

The condo was over the top, even by Lurleen's standards. Marbled walls and marbled tile were backdrops for 18th century French antiques and tapestries from the same period.

We were ushered into a grand room twenty feet from the marbled floor to the arched ceiling. A wood-burning fireplace filled much of the back wall, and a panorama of the city was visible through Palladian windows along the side. The fire was stoked by a servant. It wasn't really cold enough for a fire, and I suspected the air conditioning was on to keep the guests comfortable.

There were only a dozen of us present, a small gathering for such a large space. When everyone was settled with a glass of champagne, Savannah Evans swept into the room. She was dazzling, in her early forties, hair a shimmering tawny-gold color, cut chin length. She was even more attractive than she was on TV. Savannah was undoubtedly a size zero but she didn't look scrawny. She wore a simple black sheath, and her only jewelry was a diamond and pearl necklace. According to Lurleen, it was vintage 1920s and worth thousands of dollars.

Lurleen kept up a running commentary on everything she saw and how much it cost. As a former accountant, she couldn't keep her mind out of the numbers.

"It's a good thing her show is so successful," she whispered, "or she'd never be able to afford all this."

"There isn't a moneyed husband in the background?" I asked.

Just then, a man twice the size and twenty years older than Savannah lumbered into the room with Peter Young beside him. Peter helped him sit down on the nearest sofa where he labored to catch his breath.

"He doesn't look well," I said.

"Shouldn't," Lurleen replied. "He's recovering from his second heart attack. And yes, he is the husband with lots of money—J. Quinn Nelson. Rumor has it he'd do anything for Savannah."

Savannah bent over the couch and gave her husband a quick kiss. Then she popped up and welcomed her guests.

"So absolutely delighted y'all could come," she said. She had a refined Southern accent, like a pinch of cinnamon in chocolate cake. Nothing overwhelming, just a little sparkle. "Please introduce yourselves. Let us know why you want to participate in this cooking contest."

A plump fiftyish woman stood up first and tugged at her ill-fitting jacket.

Savannah motioned her to sit back down. "We're very informal here," she said. "Make yourself comfortable and tell us about yourself."

The woman flushed and sat down. She gave her glass to her husband, a thin, withered man, who hadn't been eating much of his wife's cooking by the look of him.

"I'm Rose Kirkwood," she said, smoothing wisps of dyed brown hair behind her ears. "This is my husband George. George has been after me for years to put my cooking to the test. He claims there is no one who can beat my banana pudding. We both love your show, so when the opportunity arose, he urged me to apply."

"Thank you, Rosa," Savannah said. "I'm delighted you could be here, and I can't wait to taste that banana pudding of yours."

"It's Rose," George said, "like the flower."

"I do apologize," Savannah said. "Rose, indeed."

We went on down the line with Izzy Moran and Pepper Young speaking about how much they admired Savannah. It seemed as if they knew her off stage as well as on.

The only person who didn't gush all over our host was an austere woman in her seventies, gray hair pulled back in a tight bun—Gertrude Flumm.

"I'm happy to participate by sharing my classic Southern recipes—with a modern twist, of course." She looked at Savannah, but it was hard to tell if she was smiling or sneering. "I can't wait to show the world what I have to offer."

"She's feisty," I whispered to Lurleen.

Then it was my turn. "I'm honored to be here. I'm not a Southerner, but I love to cook, and I look forward to coming home with lots of new cooking tips."

Lurleen was busy sizing up the field. "Five women. No men?" she whispered.

As if Savannah had been listening, she introduced the single male contestant. "James Bradshaw is a food critic who is anxious to try his hand at cooking. James is a distant cousin of mine, but you mustn't think that, because we're related, he'll have any advantage over the rest of you. The tastings will be blind. I won't know who submitted what."

Lurleen gave me a funny look. "Bradshaw has written terrible reviews of Savannah's show," she whispered. "I wonder why she included him."

James Bradshaw didn't speak—he simply raised his glass of champagne and nodded at the rest of us.

Chris Evans was introduced by Savannah as the man who kept things running smoothly. "Chris is the person who makes every show possible and ensures we have just the right mix of contestants."

Chris smiled and nodded.

Lurleen nudged me. "He looks like a young version of his namesake Captain America. Same dark hair, cute smile, blue eyes."

I gave her a blank look.

"You know, Chris Evans, the movie star?"

I shrugged. Lurleen could rattle off the tabloid stats on every current celebrity. As a classic movie enthusiast, I did better with stars from the 40s. To me, Chris looked like a kid, still wet behind the ears and soft around the middle, as if he were waiting to grow into the man he would become.

But, no matter how young he was, it seemed he'd done a good job of recruiting middle America contestants. We ranged in age from twenty-something to more than seventy, and from sophisticated to down-home.

Half a dozen waiters appeared with dessert trays.

"Please don't hold back," Savannah said. "I've brought my best offerings. What I will ask you to do on the show, is to try to improve on some of my recipes. Don't worry Rosa, Rose, you'll get your chance to best my banana pudding."

Rose smiled and blushed.

I felt obliged to taste every offering. Each was delicious—from caramelized banana pudding to apple pie biscuits. We had our work cut out for us if we thought we could improve on them.

The evening broke up around ten. No one wanted to be the first or last to leave. I noticed that Savannah's husband hadn't moved from the sofa. If anything, he looked grayer than when the evening started.

I went over to say goodbye. He barely nodded in my direction and his breathing was labored. I took his hand, which was cool to the touch. "Do you mind?" I said, checking his pulse. It was weak and thready.

"Is your husband all right?" I asked Savannah. "I'm a doctor, and I'm a little worried about him. I think you might need to get him checked out at the hospital tonight."

Savannah looked at me. "Really? He never looks well these days. We have a concierge doc. I'll call her right now. Would you mind talking with her? I won't know what to say."

"I'll be happy to do that."

Savannah made a phone call on her jewel-encrusted cell and handed it to me. I described the situation and then gave the phone back to her. Savannah nodded as the doctor continued to speak. She hung up and turned to me.

"An ambulance is on the way," she said. "Thank you so much."

"I don't need a damned ambulance," her husband managed to gasp.

"You don't know what you need, Quinn. Better safe than sorry."

I stood beside Savannah. Everyone else had left except for Lurleen and Savannah's cousin, James Bradshaw. He'd come alone and seemed in no hurry to leave. He and Lurleen stood off to the side, staring at Savannah's ailing husband.

"If you don't mind, I'll stay until the ambulance arrives," I said.

"I'd appreciate that," Savannah said. "I can't thank you enough. If anything happened to Quinn . . . I don't know what I'd do. He's my rock."

The EMTs arrived in five minutes, took one look at Quinn and got him stabilized on a stretcher with an IV started and low-dose oxygen running. Savannah left to ride in the ambulance. Lurleen, Bradshaw and I went downstairs a few moments later.

Danny was waiting in the circular entrance to the condos. Lurleen must have called him.

"Do you need a lift, Mr. Bradshaw?" I asked before I got into the car.

"No, no, I'm good. I'll check in at the hospital and see how Quinn is doing. I know Savannah is grateful for your help." He ran a hand through his head of thick white hair and stooped to close the Jaguar door for me.

When he stood I saw he was a tall man, impeccably dressed, Southern to his core. Somehow, I'd missed all that at the party. I thought he might wave a white handkerchief to signal Danny it was time to move on.

The next morning brought sad news. Quinn hadn't made it through the night. The afternoon papers picked up the story. Savannah Evans was a national celebrity, and her husband, J. Quinn Nelson, was a well-known Atlanta real estate mogul. The cause of death was said to be congestive heart failure with complications.

"Complications?" I asked, after reading the article to Mason that night.

"I heard about this earlier," Mason said, "at the precinct. It's being considered a suspicious death. There may have been a drug involved."

"Are you saying it was some kind of drug interaction?" I asked.

"Could be," Mason said, "or it could be more sinister than that."

"You mean something intentional?"

"I can't answer that right now. They're waiting on a definitive drug screen, but the death is under investigation."

I left a condolence message for Savannah at the RSVP number on the invitation, and as soon as I hung up, Lurleen knocked on my front door. Hermione did her usual rouse-the-world routine. Fortunately, the kids were sound asleep and used to Hermione's random barking outbursts.

"Have you heard the news?" Lurleen asked, rushing into the house. "You have the paper, so you know. I guess that means no contest. I'm sorry for Quinn as well. He seemed like a nice guy."

"You spoke to him?" I asked.

"I spoke to everyone," Lurleen said. "You can't have too many friends in a competition like this, and you should always size up the enemy, so to speak."

"You were on a first name basis with him?" I asked.

"He insisted. He wanted me to spend some time with him, so I did. He seemed perfectly fine. I can't believe he up and died. He offered to get me second helpings of everything, but I said I'd rather spend my time talking to him. He ate that up."

"I'll bet he did," I said. "A beautiful woman wants to spend time with an older man. You know you made his evening."

"I hope I wasn't too much for him," Lurleen said, pulling on one strand of copper hair.

"He didn't die from overstimulation, Lurleen. He died of congestive heart failure, but it isn't clear if he might have been helped along the way."

Lurleen's hazel eyes widened. "Helped along the way? As in murder? We have another murder to investigate?"

Mason had heard enough. "The police have a suspicious death to investigate. You and Ditie have no place in this. Understood?"

Lurleen nodded slowly. "It's just that I know Chris so well. I'm practically family."

"Chris?" Mason asked.

"Chris Evans, Savannah's nephew, the producer of her show. At the very least I have to call him and see how he's doing."

Mason sighed. "One phone call, Lurleen. No prying into family matters."

Lurleen nodded and didn't look Mason in the eye. I knew what that meant.

She took herself into the kitchen for a private call. She returned moments later, clearly bursting with news.

"Okay," I said, "let's have it."

"Someone may have helped poor Quinn to that grand development in the sky, but they apparently also helped themselves to Savannah's diamond necklace."

Chapter Two

Lurleen plopped down on my oversized chair next to the fireplace. It was late, but she didn't look the least bit tired. She loved delivering news no one else seemed to know.

"What have you heard about the stolen necklace?" I asked.

"According to Chris, he arrived back at the apartment this morning and found the door locked. When he went inside, the safe was wide-open and empty except for a few documents. Savannah claimed Quinn had put the necklace in the safe, and Chris said the safe was closed before the party started—he made it a point to check on that before strangers entered the condo."

"But, Savannah was wearing the necklace all evening," I said.

"The necklace you saw was actually a fake," Mason said. "I can tell you that much—that will be in tomorrow's edition of the *Atlanta Journal-Constitution*. Savannah Evans typically wore copies of her more expensive jewelry at gatherings when she didn't want a lot of security around. She usually kept her more valuable jewelry in a safe deposit box at her bank."

"So why did she keep this necklace in a home safe?" I asked.

Mason shrugged.

I stared at him. "You knew about the necklace being stolen and didn't tell me. Why?"

"You know I can't talk about an active investigation. I could see your mind working overtime when I mentioned the drug issue. This is a police matter."

"How did *you* get so much information, Lurleen?" I asked.

"When I called Chris to see how he was doing, he couldn't keep his mouth shut about it. He was upset about Quinn, naturally, but he seemed more concerned that people might think he was the one who'd stolen Savannah's necklace."

Mason rubbed a hand over his bald head. "I don't want you two involved in this."

"But, we *are* involved, Mason," I said. "Both Lurleen and I were there. Won't someone want to interview us?"

Mason nodded. "They will. I'm surprised they haven't called you already. Specific information about the drug hasn't been confirmed yet. They may be waiting on that. I'm not next on the roster, so I won't be working the case, thank goodness, and it hasn't been designated a murder. It's a suspicious death and a robbery at this point. Do either of you actually know something about the necklace?"

"I do," Lurleen said. "A pearl and diamond necklace. Edwardian, I think. The diamonds were enormous. The necklace was easily worth two hundred thousand dollars. Perhaps what I saw was a very good fake—I was never close enough to Savannah to check that out properly."

"Since when do you know so much about vintage jewelry?" I asked.

"I watch the *Antiques Road Show*, and then, of course, there was Jerome." Mason gave me a blank look.

"It can only be an old boyfriend," I said. I didn't add that it was probably an imaginary one.

"Very old," Lurleen said. "Jerome was too old for me, really, but such fun. He insisted on teaching me the trade. He was a diamond cutter in Paris and was always bringing me little baubles when he visited Atlanta."

I'd never heard of Jerome or seen any baubles, but I rarely challenged Lurleen about her exploits or her history. They always made for a lively story, and what she said about Savannah's necklace was most likely true. Lurleen knew jewelry in the same way she knew fashion and expensive furniture. She studied fine things with a passion—not because she wanted to own them—more like a hobby, the way I studied new recipes to try.

Danny knocked on my front door and then poked his head inside. "I thought I'd find you here, Lurleen. You're discussing the case, aren't you? I just got back from headquarters, and that's all anyone is talking about."

Danny used to be a plain-clothes cop with Atlanta. He got tired of the bureaucracy. Now, as a private investigator, he could pick and choose his cases and help the police or lawyers when they needed some outside assistance. He was still good friends with many of the people in the department.

While Danny made himself comfortable on my red sofa, Hermione wandered into the room. She was happy to go to bed early with the kids, but she didn't like to miss the action. She jumped up on the sofa and settled her head on Danny's lap.

"We were just discussing the missing necklace, Danny," I said. "Mason told us the one Savannah wore all evening was a fake."

"That's right," Danny said. "According to Savannah, Quinn asked her to wear the original just for him in the afternoon. She claims she did that to please him and then left it with him to put in the bedroom safe before the party started. She wore a fake for the party, as she usually did when she didn't want a security detail around."

Lurleen nodded along with Danny and spoke when he'd finished. "Chris told me he was the one who brought Savannah home from the hospital this morning, and that's when he discovered the original necklace was missing."

"So we don't actually know when the theft occurred or if it had anything to do with Quinn's death," I said. "It might have been someone taking advantage of a chaotic situation."

"That was the big discussion at headquarters," Danny said. "There was a lot of coming and going that afternoon, people bringing in food and drink for the party, then cleaning up afterwards."

"It's a current case," Mason said. "No one should be discussing it publicly."

"I know, I know," Danny said, "but you can bet if I'm hearing about it, others will hear as well."

Danny had none of Mason's reservations about talking to us. "The nephew, Chris, has a key, and he claimed he locked the apartment up after the clean-up crew was finished. Savannah asked him to do that."

"I thought there was a live-in housekeeper," Mason said.

"There is, but she was on vacation. That's what Scottie told me."

"Scottie?" Mason asked.

"You know Scottie," Danny said. "He's new on the force and my main contact there these days. He's happy to give me information if I do the same for him."

Mason grumbled something about police security, and we all let it pass.

"The safe wasn't blown open or anything?" I asked.

"Nope," Danny said. "Nothing like that, and according to Savannah, only she, Quinn, and Chris had the combination."

"Chris knew the necklace was in the safe when he locked up the condo?" I asked.

Danny shook his head. "He knew the safe was closed before the party started, but he didn't check the bedroom or the safe when he locked up. It was Savannah who claimed the necklace was in there and the safe closed."

"Then we really do have a second mystery," I said. "Who had access to the apartment?"

"The concierge, the housekeeper," Danny said. "They both have keys, but the housekeeper is in Florida with a verified alibi."

"Any of the neighbors have a key?" I asked.

"It doesn't look like it," Danny said. "The neighbors knew about the party—especially the ones living on the floor below. The building isn't as sound-proofed as they would like, and that's caused some bad blood between the Evans-Nelson folks and everyone else. Savannah and Quinn like big bashes and don't like to be told to keep the noise down. However, the neighbors claim they didn't hear anything after the party ended and the ambulance left. The condo takes up the entire third floor so there weren't any next door neighbors to see people coming and going."

"And the concierge?" I asked.

"Asleep in the back room," Danny said. "There is a recording of people entering and leaving—that's being examined as we speak."

"How exciting this is!" Lurleen said. "You know those closed room murders? A dead man is on the floor, and the room is locked from inside."

"Only this time the man died at the hospital," I said.

"You know what I mean. We know just enough to make things intriguing and seemingly impossible."

"*We* don't know anything," Mason said, "and I'd like to keep it that way."

Poor Mason. He was sounding curt, but I knew it was simply because things were churning out of his control. Once Lurleen latched onto a mystery, there was no hope of loosening her grip.

I tried to calm the waters. "Don't you think we should at least tell you what we saw?"

Danny nodded. "It makes sense, Mason. You and I both know it's better to hear the story from witnesses as soon as possible."

Mason sighed. "It's better to let the investigators do their work without interference, but I can see when my advice will be ignored. May I have some coffee and some more of those cookies you baked today?"

"The white chocolate oatmeal ones? Absolutely," I said.

"Got enough for the rest of us?" Danny asked.

I nodded. I put a dozen cookies on a plate and returned to the living room. I left water to heat on the stove.

"You have a nose for this, don't you, Danny?" Mason said.

"Ditie's cookies or the work?" he asked as he grabbed the largest cookie he could find. "Great," he said appreciatively after taking two bites. "Lurleen talked my ear off about the party last night and then again after she heard about Nelson's death."

Lurleen reddened. "Talked your ear off?"

"Sorry," Danny said. "A figure of speech. A bad one."

Lurleen would have pouted longer, but here was a new case. "I forgive you. Now, let's go over what you and I saw last night, Ditie."

"I give up," Mason said. "You gonna keep notes, Danny? We'll pass them along to the detective on the case, but there's going to be hell to pay at headquarters."

Danny took out a pen and notebook.

"Go ahead. We're listening," Mason said after he'd munched his way through a second cookie.

Lurleen and I told Danny all we knew.

"So, if the safe was found open in the morning, any of the staff might be involved," Danny said. "Maybe Quinn didn't close the safe completely when he put the necklace back, and someone saw this as a crime of opportunity with both Savannah and Quinn gone in a rush."

"What about Chris insisting it was closed before the party started?" I asked.

"People do lie," Lurleen said. "I mean I like Chris and all that, but he certainly plays up to Savannah. Sometimes it feels a little fake. Maybe he didn't close the safe after he stole the necklace, and then Savannah found it open before he could shut it in the morning."

"Or maybe more people had keys to the apartment and knew the combination to the safe," I said.

The kettle was whistling. I took coffee orders, drip version, and Lurleen distributed the cups when they were ready.

"Do you think someone created a diversion with Quinn in order to steal the real necklace?" Lurleen asked as she settled beside me.

"I'm not sure there would have been any diversion if I hadn't noticed how sick Quinn looked."

"You're right, Ditie," Lurleen said. "I thought he was just tired and needed a good night's sleep." She sipped her coffee. "I wonder if Quinn was given the bad medicine during the party."

"Poisoned at the party?" I said. "That would take some nerve. If he'd died on the spot, everyone in that room would have been a suspect unless it looked like another heart attack."

"Did you see their medicine cabinet?" Lurleen said to me.

We all looked at Lurleen.

"No," I said, "and why did you?"

"Oh, don't be such a *goody deux chaussures.*"

"Goody Two Shoes? You made that up," I said.

Lurleen ignored me. "I had a headache. Too much of that fabulous wine. So I went looking for an aspirin. *Mon dieu,* do they have medicines! At least ten bottles with his name on them. I would have written them down if I knew we were going to have a case to investigate."

"You do not have a case to investigate," Mason said.

"It sounds like an inside job," Danny said. "Someone had a key and the combination to the safe."

"You didn't see how the guests acted," Lurleen said. "They all looked suspicious if you ask me."

"Were we at the same party, Lurleen? To me, everyone seemed friendly. A few people did appear to know each other and Savannah. But, only one of them acted aloof—the cousin James Bradshaw. He kept to himself and seemed more interested in the alcohol than the conversation."

"There you are," Lurleen said, "motive and opportunity."

"I can see the opportunity—maybe," I said. "But, what was the motive?"

"You have to admit there was no love lost between Bradshaw and Savannah," Lurleen said.

"It did seem odd," I said. "One, to have a cousin in the competition, and two, that they didn't appear to like each other. No warm greetings or hugs. I don't think they even talked to one another the whole evening."

"They didn't," Lurleen said decisively. "Not until the ambulance arrived, and then Bradshaw was all solicitous—a big show if you ask me."

"The motive would be James Bradshaw didn't like Savannah, so he killed her husband and stole her necklace?" Mason asked.

"*Ce n'est pas si simple*. But, it's clear that Bradshaw didn't like Savannah, and the feeling was mutual. That's a start. That's worth looking into." Lurleen had made her final assessment on the matter. She pointed a slender finger at Mason. "There's a lead for you."

"Remember, I'm not on the case," Mason said.

At that moment his cell phone rang. He got up and took the call in the kitchen. A moment later he returned. "Gotta go. I *am* on the case. A preliminary drug screen showed a high dose of a chemotherapy agent in Nelson's system with no record he was being treated for cancer."

"What drug?" I asked.

"Possibly doxorubicin," Mason said, checking his notebook. "Apparently Quinn's urine was red and not from blood. That tipped one of the nurses off, so they're confirming the drug through more specific tests."

"The Red Devil. It's a chemotherapy drug used to treat aggressive cancers. It's given intravenously, as a drip," I said. "There's no way he got that drug during the party."

Chapter Three

I followed Mason to the door. Danny and Lurleen were right behind me.

"When and where did he get the dose of doxorubicin?" I asked. "He didn't get it at the party, and he was already sick when he went to the hospital. If his urine was red, that side effect only lasts a day or two."

"That's what the medical examiner concluded," Mason said.

"Of course, we don't know how many doses he'd already received," I said. "That drug has a lot of nasty side effects and can cause irreversible heart damage over time."

That stopped Mason for a moment. "You're saying Quinn's heart failure could have been the result of poisoning with—" Mason searched his notes once more—"with doxorubicin?"

"It's possible. Or it could have made a fragile heart stop functioning."

Mason grabbed his jacket from the coat rack beside the front door. "According to Quinn's concierge doc, he didn't have cancer and neither did Savannah. Who would have given it to him and why? I doubt it's a drug you can pick up at a local pharmacy, so where did someone get it?"

"Most likely at a hospital or a cancer treatment center," I said. "The drug's given IV over several minutes, and it's very expensive. I don't see how a lay person could get hold of it or know how to administer it. A person would need some medical knowledge—at least enough to start an IV."

"You called it The Red Devil. Why that nickname?" he asked. "Other than the red urine."

"It's the bright red color of the drug itself and the serious side effects. It can cause inflammation or damage at the site of the injection. That's why people being treated for cancer often have a port put in."

"A port?" Lurleen asked.

"A port is a medical device that sits under the skin and connects with a large vein feeding directly into the heart. Medicine is given through a needle into the port and saves wear and tear on the tissue or on smaller veins. Did Quinn have a port?"

Mason looked over his notes. "No. The medical examiner commented on that. He expected to see it if Quinn were being treated for cancer."

"No doctor would give that drug to a man after two heart attacks," I said. "It's likely it contributed to the congestive heart failure that killed him. If he got several doses over time, he would have been pretty miserable— nauseated and losing his hair. It's likely Savannah would have noticed that."

Mason nodded. "Thanks, Ditie. I'll follow up with her."

He gave me a kiss and left.

There wasn't more to do that evening, and we all had the start of a new week coming up. Danny had an ongoing case he was wrapping up, and I had a busy Monday at the refugee clinic. Lurleen had a workout with her personal trainer, Wendy, and whatever else she had planned for her day. She'd pick up the kids from school for me, as she did most afternoons.

"I'm not sure I can sleep," Lurleen said as Danny urged her out the door. "This is too interesting."

"It will keep until tomorrow," Danny said with a yawn. "Thanks, Ditie, for the cookies. If you need any help finishing them off before they go stale let me know."

Next to Lurleen, Danny was my biggest cheerleader. I brought him a plastic container with the rest of the cookies.

"Thanks. This will help me on my stake out," he said.

"Tonight?"

"Nope, tomorrow night—that's when the husband in question tends to get home late from work."

When they left, I checked on the kids once more. Hermione took the opportunity of an open door to jump onto Lucie's bed and curl up at her feet. Lucie never stirred.

I took a quick shower and settled myself under the comforter. Majestic leapt onto the bed and nudged up against me waiting to be stroked. He rewarded my petting with a loud continuous purr. If I ever suffered from jangled nerves, that purr always settled me down and helped me think.

It *was* too interesting as Lurleen had said. Doxorubicin wasn't a drug you could pick up at the neighborhood pharmacy, so who would know where to get it or how to use it?

My cell rang—a number I didn't recognize.

"Thank goodness I got you." It was a familiar voice with the soft tones of a cultured Southern accent. "Savannah here. I know it's late, but I had to call you. You tried to save Quinn's life." Her voice broke. "I can't believe he's gone."

"I'm so sorry," I said.

"They're saying Quinn might not have died from natural causes. They say he had some drug in his system that shouldn't have been there. Something that started with a D."

"I heard that as well. It seems Quinn had an anti-cancer drug in his system—doxorubicin. Did he have cancer?"

"No," Savannah said. "The police asked me. How did you hear about the drug?"

"The medical rumor mill," I said. I wasn't sure Mason would want me broadcasting what he'd told me in private. "Did Quinn suffer from nausea or start losing his hair over the last couple of months?"

"What a strange question. He did seem to be failing in general, especially after his second heart attack. He felt sick sometimes, but I assumed that was from his heart. And now that you mention it, he did say to me his hair was falling out. He wondered if he should talk to our doctor. I didn't think much about it since Quinn's father went completely bald. I assumed that was what was happening to him."

"Do you know when that started—Quinn's hair loss I mean?"

"You have so many questions, Ditie. You'd think you were the one who called me and not the other way around. I think maybe Quinn said something about it a month or so ago. He said it was coming out in clumps. Why do you ask?"

"It might say something about when he started getting doxorubicin treatments, although it doesn't answer the question of why he would need them. If he did have cancer would he have kept that information from you?"

"It's possible. He kept a lot of secrets from me. That could have been one of them. If he did, it was to try to save me pain." Savannah was silent for a moment. "Quinn and I loved each other, and I have to find out who murdered him."

"The police are on the case."

"I know. I read about what they're doing in the newspaper, but publicity is the last thing I need right now."

I wondered if that was true. Lurleen had told me that according to the gossip magazines, Savannah's show was losing viewers and might not be renewed for the next season. Surely, this kind of publicity would garner sympathy for her and ratchet up her ratings. I put that thought aside as she continued in a voice that sounded strained with emotion.

"I'm frightened. I've been threatened in the past. What if someone decided to do more than talk?"

"What do you mean?"

"A few years ago, I got nasty letters that threatened me. Then they stopped until several months ago."

"You've told the police about this?"

"Of course, but it comes with the territory of being famous. They say they'll look into it, but I need more. I need you to help me."

"What can I possibly do?"

"I know who you are. I read about you in the paper—the Sandler case and then the Civil War reenactments. You've solved cases that baffled the police."

"I don't do that for a living," I said.

Savannah continued as if I hadn't spoken. "I knew something bad was going to happen. Quinn seemed anxious all the time."

I had an unpleasant insight. "Did you include me in your contest because I've helped solve a high-profile murder in the past?"

Savannah hesitated. "I loved your tea cakes and so did my nephew, Chris. It was a perfect fit. I thought you would be a wonderful contestant and might also help me figure out who was sending the threatening letters. Obviously, at the time, there was no murder to investigate. When Lurleen asked if her private eye boyfriend might come along for a short vacation, I felt it was meant to be."

"Did she mention *my* boyfriend? Detective Mason Garrett? Atlanta Police Department?"

"No, she left that out."

Savannah was quiet.

"He's been assigned to the case and he'll find out what's going on," I said.

"Hmm," Savannah said. "I guess that means I can't ask you to look into things on your own and keep what you learn private."

"I couldn't possibly do that. Mason won't leak anything to the press if that's what you're worried about, but he's the one you should be talking to, not me."

Savannah was quiet again.

"All right. But, the other reason I'm calling is to let you know the contest is still on. It's the only way I can cope with this terrible loss."

"Will the police let you do that?"

"The filming will take place at my house in South Carolina, near Beaufort, and the Atlanta police have no jurisdiction there."

"I'm sorry, Ms. Evans, I can't come. Your husband has been murdered, and I have children to think about."

"If you're worried about *your* safety, don't be. Whoever did this accomplished what they set out to do. They killed Quinn. They knew he was my lifeline and that I'd be devastated by his death."

"As long as there is an unknown murderer out there, I can't participate. My children have already been through too much."

"I know. Jason and Lucie. I know their mother, your childhood friend, was murdered."

I had a creepy feeling that Savannah Evans knew far too much about me. "How could you know about them?"

"Chris does a thorough bio on every contestant we consider. That's to make sure we have a varied group of participants and no one comes with any surprises. We included a short bio of everyone at the back of the packet you received."

I pulled out the packet from my nightstand as she was talking and found the bios at the end. There was a picture of me and three sentences about my love of cooking, my work as a pediatrician, and my two children, Lucie and Jason. There was nothing about what had happened to them or their mother.

"You will be perfectly safe here," Savannah continued. "No one wants to hurt *you*. I have my own security detail. Quinn made some enemies over the years, and some people are jealous of my fame. Please, please think about it for a few days, and then let me know your decision."

"I'll do that, but it's unlikely I'll change my mind. You must understand that if I do decide to come it's as a cook and not an investigator."

"You've made that clear," Savannah said. "I'm eager to taste what you have to offer. I know Lurleen wants to come—we spoke before I called you—and perhaps that boyfriend of hers could come—as my guest, of course."

"You aren't giving up on getting us involved, are you Ms. Evans?"

"You must call me Savannah. We'll be old friends or new enemies by the time this is over." She sighed into the phone. "I really need your help, Ditie, I really do."

She used the magic phrase, the phrase my brother claimed was like a post-hypnotic suggestion. "I need your help."

"I'll do what I can. I have to warn you that anything you tell me, if it's relevant to the case, anything I find out, goes straight to Mason Garrett."

"I understand. I can live with that. At least I hope I can."

"What do you mean?"

"I mean that I'm not sure the murderer is done. I'm afraid I might be next."

"What are you talking about?"

"The threats I mentioned. Your Mason Garrett will have them on file. They are against me as well as my husband—never traceable—typed on a computer and then mailed from all over the country and always signed, 'A disgruntled fan'."

"And what do these threats say?"

"That I had harmed the person and their family in some way, and that I would feel the same hurt they felt. Now, I know what they mean. Another threat came yesterday. I have a copy." I heard Savannah rustling through some papers. "Here it is. 'Now, you have a taste of pain with more to follow. Enjoy,'" she read. "Enjoy is *my* sign-off line."

"I know," I said. "My daughter, Lucie, and I watch all your shows. Are you safe where you are now?"

"Yes. I have my staff and a bodyguard here. By the way, the staff had nothing to do with the missing necklace. Chris told me he mentioned that to Lurleen. Most of my staff have been with me for years. They are loyal and well-paid."

"I'm going to call Mason after we hang up. He may be in touch with you tonight."

"Fine. I'm not sleeping anyway."

We hung up. I called Mason and filled him in on the conversation. He hadn't heard about the latest threat. He wasn't pleased about my interviewing Savannah regarding Quinn's health.

"I don't want you asking questions, and I don't want you going to that contest," he said. "I have no authority in South Carolina. I can't keep you safe. Ms. Evans should call it off."

"She's not going to. She wants Lurleen and Danny to come as well. I've already told her I probably won't participate for the sake of the children."

"Good," Mason said. "I'll contact Ms. Evans tonight."

That was the end of the conversation. No 'I love you.' All business and worry. It unsettled me.

A moment later the phone rang. "I do love you, Ditie," Mason said. "I just don't want you involved in this."

Now, at least I thought I could sleep, but I was mistaken. My mind went into overdrive as it did sometimes when I was worried about a patient or uncertain about a diagnosis.

Did any of the contestants look suspicious, as Lurleen suggested? Were the staff as trustworthy as Savannah claimed? Was the stolen necklace a crime of opportunity or connected with the murder in some way?

There was no telling how quickly or effectively doxorubicin might kill someone. In fact, it might not be fatal at all, except that Quinn had a bad heart.

And why would Quinn agree to take a drug like that intravenously? He wouldn't feel well after he got it, and it was likely to cause damage or discomfort at the IV site. He must have thought it was something else, something he needed enough to tolerate the side effects.

I wasn't about to sleep with so many nagging questions.

I went downstairs to read and poked my head into the children's rooms once more. Jason was scrunched in one corner of his bed, his toy transport truck on the other side of him. Six little cars were spread out beside the truck. It was Lurleen's most recent gift, and I knew he played with it every night before he went to sleep. I put the cars back in their compartments and moved the truck to his toy shelf. Then I brushed his straight dark hair away from his face and kissed him goodnight. He opened his eyes briefly, smiled, and closed them again.

I could see a light under Lucie's door. She turned it off when she heard my footsteps in the hall.

I opened her door and walked over to her bed. "Not asleep, Luce? It's late."

"I was asleep, but something woke me up. I thought I heard something outside my window."

I went into the hall, turned on the deck light and drew back her curtains. I looked outside and motioned for her to look as well. "I'll send Hermione out to check."

Hermione was snoring peacefully on Lucie's bed, but she was more than willing to wake up when I called her. She went out back, stood at attention for a moment, her nose sniffing the air. Then she trotted down the stairs to look around the garden. After five minutes she returned and waited patiently by the back door for me to let her in.

"Nothing there, Luce," I said. "You know Hermione would have started barking if she'd found anything wrong."

Lucie smiled and climbed back into bed.

I brought Hermione into the house, gave her a treat, and she followed me to Lucie's room. As if to prove a point as Lucie's guard dog, she jumped up on Lucie's bed and curled up next to her. I pulled the covers around Lucie and stroked her silver blond hair. She was asleep before I left the room.

Every now and then I needed a reminder about how much care my children needed. All children needed care, but most hadn't been through what my two had.

I couldn't take off for South Carolina even if I wanted to. I wasn't footloose anymore. I had children now who had suffered too much loss and who meant more to me than anything or anyone else in the world.

Chapter Four

The next morning, I read about plans to celebrate the life of J. Quinn Nelson at the end of the week. "Celebrate" was from a direct quote by Chris Evans who spoke about how much Quinn meant to the real estate community and to the city of Atlanta. Nothing was said about the way he died except that he'd been ailing for some time. The announcement took up most of the obituary page of the *Atlanta Journal-Constitution*.

On the front page of the AJC, above the fold, was a long piece about the missing necklace and some suspicion that Quinn might have been poisoned. They didn't name the drug involved—somehow Mason managed to keep that out of the newspaper.

Lurleen stopped by as I was putting pork tenderloin in my slow-cooker for dinner that evening. Lucie and Jason were sitting at the table, finishing breakfast.

She burst into the kitchen ready to talk and then heeded my look.

"Oh, the kids," she said, smiling at Jason and Lucie. "I just dropped in to say hello. I was missing you and realized I just couldn't wait until this afternoon to see you."

Jason gobbled it up, but Lucie looked wisely suspicious.

"Did you bring us something?" Jason asked. "Something for Halloween? You know it's in…" he counted on his fingers—"three days."

"I do know that," Lurleen said, "and when I pick you up from school, we'll do a little Halloween shopping."

She left with a nod in my direction. "I'll call you later."

Jason couldn't stop talking about plans for the afternoon. He already had his Black Panther costume. "Mommy, can I wear it to school?" he asked.

I did love the sound of that 'mommy,' but I didn't mind a bit that Lucie still felt best calling me Aunt Di. Whatever worked for them worked for me. "I think they're having a parade Halloween morning," I said. "You can wear it then. What about you, Luce? Do you want to wear your costume to school?"

I knew she was going as Katniss Everdeen from the *Hunger Games.*

"No, Aunt Di. No one in fourth grade is wearing a costume to school. That's for the little kids."

Happily, Jason didn't register that he was being called a little kid. Instead, he wanted to know where Lurleen would take them in the afternoon and what she might buy.

"There's a Halloween shop Lurleen told me about, so I bet that's where you'll go."

Jason ran back to his room to get his Black Panther's comic book for show and tell.

While he was gone, Lucie raised one eyebrow and said, "Lurleen didn't come to talk to you about Halloween. She came to talk about the party you went to and the man who died and the necklace that was stolen."

Sometimes Lucie unnerved me, and I wondered if in that nine-year-old body lived a miniature adult. "Did Lurleen say something to you about that—and since when can you raise one eyebrow?"

"I've been reading the paper and listening to the news. I'm not a baby anymore."

"I'm not sure you ever were."

Lucie smiled proudly. "I've been practicing raising one eyebrow. Uncle Danny tried to teach me how. When Uncle Mason does it, everyone around him—even you, Aunt Di—gets quiet and waits to hear what he has to say."

I nodded. I'd never thought about it, but it was true. When Mason raised one eyebrow it meant he was very serious about something.

"All right, Lucie, I think you are exactly right. I think Lurleen was hoping to catch me alone, so she could tell me something. However, I also think she plans to take you shopping this afternoon, so we can get our yard and house ready for a fantastic Halloween."

Jason came back, and Lucie didn't say anymore. I took the kids to school and headed for the clinic. Lurleen called me before I arrived.

"Did you drop the kids off?" she asked. "Are you in the car?"

"Yes."

"People are having a field day with the idea Quinn was poisoned. They're speculating that Quinn and Savannah were about to divorce and that she might have poisoned him to get him out of the way. They said she was the one with all the money at this point and maybe she didn't want to pay him alimony."

"Did you read that in some supermarket tabloid?"

Lurleen was quiet.

"You did, didn't you?" I said.

"It doesn't mean it isn't true. I still have friends at Sandler's Sodas, and several of them called me yesterday. They said when Savannah had a party recently, Quinn wasn't there."

"Maybe that was because he was too sick to come."

"I think it's worth looking into," Lurleen said.

"You do know Mason has forbidden us to look into anything."

"Yes, but maybe he hasn't heard the rumors."

"Then I'd say give him a call or get Danny to do it for you."

"Are you really going to stay out of this?"

"Lurleen, I have to, for the children's sake. And you should too, for their sake as well."

I could hear Lurleen sigh. "You're right, Ditie. Mason will figure it out. Besides, we have Halloween to think about."

"We do, and the kids are very excited about this afternoon. I gotta go, I'm at the clinic."

I parked the car, walked up to the double doors of the building and then passed by the reception desk to the elevators. Down to the basement. Then I walked quickly through the hallway, and I could feel my focus shifting.

The red plastic chairs in the waiting room were filled with families as they were every Monday morning. I always scanned the room to see if any of the children looked especially sick. It was the first thing I did, even though I knew our triage nurses would have caught anyone who needed immediate attention.

Vic stopped me as I dropped off my jacket and purse in my office. She was the director of the clinic, but she acted more like a colleague than my boss. "I heard all about the party you went to at Savannah Evans's penthouse. Now, they think Quinn Nelson didn't die of natural causes?"

"That's right. It's even more bizarre than that. They found traces of doxorubicin in his system, and he didn't have cancer."

"Good lord," Vic said. "That is weird. I assume the cooking contest is off?"

"Savannah wants to do it. She says it's the only thing that will take her mind off Quinn, and she wants me to come as some kind of undercover detective. It was unnerving what she knew about me and the kids. I told her I couldn't come as long as the murderer was on the loose."

"That makes sense," Vic said.

"How does the day look here?" I asked.

"Manageable," she said. "We have a full house, but we've got our volunteer CDC docs here this morning, and a contingent of med-school students coming this afternoon."

"They're a good group," I said.

"They are."

Vic handed me the roster, and we went over how we would divide up the patients.

I loved the clinic for a hundred reasons. It grounded me and kept me focused on the things that really mattered. Patients and their families were always grateful for the help we gave, and it felt like *my* world community—a world in which we all helped one another. I knew I could count on the staff. If they ever had a question about why I made a decision, they'd ask me, and we'd talk about it.

The day flowed easily and passed quickly.

I was home by five thirty to the other half of my life that kept me grounded. Jason was bubbling with excitement. He met me at the door. I saw Lurleen sitting demurely in my grandmother's rocking chair.

"You should see, Mommy, what Lurleen bought," Jason said. "She said it was a surprise and I couldn't tell you. Do you want to know?"

I looked over at Lurleen who smiled and nodded.

"It's a big, big monster. Wait till you see! You might be scared, Mommy. Uncle Danny has to blow it up."

I couldn't help but smile, Jason was so excited. "Does it scare you, honey?"

"Not me, but it might scare Lucie."

Lucie just grinned. "Lurleen bought me an archery set so I could look like Katniss Everdeen with a real quiver and arrows. She said she'd learned how to do archery from her boyfriend Artemus who went on to be in the Olympics." Lucie leaned in and whispered, "I don't think that really happened because Lurleen didn't know the bag that holds the arrows is called a quiver."

"Hmm," was all I said.

We worked together to make a dinner of pulled pork, coleslaw and fresh corn on the cob. The pulled pork had been simmering all day, and the house was full of good smells and good humor. We made enough for Danny and Mason, but neither one showed. They each called before I put the kids to bed.

I rarely saw Mason over the next forty-eight hours, but my hands were full with busy days at the clinic and preparation for Halloween.

It was my favorite holiday—probably because of the candy and the innocent scariness—and now, I had children to share it with!

Lurleen and I decorated the house. On the door we put a six-inch spider, which crawled and made a scary noise when anyone jangled it. In the yard, Lucie and Lurleen made several life-sized ghosts, attached them to sticks and had them peering out from inside my magnolia tree. I helped with another group of ghosts that we pinned to a long silvery string stretching from a hook on the porch to a fence behind our rose bushes. My supply of white sheets was decimated, but that was a small price to pay for how glorious the yard looked and how much fun we had.

Danny blew up the monster with a bicycle pump, and then we worried it might scare away the little kids. Lurleen painted a smile over its blood red lips and that made it a lot less threatening.

Jason was so excited to wear his Black Panther costume to school on Halloween that he barely slept the night before.

Lurleen planned on being a witch but looked far too frightening. Even Jason came up and asked her if she really was Lurleen. She changed into a Wonder Woman costume. With Lurleen's body and long legs, she looked spectacular.

I dressed up as a chocolate chip cookie.

I took the kids around the neighborhood after an early supper. Lurleen distributed candy until our return.

We all slept well that night, full of sugar and chocolate.

The following day, more news from the *Atlanta Journal Constitution* brought me back to current events.

Quinn's burial was to be a family service scheduled for Friday with a private gathering that afternoon in Savannah's condo. A more public memorial would be held on Saturday night at an exclusive venue near Piedmont Park to be attended by every dignitary in Atlanta. Apparently, Quinn was not one to shy away from publicity, even in death.

Savannah said she would not make a public appearance at this time, so it was Quinn's developer friends who planned the evening event. Mason and Danny attended both the public and private gatherings.

The guest lists for both engagements were sent to the Atlanta Police Department. Two hundred fifty people were invited to the evening ceremony. Guests included the mayor, several CEOs of major Atlanta companies, and of course the real estate community.

Security was tight. According to Danny, half the waiters were actually security guards hired by the mayor. Danny said a number of them hung out in the kitchen to make sure no one tampered with the food.

Danny was willing to tell us all the colorful details, particularly when I offered him his favorite dessert—lemon meringue pie. It didn't hurt that

Mason was working late. He kept information close to the vest when he was working on a case.

Danny, Lurleen, and I talked after I made sure the children were asleep.

"During the public event," Danny said, "one man kept asking about Savannah Evans. Why wasn't she present? Didn't she care enough about her husband to show up?

"Everyone was drinking, and no one seemed especially upset over Quinn's death. They drank to him. They drank to Savannah, to her company, to his company, and then they moved on to other topics. It was only this one guy who kept asking questions. He got louder and louder until security asked him to leave.

"He wouldn't go. He headed for the dais where several dignitaries were getting ready to talk about Quinn. He grabbed the microphone from the first speaker. Said he'd been waiting for this moment for years, and he wouldn't be put off. He got as far as claiming Quinn was a murderer who deserved to die. Then the police dragged him off the stage."

"Whoa," Lurleen said, her eyes sparkling. "I read something about that in the paper, but they didn't name the man."

"His name is Timothy White. He was on the list as a representative of the hospital that treated Quinn for both heart attacks. Scottie told me they'd just found out White wasn't part of the hospital delegation. He'd been employed by the hospital in the past but was fired and jailed for stealing drugs from the hospital pharmacy. He got out a few months ago."

"Scottie, your new informant?" I asked.

"Yes. Mason's playing by the rules, so I'm not getting much from him. You aren't either, I'm sure."

We shook our heads.

Newspapers broke the story the next morning after White was brought in for questioning. According to the article, he was a former oncology nurse, and yes, he knew the drug doxorubicin. He knew how to administer it. He also had a grudge against Quinn Nelson. In an interview with the press, he admitted he didn't like people with money who threw their weight around. He didn't like the power team of Savannah Evans and Quinn Nelson, but that didn't mean he went around threatening them. Or killing them for that matter.

Between the newspaper and Danny, Lurleen and I managed to get the full story over the next few days. Apparently, Mason was about to let White go when an anonymous tip sent him in a different direction. A phone call from an unnamed source stated that White's mother had been employed by Savannah Evans. She'd been fired while undergoing treatment for cancer, but she couldn't afford the medicine when she was out of work. White's mother died, needlessly, painfully, cruelly, in his eyes.

Danny seemed happy to tell us what the newspapers didn't know yet.

"White never admitted to killing anyone, but he confessed he might have written a threatening letter or two. He also said he was glad Quinn had suffered in the same way his mother had—ironically from receiving the treatment his mother could not afford."

"You sound as if you were in the interview room with Mason," I said.

"I wasn't, but Scottie was." He looked at Lurleen. "Mason will kill me if he knows I'm talking to you. This can't go anywhere else."

"Cross my heart, Danny, I'll be quiet as a mummy," Lurleen said.

Bit by bit, the full story came out in the paper. It was front-page news for a week. Lurleen and I were off the hook in terms of keeping information private.

It appeared the case was essentially closed, and we all felt relieved. The anonymous tip was one loose end. Danny said Mason was looking for the source and attempting to gather more details such as where White got the doxorubicin and when and how it was administered. But it seemed the murderer was in hand.

Lurleen was ecstatic. "It's over," she said. "Now, we can go! I already called Chris, and he put me through to Savannah. She was so pleased to hear your decision."

"My decision?" I said.

"You know what I mean. There's no danger in going now." Lurleen was practically dancing on poor Quinn Nelson's grave. "I'm not being disrespectful," she said. "I'm just so happy we get to go. It will do Savannah a world of good. She said so herself. Our job will be to cheer her up. Help her find her *joie de vivre*."

I agreed with Lurleen's sense of our mission, although I knew it would take more than a cooking contest to ease Savannah's grief if she loved Quinn as much as she said she did.

"So where exactly are we going in South Carolina?" Lurleen asked. "I assume it's Charleston—Savannah always talks about how much she loves Charleston cuisine."

"It's a little town called Veracrue—just outside Beaufort," I said. "'Beautiful Beaufort by the Sea—that's how you can remember how to pronounce it."

"What?" Lurleen asked. "Beaufort?"

Her face drained of color, and I thought she might faint.

"Are you sick?" I asked.

We were in the kitchen where I had just pulled out a favorite Southern cookbook from my book rack. I sat her on a stool and brought her a glass of water.

Lurleen said nothing while she drank. Slowly her color returned. "I'm not sure . . . I can go with you, Ditie."

"But, you're the reason I'm going. What's wrong?"

"I didn't know the contest would be in Beaufort," she said.

"It's in Veracrue, a small town outside of Beaufort."

"I know where it is," Lurleen said.

Then she burst into tears.

"I just can't come, Ditie. I'm sorry."

"It's all right," I said. I hugged her. I didn't know what was wrong but clearly something was. "You know Beaufort?"

Lurleen nodded, unable to stop the flood of tears. I grabbed some paper towels, and she hid her face in them.

"You lived there?" I asked.

Again, Lurleen nodded.

I didn't press her for more. I'd always known Lurleen had some secret in her past, something she never wanted to share with me. Now, I knew it had to do with South Carolina, in or near the town of Beaufort.

I led her to the sofa in the living room and put my arm around her while she cried. The children were in school, thank goodness. Hermione came up and put her head in Lurleen's lap. Hermione was an old soul. She knew when one of us felt bad and needed comforting. Even Majestic wandered in. Despite his disdain for most humans, he seemed to have a special fondness for Lurleen. He jumped on the sofa and settled between us.

When the tears subsided, Lurleen looked at me—red-eyed, mascara running. "I must look a fright."

"A little, but underneath it all, you still look beautiful. Can you tell me what's wrong?"

"Ditie, I've tried so hard to put the past behind me. Just when I think I've succeeded, something brings it up again."

"Maybe it's time to face it, Lurleen," I said. "Secrets make people sick."

She nodded but didn't speak. After a few seconds, she sighed. "I'll go with you."

Chapter Five

When I saw Lurleen the next day, she'd recovered her equilibrium. It was clear she didn't want to talk about what was troubling her, and I'd known her long enough not to press her about it.

A week later, I sat in her bedroom for half an hour while she finished packing.

"I guess we've wrapped up another murder," she said as she closed her second suitcase. She looked around the room. "It's so hard to know what we might need at an estate in South Carolina."

"*We* haven't wrapped up anything," I said. "Mason got his man with the help of an anonymous tipster." I looked at Lurleen's suitcases. "We're only going for a week, and Savannah emphasized that dress was casual. She said there would be one gala event when we arrived and another to award the winner his or her prize."

"No worries, *chérie.* I'm not getting carried away. I haven't seen a television series in production. I'll be in the audience and you never know when the camera might capture me there. I'll have to wear something different for each shoot."

Along with many of the clothes from her closet, Lurleen had managed to pack away whatever was troubling her.

"If you should get eliminated, Ditie, which you won't, you'll probably get to be a taster. Are you sure *you're* bringing enough clothes?"

I shrugged off that worry. "I do like the way Savannah runs her contests. If you're eliminated, you don't have to disappear or walk down a long corridor muttering to yourself about what you or the judges did wrong."

"Savannah's *une bonne âme,* although not everyone thinks so."

"A good soul? What do you mean, Lurleen?"

"Some people think she's a really fine person, but others disagree. You know how people are, *cherie*. When someone is famous, everyone picks at them—other chefs, old school chums, the usual."

"How do you know all the gossip?"

"Social media, naturally. It's all there. About everyone. You should Google yourself."

"No thanks," I said.

Danny called up to us. "You two ready? If we don't leave soon, we might miss dinner."

"Coming," Lurleen called down. "We can't be late," she said to me as if I were the one holding up things. "I refuse to miss one morsel of food served by Savannah Evans. This is our welcome dinner. I haven't eaten a thing all day."

I offered to help Lurleen with her luggage, but Danny bounded up the steps to take the two large suitcases and her overnight bag. He was a big guy, muscular, and could have handled twice as much luggage without breaking a sweat. "Good thing we're taking my car and not your Citroën, Lurleen," he said.

I climbed in the back seat of Danny's Honda so Lurleen could stretch her long legs in front. I'd already put my single suitcase in Danny's trunk and said goodbye to the kids.

Tommy and Josh had scooted the children off to a matinee right before we left. Eddie promised to bring her dog, Schnitzel Doodle, over later in the afternoon. Hermione and the kids would be in heaven. Majestic would be less enthusiastic.

Secretly, I was looking forward to a long drive in which I might quietly daydream. Lurleen and Danny could carry on their usual lively conversation.

I'd miss the kids, but it was only for five days. It would be a good bonding experience for my brother and the children.

The logistics were complicated—making sure Tommy knew where to drop the children at school, when to pick them up, how to get Lucie to afterschool art lessons and Jason to karate. And of course, work was only slightly less hectic. I did my best to settle things at the clinic so that no one would have to take over my cases while I was gone. But, emergencies happened. My boss, Vic, was as reassuring as always. "We'll survive, Ditie," she said.

I'd been so busy with preparations to be away, I'd had only a little time to think about the contest or test out recipes. Savannah was good about that. She provided a list of the categories for the show and didn't mind if we worked on our own variations before we arrived. The technical challenges remained a secret. We would each have the same recipe for those, and the challenges were to test our basic cooking skills. For me it was no big deal. I wasn't one to get nervous.

I read over the rules as we rode. There would be one to two shoots a day, depending upon the time required to prepare the food. We had one free day to catch up on anything that needed a reshoot. Savannah and her assistant chef, Anna Hayes, would have all needed ingredients available to us. If we wanted something highly unusual, we were to let Anna know ahead of time so it could be purchased and on hand.

Savannah would not watch the preparation, and the tastings would be blind. She'd show up when the six numbered offerings had been placed on the table. We were given a list of favorite Southern foods for the week of shooting. The contest was to see who could make the best variation on the theme, starting with banana pudding.

I got the feeling Savannah wanted everyone to do well. The show wasn't about humiliating anyone.

I wasn't sure where the drama would come from, but, naturally, there had to be some. I'd watched enough of her shows to know some contestant would have a meltdown in the last thirty seconds before time was called.

Lurleen had binge-watched *The Great British Baking Contest* and gave me pointers on how to seem charming and vulnerable as I rolled over the competition. Her words not mine.

Once we entered South Carolina, I started to get excited. This was going to be a lot of fun, and the stakes for me were very low. I loved to cook and if people liked what I made, great. If not, that would be okay too.

I didn't really care if I got eliminated on the first round. That would simply give me more time to taste everyone else's offering and watch their techniques. Unlike Savannah, we didn't have to stay out of the kitchen as others worked.

I skimmed through the rest of the package and took five minutes to read the bios of the other contestants. None of them were more than a few lines.

Rose Kirkwood, married with one grown daughter, was described as a housewife who won prizes in local fairs for her cakes and pies.

Pepper Young, married, was a former drug rep who now spent her time organizing charity events in and around Atlanta.

James Bradshaw, single, a local food critic, had recently retired as a pharmacist to devote himself full time to Southern cuisine.

Izzy Moran, married, was said to be a former hospital administrator, now busy with her young son and deeply involved in farm-to-table organic food programs.

Gertrude Flumm, single, was a cafe owner in Beaufort known for her authentic low- country cuisine.

Not much there to go on except that I suspected Gertrude Flumm might have the edge on the rest of us.

Then, uninvited, my thoughts turned to Quinn's death. The Atlanta police believed they had their murderer, but what if they were wrong about that. Who called in the tip about Tim White and why did they do that? At least three of the contestants had some medical background, including Bradshaw, a pharmacist who appeared to be none too fond of Savannah. What if the murderer wasn't White after all?

As we neared Beaufort, Lurleen grew quiet. She'd never said any more to me about the trip and what it might mean to her. Instead she'd sealed up like a shrink-wrapped package of fresh produce.

I could hear her taking slow deep breaths in the front seat. I could also see her glancing out the window and then turning away as if she were looking at a train wreck. I reached between the front seats and squeezed her arm. She touched my arm with her right hand. Her hand was cold.

The low country surrounding Beaufort was just that—close to the sea and flat. Dozens of islands dotted the space with bridges connecting them to each other and the mainland.

"We'll take a tour," Danny promised, "during a break in the shooting. There's so much history here. I'll bet Savannah Evans's home was a summer house of a plantation owner. The owners made a fortune off of Gullah slaves growing Sea Island cotton on those islands and spent their summers on the bluffs of Beaufort and Veracrue to avoid mosquitoes and the miserable heat."

Lurleen remained silent. When Danny was done talking, she turned to me in the back seat and pasted on what looked like a determined smile.

"Have you thought about what you'll do, Ditie, for the banana pudding?" she asked. "I mean, I love your banana pudding, but there is that one contestant. It's her *spécialité*. And that caramelized banana pudding of Savannah's—*ooh, la la.*"

"Are you losing faith in me?" I asked.

"*Jamais, chérie.* I'm just not sure you're taking this seriously enough."

"Sweet Lurleen, I don't want to be a famous chef. I want to have fun and learn a few tricks of the trade. Nothing wrong with that, is there?"

"Nothing at all."

For the next fifteen minutes of the trip, Lurleen didn't speak. Danny was clearly aware of her anxiety and spent the time continuing his story of the rise and fall of Beaufort. "Union forces managed to defeat the Confederates in a sea battle outside Beaufort early in the war. They occupied the town and plantation owners fled. Many of the slaves remained and worked the land. After the war, the living was hard. Old mansions were given away for a song, and most plantation owners didn't return. Many of the freedmen were given parcels of land, so they became land owners."

Danny talked about the more recent revival of the town with its focus on tourism and told us about some of the movies that had been shot there— scenes from *The Great Santini, The Big Chill, Forrest Gump.* "When you see Tom Hanks running across the Mississippi River as Forrest Gump, he's actually running across the bridge from Beaufort to the sea islands—we'll see it when we get in town."

This was the kind of information Lurleen would normally have supplied or at the very least enjoyed hearing, but her mind was obviously elsewhere.

"You know Pat Conroy taught English in Beaufort and married someone from around here," Danny said.

That seemed to catch Lurleen's attention.

"I've read all his books," she said.

"Did you like them?" I asked.

"Painful. Every one of them."

Savannah lived a few miles from Beaufort, close to the water. A single sign welcomed us to the town of Veracrue, population 1000. We arrived at the gate to Savannah's estate around 5:00 pm.

A uniformed officer emerged from a small guard house. Danny handed him the official invitation, and the guard called the main house. A moment later the gate opened automatically, and Danny drove down a short private drive in which a giant oak tree draped in Spanish moss hid the mansion behind it. The atmosphere was irresistible, full of mystery and romance.

Danny couldn't stay quiet. "You do know Spanish moss is neither Spanish nor moss."

"I heard that," I said. "It's a flowering plant that doesn't hurt the tree unless it provides too much shade for the tree to grow well. It originated in South America, some place like that I think."

Danny looked at me in the rearview mirror. "I forgot you were a closet horticulturalist."

"Not really, but my first trip to the Southern coast brought me face to face with trees dripping in Spanish moss. There's nothing like it."

At a circular drive in front of the antebellum mansion, Danny pulled to a stop. It was a beautiful home with verandas stretching end to end on the second and third floors. A servant opened doors and took out our luggage. A second offered to park Danny's car for him in the garage. On the landing atop ten marble steps stood Savannah Evans, looking wan but lovely, in a pencil skirt and sweater set that matched her tawny hair and rich skin tones.

She greeted us warmly as if we were the only guests who mattered. "I am so glad you're here. Your rooms are the first three down the left corridor on the second floor. The staff will show you and bring up your suitcases. Freshen up and come down when you wish. We're having drinks in the main parlor at six."

As I entered, she said, "If you have time after you freshen up, Dr. Brown, I'd love to talk to you privately."

"Of course."

"I'll be on the back terrace."

I checked out the room, magnificent with a canopied bed and ornately carved mahogany furniture. The adjoining bathroom was all marble and as large as my living room. The bedroom window looked out on a terraced garden. This was going to be a restful vacation.

I took a luxurious bath in a clawfoot tub and changed into a simple wrap dress in a deep blue print. It flattered my figure, which was plush-size, nicely squeezable according to Mason and my daughter Lucie.

Half an hour later, I was downstairs in search of the back terrace when a thin gentleman in gray approached me. "May I help you, madam?"

"I was looking for Ms. Evans and the back terrace."

"This way, please." The man was perfectly polite and perfectly British. He was well-dressed although his jacket seemed a size too large for him.

"Are you visiting from London?" I asked.

The man smiled, a broad smile that brought color to his pale face. "Not visiting exactly, miss. I've worked for Ms. Evans and Mr. Nelson off and on for ten years. I worked as a butler until my employer's death last year. Now, I work here full time."

I smiled back. "You're a lot more forthcoming than Mr. Carson was on *Downton Abbey*. It's refreshing."

"I'm glad you don't mind. I'm a talker, something my former employer tried to drum out of me. As you can see, he wasn't successful. I don't think he minded really. He kept me on for twenty years and left me a tidy sum."

The gentleman in gray coughed and then apologized. "I'm susceptible to allergies here I'm afraid. The back entrance is through this hallway."

"Thank you," I said. "What shall I call you?"

"Dorian," he replied.

"As in Dorian—"

"Yes, Gray. I don't think you'll forget me now," he said with a slight bow.

"I don't think I'd forget you anyway."

Dorian opened the heavy wooden door for me and closed it after I'd passed through. Savannah jumped up from a teak lounge chair. She rushed over to greet me.

"Thank you for meeting me here. I see you've met Dorian. He's quite a character and a dear. He used to help with our holiday parties, but now he's part of my permanent staff. Don't be fooled by his formal ways. He'd do anything for anyone."

At the mention of holiday parties, Savannah teared a little. "I can't imagine I'll want to have another Christmas party. I'm not even sure I'll want to keep this house. Quinn always said it was the place we belonged, but I don't know how it will feel without him."

"It's a beautiful house," I said.

"Yes, and you haven't seen the best part, the kitchen. Quinn helped me design it, just so we could shoot some of the shows here." Again she teared. Every memory seemed to bring her back to Quinn's death. "Please sit down beside me. Would you like something to eat or drink?"

"No," I said. "You wanted to talk to me. I doubt we'll have much private time."

"You're right. If anyone joins us, we'll pretend we're talking about the gardens. Lurleen told my nephew, Chris, you are quite a gardener in addition to your abilities as a cook."

"I'm afraid Lurleen exaggerates my talents. I love a pretty garden but I'm no expert."

I stopped talking and waited for Savannah to tell me what was on her mind.

Savannah took a deep breath in and let it out slowly, yoga style. "I know the police think they've caught the murderer, but I'm not convinced."

This time I was the one who sucked in air. "Why?"

"I've known Tim White for years. I didn't let his mother go because she had cancer. I let her go because she was stealing things. At first it was small things, like a silver tea pot from the 1800s—something I rarely used and would never have missed if my assistant Anna, hadn't told me it was gone. Then it was items of more and more value—a silver punch bowl stored in the attic.

"It was her cancer that made me keep her on. I asked if she took things because she needed money to pay for treatments and she said no. She denied stealing, but eventually I had no choice but to let her go. Tim knows the whole story. He knows my husband wanted to prosecute and I said no. He also knows I made sure his mother had the best possible treatment."

"And yet, according to the police, White hates you."

"It's true. He blamed me and Quinn for taking his mother away from him, both when she worked for us and later when she died. He was a young man at the time of her death with no father. He ended up living in a boarding house, I think. But, I don't believe Tim is a murderer. He got into drugs, using and selling, according to my sources. He may even have sent some hate mail to us. But, murder Quinn? I don't think he had it in him."

"So you believe the murderer is still out there?"

"I'm afraid he might be. I've made people angry in my time, lots of people. You can't have the success I've had and not make enemies. Look at Martha Stewart. Some people were delighted she went to prison and sorry when she got out."

I nodded. "Still there is a big difference between jealousy and murder."

"Perhaps not for everyone. The hate mail would take your breath away, along with the vicious critiques."

"I hope you've said all this to the police."

"I have. I spoke at length to your delightful Mason Garrett over the phone. He listened and promised he'd investigate every person I put on a list of potential suspects. But, time is of the essence, Ditie. I can see how things are escalating. I'm worried Detective Garrett won't have time to find the murderer before it's too late."

"Too late?"

"You know—before someone tries to harm me."

"Are the police here investigating?"

"The chief is a friend of mine. But, what can he do? The police think they've found the murderer."

"I see. You're fine if I talk with Lurleen and Danny about what you've told me?"

"Naturally."

At that moment we were interrupted by James Bradshaw.

"You're early, James," Savannah said.

"I couldn't stay away, my dear. Not with all you've been going through."

"I'm delighted to see you," she said, but there was no warmth in her voice. "You remember Dr. Brown, one of your fellow contestants."

"Absolutely. Couldn't forget such a lovely face and such a formidable opponent from what I've heard."

"Please, call me Ditie. I'm afraid you've been talking to Lurleen. She's my biggest fan."

"Always nice to have one of those," Bradshaw said.

I stood. "I'll leave you to catch up on things, Mr. Bradshaw," I said. "I remember you and Savannah are family."

"Cousins. We go way back. Some might say too far back," Bradshaw said. "But, you must call me James."

I left with the peculiar sensation I was leaving Savannah in the lion's den. James Bradshaw had a way of turning every comment into something slightly sinister. I wondered if he was on Savannah's list of suspects. I'd ask her about him when I got the chance.

In the meantime, I needed to call Mason, right after I checked on the kids.

"Got them in hand, even as we speak," my brother, Tommy, said. "Eddie is here as well, fixing us a wonderful dinner."

"Don't forget their homework," I said.

"I've got it covered," Tommy said. "And if I didn't, Lucie would straighten me out in a heartbeat."

I could hear Lucie giggling in the background.

I spoke to each of the children and told them how much I missed them.

"Uncle Tommy is teaching me magic tricks," Jason said.

Lucie was equally enthusiastic. "You should see how much fun Hermione is having with Schnitzel Doodle!"

"I wish I could see that. I suppose Majestic has simply disappeared."

Lucie laughed. "No, Aunt Di. Majestic swatted at Schnitzel Doodle and then settled down on the front porch to keep Doodle away from his territory. Doodle is what Grandma Eddie says we should call her dog—he's too small a dog for his full name, she says. But, really, Aunt Di, he's almost as big as Hermione."

Tommy got back on the phone.

"I owe you," I told him.

"Other way around. I get to have fun, and Josh and I get a home-cooked meal every night. No worries. Make us proud."

Next, I called Mason, and that conversation was a lot less carefree. I repeated what Savannah told me. He listened. "She may be right. White continues to claim he's innocent and we haven't traced any missing doxorubicin from Georgia pharmacies or hospitals."

He was quiet for a moment.

"It appears Quinn came directly from South Carolina to the party. It's unlikely he would have had time to get the infusion in Georgia, and we don't think White traveled out of the state recently. South Carolina may be the place I need to be. That's where most of Savannah's suspects are." He was briefly silent again. "I'm coming down there."

"You said you have no jurisdiction here, and what about your other cases?"

"This is my major case. I can be invited by the local police," Mason said. "I know my captain will go along with it. You said Savannah Evans was good friends with the chief of police there. I'll get in touch with him."

I had just enough time to talk with Lurleen and Danny before cocktails were served. Both of them listened intently.

"We must be discreet," I cautioned.

"You know me, *chérie*. I am the essence of discretion," she said. "When I worked with the FBI—"

Both Danny and I gave her a look.

"You know, when I was dating Earl, my first American boyfriend. He was protecting the Secretary of State and I went along as a decoy."

She saw me glance at my watch.

"*Eh bien*, it's a long story. Maybe later. Anyway, I can be discreet."

Lurleen looked about as discreet as a peacock pretending to be a wild turkey.

Danny couldn't keep his eyes off her. "You look good," he said. "I mean really good."

"Down boy," Lurleen said sweetly. "We have work to do."

We were just about to leave Lurleen's bedroom, when Dorian knocked brusquely on the door.

"So glad to find you here, Dr. Brown. There's been an incident in the drawing room. I wonder if you might come down immediately. With your medical bag if you brought it."

Chapter Six

I always brought my bag with me when I traveled. Emergencies, especially kid emergencies, could happen at any time, in any setting. I grabbed it and ran downstairs to the parlor. It wasn't hard to see who needed help. Izzy Moran lay on the oriental carpet struggling to breathe. The other guests stood in a semicircle around her.

Her husband, Frank, was on his knees, gripping Izzy's hand. "She has a peanut allergy," he said. "Someone must have given her something with peanuts in it." He looked up at me wild-eyed. "Do something. I don't know where her EpiPen is."

"I've got one," I said, and I could see Frank start to breathe again.

I grabbed it and asked Dorian to call 911. "Is she allergic to any medications? Does she have any heart problems?"

Frank said no.

I motioned Lurleen to stand near Izzy for privacy as I raised her dress to gain access to her thigh. I injected the epinephrine and in a moment the woman's breathing became less labored. The EMTs arrived seconds later.

"That was fast," I said to Dorian.

"I called them as soon as I saw the situation was serious."

"Thank you. You helped save a life."

"It was entirely you, Dr. Brown."

"I agree," Savannah said. "You saved her life and probably mine as well. I also have a peanut allergy. I allow no peanuts or peanut oil in my kitchen. You must have read that in the contest rules."

"I'm sure it's there. I haven't had time to pore over all the details."

The EMTs got Izzy on a stretcher and out the door to the waiting ambulance. Frank followed behind. Everyone remained silent until they left and then gradually settled into the numerous couches and armchairs around the room. Savannah waved away the hors d'oeuvres, and they were taken back to the kitchen. "This is all a ghastly accident, and I hope no lasting harm has been done."

"Don't dispose of any of the food," Danny said to the staff. "We'll need to see what's in it."

Savannah turned to me, her back to the others. "Now, you see what I mean," she said quietly. "Someone's out to finish the job they started with Quinn. Izzy Moran wasn't the intended victim. I was."

I put a hand on her arm. "I spoke with Mason earlier today, and you are about to have another house guest."

"Detective Garrett is coming—the one investigating my husband's death in Atlanta?"

I nodded.

"I'm so glad to hear that. But, why is he coming?"

"He thinks the key to your husband's death may lie in South Carolina. When he hears about this incident, he may be more convinced of that."

"I know this was no accident, and Buddy Lewis, the chief of police, will welcome his help—as long as Detective Garrett doesn't try to direct the show. Chief Lewis can be a little sensitive about that sort of thing."

"Mason knows he has no jurisdiction in South Carolina. He plans to call your chief before he comes and make sure he's welcome."

Danny was busy securing the scene of the possible crime. "No one should touch anything or leave the room. Mr. Gray, please call the police."

"Already done, sir." Dorian nodded to Savannah. "Ms. Evans had me on the phone as soon as she realized what had happened."

"You're treating us like criminals, and I, for one, won't stand for it!" This came from James Bradshaw. He straightened himself to his full height, six feet two I would guess, shoulders back, as he stood rigid in his indignation. He flicked his fine white hair away from his face.

Danny walked across the room to stand next to him. He was taller than Bradshaw and thirty pounds heavier, all of it muscle.

"Take it easy, Mr. Bradshaw," Danny said. "We're not accusing you of anything."

Savannah ignored James's comments except to nod toward one of the staff who offered Bradshaw another drink. She looked around the room. "I know this has been upsetting to everyone, and we'll sort things out as quickly as we can. I'm sure you can appreciate the need to protect Mrs. Moran's privacy. You all have smartphones, but please, don't send out any photos you may have taken this evening," she said.

People murmured their assent. Chris Evans was present with a member of his crew. They'd taken shots of the opening gathering. I heard him warn his photographer that no pictures were to be released to the press.

Savannah whispered to me, "You can imagine what this would do to my reputation if someone leaked photos to the newspapers. 'Woman fights for her life after being poisoned by Savannah Evans.'" She shuddered.

Danny overheard the conversation. "The police will want all the phones and cameras. We'll wait for the chief to decide how to proceed."

Dorian announced the arrival of Chief Lewis. The chief walked in as if he owned the place. He was a large man in his late forties I would guess. He was not especially tall but well fed with what could only be called an impressive beer belly and a conservative crew cut of brown hair touched with gray. He took charge of the situation, confiscated the phones and interviewed those present.

After an hour, he took Savannah aside. I could hear him reassuring her it was probably an accident when Mason arrived.

"I got away a lot sooner than I expected," Mason said after greeting me inside the front door.

He looked into the large parlor through opened pocket doors and saw nearly a dozen well-dressed people staring silently back at him. "What's this?"

I told him what had happened to Izzy Moran. "Savannah is certain the food was meant for her."

"Peanut allergy? That must be a hard one for a chef," he said.

"Or a ticket to success," I said. "Savannah prides herself on avoiding common allergens in her cooking. Kid friendly by taste and healthy as well, no peanuts, no dyes. She uses simple, organic ingredients. It's one reason I love her shows."

"She must have an EpiPen nearby," Mason said. "It wouldn't be a very effective way to commit murder."

"No, it wouldn't," I said.

Chief Lewis found us in the hallway. "I'm the Chief of Police for Veracrue, Boyd Lewis. Who are you?" he said to Mason.

Savannah joined us in the hallway, and I made the introductions.

"So you're the Atlanta cop I spoke to on the phone," Chief Lewis said to Mason. "You're the one investigating Quinn Nelson's death."

He kept nodding his head as he spoke as if he were sizing up Mason. Two young officers stood beside him.

"We're it for the town of Veracrue," he said when Mason asked about the number of men Chief Lewis had available. "We have more volunteer officers if we need them, and we can always draw from Beaufort. I'm glad you're here—I can use you."

Mason introduced Danny Devalle. "He used to be on the force in Atlanta until he left to work on his own. He's well trained."

"I know. We met when I came in," Lewis said.

Danny must have seen the bulldog keychain on the chief's belt. "You a Georgia Bulldogs fan?"

The Chief nodded. "Graduated from the University of Georgia twenty-five years ago."

Danny wasn't one to boast, but he could see the way to this man's heart. "For me it's ten years. I was a tight end, played all four years."

"Damn straight." The chief stopped talking and stared at Danny. "You're 'Dan the Man,' best tight end Georgia ever had! I can't believe I didn't recognize you. My name's Boyd, but my friends call me Buddy."

"I'd like to help y'all in any way I can, Buddy." Danny always had a soft Southern accent, but he could slip into a down-home variety when it was called for.

The chief beamed back at him. "You're my boy. Someone raised you right."

"I'm also here to help," Mason said. "I'll fill you in on the investigation in Atlanta."

The chief turned to Mason. "You don't sound like you're from the South, Detective Garrett."

"I grew up in Atlanta, and I'm Southern all right."

"Atlanta ain't hardly the South, but we can't all be born in God's country," Buddy Lewis said. "I forgive you." He let out a hearty laugh as if he'd just made the best joke in the world.

An attractive woman, in her thirties, entered the parlor to announce that dinner was ready. She was understated, her raven-colored hair pulled back in a tight bun. Her dark eyes registered concern.

"Thank you, Anna," Savannah said. "Anna Hayes does most of the cooking for guests and often creates recipes for my show. She's a godsend."

Savannah turned to the group of contestants and their spouses. "The best thing we can do right now is have a good dinner. No one other than Izzy Moran reported an allergy on the form I asked you to fill out. Do any of you have one you forgot to mention?"

There was a murmur of nos and a shaking of heads.

"Excellent," Savannah said. "After dinner we'll discuss plans for tomorrow. Please start without me. I'll need to speak with the chief for a few minutes."

The rest of the guests walked through the grand hallway and into the dining room. Lurleen and I remained at the door, allowing the others to pass inside. What appeared to be an antique lace table cloth covered a large mahogany table, in the middle of which was a tiered silver centerpiece holding candles in small crystal cups.

"Ah," Lurleen gasped. "An epergne, an old one by the look of it and valuable."

"A what?" I asked following her gaze. "An apern?"

"Epergne. The centerpiece," she said.

"It *is* old," Savannah said. "You have an excellent eye, Lurleen. It's been in this house since before the Civil War. It's my oldest and most prized possession."

Whatever it was called, the centerpiece was beautiful. A cut glass chandelier overhead gave a soft glow to the bright silver.

Clusters of red roses nestled in small bowls behind each place setting.

If not for what had happened in the drawing room, the dining room would have provided a lovely image of fine Southern dining. As it was, guests entered slowly, found their places and sat down without comment. Anna quickly removed the place settings for Izzy and Frank Moran.

Lurleen and I remained in the hall near Savannah, the chief, Mason, and Danny.

"I can't possibly eat dinner," Savannah said. "Who knows what might be in the food no matter how careful Anna is? If someone managed to get peanuts into the hors d'oeuvres, I'm sure they could do the same with my entree."

"You do have an EpiPen?" I said.

"Naturally. There's a first aid kit in the kitchen, but who's to say the person who did this might not try to put something else into my food. If you don't mind, I'd like you to stay near me."

I nodded.

"I'll have Anna fix us something simple," Savannah said, "enough for the chief, his officers, and Detective Garrett. We'll eat in the parlor, if that's all right with you."

At Mason's request, Danny and Lurleen joined the other guests in the dining room. They were to keep an eye on people at the table.

The rest of us found a comfortable corner of the parlor where we could talk while we waited for dinner. Mason filled the chief in on what the investigation in Atlanta had yielded.

"I know that kid Tim White," the chief said. "He was always a little off kilter. I'd say you have your man."

"We were confident he was the murderer until some details couldn't be nailed down," Mason said. "We don't know where or how he got the doxorubicin, and no one has seen him in South Carolina recently. He's had a job in Atlanta as a visiting nurse and never missed a day of work according to his employer. Now, we have this new incident. I'd like to run a check on the pharmacies and hospitals in South Carolina to see if any doxorubicin is unaccounted for. We couldn't trace it to Atlanta or Georgia."

"We'll get on it," the chief said, but he gave Mason a long look. "You here to help or take over the investigation?"

"Help," Mason said quickly. "I have no authority here. It's your case, Chief. I'm here to be an extra pair of eyes and ears."

Savannah and I were close enough to listen to the entire exchange. A small town chief of police and a big city detective could be a prickly pair.

Savannah swooped in. "Thank goodness you're both here." She put a hand on the chief's arm. "Quinn would be relieved to know you're protecting me. Thank you both."

That seemed to do the trick. The chief patted her arm and shook hands with Mason as if he meant it. "We'll keep you safe, Savannah."

"May we go on with the contest?" Savannah asked.

"That's up to you," the chief said. "You got an opinion, Detective?"

"It may be dangerous for you, Ms. Evans, whatever you decide."

"Yes." She was silent for a moment and then sat up straight. She had the look of a very determined woman. "I can't live in limbo, and I don't want to disappoint my fans. I'd like to go ahead with the filming. Perhaps I'm overreacting. The peanuts could have been in a candy bar Izzy had, you know, processed in a plant with peanuts. Of course, I'll make it clear that anyone who wishes to drop out of the contest may do so."

As it turned out, no one wanted to leave. The shooting was delayed for a day until Izzy was fully recovered.

Izzy didn't seem especially fazed by her near-death experience when she returned to the house the following morning. "I had my own EpiPen upstairs. I just forgot to bring it down with me."

Monday was spent getting us used to the lights, the cameras, the rules. The actual contest would start on Tuesday morning. Early. Because of the delay, four episodes would be shot that day. That meant two technical and two contest challenges. Savannah advised everyone to get a good night's rest.

Chris delivered the bad news to Savannah after dinner that night. Lurleen and I were standing next to her.

"Have you seen the evening papers?" he asked.

Savannah shook her head.

Chris took her arm. "I think we should talk privately."

Savannah motioned for us to come along. Chris turned on the TV in Savannah's private suite upstairs. She watched as a local news anchor announced the scandal brewing at Savannah Evan's estate. "First a husband dies mysteriously, none other than Atlanta real estate mogul J. Quinn Nelson, and now a guest has fallen ill after eating food prepared by Savannah Evans. Were both of these people poisoned?"

An amateur video showed a woman on the floor of Savannah's grand house with close-ups as Izzy was whisked away in an ambulance.

"The woman, a contestant on Savannah's *Southern Comfort Cooking Contest*, is said to be in good condition and was released from the hospital this morning."

"Oh no," Savannah said. "How could this have gotten out? What do we do now?"

"I don't know how it got out," Chris said. "We confiscated all the phones. In any case, it's best if I give the news media the true story after I run it by the chief. You better steel yourself. They won't leave this alone."

As if to verify what Chris was saying, Savannah got a call from the guard at the gate. "We've got a dozen news trucks setting up camp here. Want me to do something?"

"Just keep them outside, Emmett. It's all we can do."

Chief Lewis sent his officers to make sure the reporters stayed outside the gate. Danny went with them.

That gave Mason and me a chance to catch up. I wanted to know how the kids were doing, and he wanted to know that I was fine.

"I wish I could get you out of here," he said.

"I feel a lot safer staying put now that you're here."

Danny found us in the parlor fifteen minutes later.

"It's a zoo out there," he told Mason.

We moved to the front porch where Lurleen was already sitting. We could see lights beyond the gates and hear some noise but nothing distinct.

"There must be twenty trucks, and I'll bet more will come tomorrow," Danny said. "Buddy says not much exciting happens around here, so this is a big ticket item. I walked around the walls of the estate—probably a mile around. There's a road that winds outside it. The walls are solid stone, but only six or seven feet tall with a locked gate at the back. If someone was really determined to get in, I think they could. Buddy said he'll station his men outside tonight, but he'll need more than just one man on the front and back porch."

"I saw all the live oaks in the front with the Spanish moss as I came in," Mason said. "It could hide anyone coming through, but I can't imagine they'd try to get inside the grounds that way—Savannah has the house well-lit in the front. How's the back?"

"That's a different story," Danny said. "There are the formal gardens just off the back deck—easy enough to spot someone there, and I told Savannah to leave the garden lights on all night. But, beyond that is a strand of loblolly pines with lots of undergrowth. It'd be hard to see anyone there, and it's only a quarter moon tonight. "

"No sentinel dogs?" Mason asked.

Danny shook his head. "Savannah uses this location so often for shoots and parties, she didn't want to risk anyone getting bitten, so the answer is no."

"Then anyone could get in, maybe *did* get in to cause the peanut crisis," Mason said.

"It's possible," Danny said, "but according to Savannah the house itself has tight security. Quinn saw to that before he died."

"Savannah has enough staff that they would have reported a stranger on the grounds," I said.

"If they weren't involved," Mason said. "But, if one of them had a grudge against Savannah, it'd be easy enough to help a stranger come in—maybe as a delivery boy, something like that."

"I'll check that out," Danny said, "once I get the okay from Chief Lewis."

Chief Lewis joined us on the front porch. "Okay for what?" he asked.

"We were wondering if someone could have gotten into the house and tampered with the food," Danny said.

"You know," Chief Lewis said, "the incident could have been anything or nothing at all. Savannah's always been jumpy, and Quinn's death has only made her worse. I'll bet it was all an accident. You have to understand about Savannah. She's become a real TV personality, and for some reason she's picked up Quinn's paranoia along the way. Quinn was always looking over his shoulder, and now Savannah's doing the same."

"Quinn was murdered," I said, "so maybe his paranoia was justified."

Chief Lewis gave me a hard look. "Quinn made himself a lot of enemies—it could've been anyone who wanted to finish him off. Someone in Atlanta I'd bet—like that nutcase Timothy White. But, Savannah, she sees a problem around every corner. I've known her since she was a kid. Always high strung—the theatrical type, you know? You can't take half of what she says for fact."

Buddy Lewis settled himself in a rocking chair beside us and looked out at the wide circular driveway and the central live oak drooping over it.

"Ain't nothing like a fall evening to put your mind at rest. Or stir it up if you happen to be Savannah Evans. Has she told you this house is haunted?"

We shook our heads.

"You wait. She'll get to that. She'll have you seeing a haint every time you turn around."

"A haint?" I said.

"You're really not from the South, are you Miss Ditie? You know, a good old Southern ghost. They hang in all the best Southern mansions. It's why people paint their porch ceiling blue, like this one, to keep them away. Savannah would say it didn't work in her house. In any case, we're secure for the night. I know most of the reporters out there. They'll respect Savannah's privacy. I told them there'd be hell to pay if they didn't. We got this covered."

As it turned out the chief was wrong about that. One of his officers reported he thought he saw a man lurking outside the wall at the back of the estate, but when he went to check, no one was there.

Chapter Seven

Danny and Mason found us on the back deck a little after seven Tuesday morning. Lurleen and I were drinking coffee and soaking up the early morning sunshine. The first shoot was scheduled for eight, and we were both dressed and ready to go. Lurleen was giving me some last minute pointers on how to play to the camera.

Danny looked like he'd just stepped out of the shower, which he probably had. Mason appeared more crumpled, as if he'd slept in his clothes.

Danny said neither one of them had gotten much sleep. "I suspect you two will want to hear this," he said.

Lurleen nodded eagerly and made a place for Danny beside her.

Mason sighed and sat down next to me. He looked exhausted.

"I was near the front gate when one of the officers reported seeing a man at the back of the estate," Danny said. "It was around 11:30 last night. By the time we got there he'd disappeared. I called Mason to let him know about the situation."

"And I called the chief," Mason said. "Woke him up from a sound sleep apparently. It was after midnight, but he got over here in twenty minutes with some portable search lights."

"The chief did a good job of covering the area," Danny said. "He had us searching quadrants of the estate using the lights. I wouldn't be surprised if we woke up half the guests."

Lurleen shook her head. "Anna had coffee available at 6:30, and I'd say most of the folks stopped by to get some. They talked about being nervous with the contest starting this morning, but no one mentioned searchlights or noise last night."

"Good," Mason said.

"Maybe," Lurleen said, "they just thought it was normal life on the estate of a celebrity, lots of security, lots of light."

"Did you find the man?" I asked.

"Nope," Danny said. "Nothing appeared to be amiss and there was no sign of anyone. All outside doors were locked with no evidence of a forced entry. Buddy went back home around two. Mason and I split up and walked the perimeter for another hour. As far as I know the two officers stayed at their posts all night."

"I wouldn't be so sure of that," Lurleen said. "I saw the cute younger one with all that dark curly hair asleep on a sofa on the back deck, dead to the world."

"What time was that?" Mason asked.

"It was 3:00 or 4:00 am. I woke up—not sure why— and I wandered to the portico at the end of the hall. There he was stretched out on the deck below me."

"You didn't see or hear anything else?" Mason asked.

"No," Lurleen said. "After that I went back to sleep."

"Looks like it was all a false alarm," Danny said. "Might be some reporter wandered off for privacy and then came back unnoticed."

The four of us were sitting clustered around a low teak coffee table, and we kept our voices down. News traveled fast in this environment, and we still didn't know who had leaked the photos of Izzy Moran to the press. That meant someone might be eager to hear about the latest rumor of an intruder roaming the grounds at night.

Savannah joined us. "Thank you both for what you did last night," she said to Danny and Mason. "Buddy told me that someone was seen near the back gate. I'm relieved it turned out to be nothing."

I glanced at my watch. It was 7:20, and I was suddenly ravenous. Perhaps I did get nervous after all. I followed Savannah inside and back to the dining room with plans of grabbing a muffin.

"Don't eat," Lurleen called after me, "I just fixed your make-up."

A separate breakfast room had been set up in a back parlor with several small tables. I watched Savannah chat with participants at each one, assuring them they looked wonderful and were about to have a great time. "Just be yourselves, and you'll be fine."

I noticed she didn't pause at the table where James Bradshaw and Gertrude Flumm were seated, chatting, heads together. They stopped talking as Savannah walked by. Neither one of them looked up. Gertrude wore a sour expression, as if appearing in the contest brought her no pleasure. Her hair was pulled back in a bun and covered with a net. She was slight and maybe an inch or two taller than me, but she looked as if her backbone had a steel rod in it. James slumped over his coffee. I remembered how he'd looked at Savannah's party—tall and elegant, perfectly coiffed. Now, his hair was in disarray and his outfit was decidedly casual—tan khakis and a maroon polo shirt.

Flumm and Bradshaw were both locals but had chosen to stay in the house as guests. I suppose it made sense. That way they could focus on the contest.

After breakfast the entire atmosphere changed from relaxed to business-like. Savannah had a make-up and hair specialist available on set to take care of last minute concerns.

The kitchen set was enormous. Contestants had their own islands on which to work that included an oven and stove top to one side. We had a prep table behind us for supplies. It looked as if Savannah had studied the set-up from the *Great British Baking Contest*, except we weren't housed in a tent outside the mansion.

Shooting was to start promptly at eight. Savannah was always prompt according to Chris Evans. He told me it was part of what made her empire such a success. Everything started and ended on time. He said the other key to Savannah's success was Anna. She was the power behind the throne—the chef who could take any set of ingredients and produce an outstanding and original creation.

"If Anna ever gets her own show," Chris said as he checked my station, "Savannah might be out of a job." He glanced around as if afraid someone might have overheard his comment. "Don't get me wrong, Savannah's an amazing entrepreneur. She deserves every bit of success she's achieved—she's just not a great cook."

"Funny you should say that," I whispered back. "A friend commented that she'd never seen Savannah do much cooking on her shows."

"Your friend is right. Just don't spread that around."

Chris glanced at his watch and became mister professional. "I have two more stations to check. You're good. Please don't wander off."

At two minutes to eight, Savannah reappeared. She began speaking after a signal from Chris. "We'll start the contest with a technical challenge. Your first task is to prepare a chocolate pudding cake. That will get you warmed up for your next assignment, banana pudding."

She smiled broadly for the camera.

"You have the ingredients on the sheet in front of you. You have one hour. What I want to taste is a crunchy chocolate layer over a bubbling ooze of luscious decadent chocolate pudding. On your mark, get set, create."

I studied the ingredients. This didn't sound too hard. I'd made a flourless chocolate cake in the past, and this list of ingredients looked similar. The hour flew by.

The lights were a lot brighter and hotter than I expected. Air conditioning going full blast made the set tolerable. The cameras didn't bother me much, but I could see other contestants either nervous or happy to see the camera when it focused on them.

Pepper Young was one of the ones eager to catch the cameraman's eye. When she did, she was all smiles. Did she have higher aspirations than a cameo on the Savannah Evans's show?

Chris posted minutes left and then told us to step away from the table when the time was up. The cameras were stopped as we placed each of our entries on the tasting table with a card face down that had our name on it.

Savannah swirled into the room and stood behind the table. "None of you will be eliminated from this round, but you will receive positive or negative points based on how well you executed the technical challenge. She took her time sampling each entry with comments as she proceeded down the line. "This one looks a little overdone. I can't seem to find any of that gooey pudding I was hoping for." She'd turn over the card, and the camera would catch the contestant's expression. Mine was last. "Now, this is what I'm talking about," she said after she'd taken a bite. "Chocolaty crunch on the outside and irresistible dark pudding coming through with each bite. Outstanding."

I smiled, and Lurleen, seated in the front row, beamed back at me. She would have hooted and hollered if Chris had not been very clear about silence from the audience. Gertrude Flumm and I tied for first place. I thought for a moment Gertrude might contest the decision. Instead, she graciously shook my hand. "Well done."

James Bradshaw and Pepper Young tied for last place. James was all soup and no crust. Pepper's was dry. "Cooked to within an inch of its life," Savannah said, not too kindly.

We were given a half-hour break to freshen up and grab a snack. Lurleen started speaking immediately. "You were fantastic," she said, "such a pro. So calm under pressure. I guess it didn't hurt that Jason and Lucie love your flourless cake."

"It didn't hurt a bit. Let's find the boys."

"The boys, Mason and Danny, were with Chief Lewis in the front parlor. "All quiet here," the chief said. "Nothing to worry about. You boys look dead to the world. Now, Danny, here, he's a young man, don't need his sleep. But, you, Detective Garrett, you look like you could use a nap. A man your age can't stay up all night and not pay for it."

Mason and Buddy Lewis were contemporaries. If anything, the chief was probably a year or two older, I'd guess. Mason didn't respond.

"I won't budge from here before dinner," Chief Lewis said.

"I'll take you up on the idea of a break, chief," Mason said, "after I hear how the morning went. How was it, Ditie?"

"Ditie won the technical challenge! First place." Lurleen said.

"A tie for first place," I said. "I'll walk you upstairs, Mason."

Mason had been given a bedroom at the end of the hall where Lurleen and I were staying. I lay down with him, hoping we might talk for a few minutes. Mason fell asleep before I could say a word, so I left him to take his much-needed nap. The door across the hall was open, and I heard Peter and Pepper Young talking. Arguing was more like it.

"She likes you, maybe too much, but she certainly doesn't like me," Pepper said. "She went out of her way to humiliate me."

"Savannah's all right," Peter said. "You're taking this contest too seriously. You need to settle down."

Peter saw me in the hallway. He looked annoyed and then pasted on a fake smile, as he closed the door. I walked to the end of the hall and entered the small enclosed porch Lurleen had found the night before, the one that looked out on the back of the estate. The formal gardens were lovely with water flowing from a multi-tiered cast iron fountain in the center of the garden. Beyond that were raised beds of flowers, and past that all I could see was a strand of trees, loblolly pines and other ones I couldn't identify— thick enough to hide a man or an army of men. A barely discernible path seemed to meander through the woods toward the back of the property.

I hoped Danny was right —that the sighting of someone outside the back gate was nothing to be concerned about.

Chief Lewis described Savannah as overly dramatic, but she didn't make up the fact that Quinn had been murdered or that someone had introduced peanuts into hors d'oeuvres that were meant to be allergen free.

I wandered back to the set ten minutes before the next shoot.

This time it was Anna who came around to make sure we had what we needed. My recipe for banana pudding was simple. I had a friend in Atlanta who made the best banana pudding I'd ever eaten. I decided to tweak her recipe with cardamom and coconut. One of the Middle Eastern refugee families I treated in the clinic often used cardamom and banana in their recipes and sometimes brought me a dish as a treat. Everything they offered me was delicious. I thought coconut might add another complimentary taste.

Anna congratulated me on the technical challenge from the morning. "I watched you on the monitor. You were very relaxed, and I sampled some of your pudding cake. It was delicious."

Chris got us ready a little before ten.

Savannah introduced the next segment—to improve on her banana pudding. She smiled broadly at the cameras and at us. Then she left the set.

I made sure all my ingredients were in place, checked my watch, and saw that I had time to make my own vanilla wafers. I'd practiced this at home, and I knew I could get things done in the hour we had.

We took a five-minute break in the middle of the shoot, which gave us time to wipe the sweat off our brows and drink a little water. Chris came up to me. "Any chance you could look a little more anxious? Maybe glance at your watch from time to time?"

Lurleen was standing beside me at the break. "You don't know Ditie," she said to Chris. "The more nervous she gets the calmer she looks. And baking never makes her anxious in the first place."

Chris nodded and moved on.

When time was up, the six of us brought our presentations to the long table where Savannah would sit and taste. We were told to make two portions.

The presentations came in all varieties. One person used a parfait glass with layers of banana, wafers, and custard. Another had concocted what looked like Baked Alaska. It seemed to me I might be the one eliminated in this first round.

We were told to leave the kitchen for the next part of the contest. Savannah was not to get any clues from us as to whose dessert she was tasting. I was more than happy to move into the comfort of the dining room.

Lurleen joined me there. She'd been seated in the kitchen audience along with the spouses of the other contestants. "Savannah asked me to be a taster for the first segment! I'm so excited, but you must realize I can't choose you simply because you're my best friend."

"I understand, Lurleen. You will need to vote for the rightful winner—no hard feelings, I promise."

On a cue from Chris, Lurleen checked herself in a mirror in the dining room and walked back onto the set. Anna ushered us into a small office adjacent to the kitchen where we could watch what was going on through closed circuit TV.

Savannah introduced Lurleen as a dear friend from Atlanta who had volunteered to help with the difficult decision for this first round. Lurleen nodded to the camera.

Savannah and Lurleen took a bite of each dessert.

Savannah discussed the pros and cons of the submissions. She was clear, kind, and direct. Then she conferred with Lurleen and labeled submissions one, two, and three. We were brought back in.

Rose Kirkwood took first place. Her husband was right. She made very fine banana pudding apparently. I took second. Gertrude Flumm took third and looked miffed that she hadn't won. We three were allowed to leave the room. The remaining three contestants stood together—James Bradshaw, Izzy Moran, and Pepper Young.

Savannah brought out the banana pudding she liked least. "While it has some fine qualities, the custard is a little too sweet and the bananas were not cut with enough care." She opened the envelope that revealed the name of the baker. "I'm so sorry, Pepper, but you have been 'panned' from the competition. You'll help me taste."

Pepper blushed. "Banana pudding isn't my specialty. I was hoping for cobbler."

The second episode ended.

Savannah thanked everyone for their efforts. She said lunch would be served in half an hour, and a third taping would begin at two.

Before lunch, Chief Lewis asked if we might meet in Savannah's office upstairs. By "we" he meant me, Mason, Danny, and Savannah. Lurleen looked so hurt at being excluded that the chief agreed to let her come along.

"I want to bring you up to date," the chief said. "As you know the rumor of a man on the grounds has not been confirmed. As to the peanut incident and the leaking of photos to the press, that's another matter. We're doing background checks on all contestants and the staff. So far we haven't turned up anything."

"You won't find anything on my staff, Buddy," Savannah said. "They come vetted. If, for any reason they're not suitable, they're gone within thirty days."

"Can we get a list of the ones that didn't make the cut?" Mason asked. "The ones that might bear a grudge against you?"

"Certainly. I'll have Anna prepare it for you."

"You have a large staff?" Mason asked.

"It's a big empire, but I'm very hands on. I know what everyone is up to. Nothing gets by me."

"I hope you're right," the chief said, "but that don't mean we won't check on folks."

"I understand, Buddy. Someone wants to bring me down. They've already robbed me of my life blood. Quinn was everything to me."

Savannah started to cry.

Chief Lewis led her to the sofa. "You sit down here, Savannah. I'll get Anna and she'll know what to do."

Instead, it was Lurleen who seemed to know what was needed. She sat beside Savannah and put her arm around her, offering her tissues as she cried.

"Lurleen, I'm so glad you're here," Savannah said. "You men can go about your business and don't bother Anna. She has enough on her hands managing lunch for twenty. Ditie, Lurleen, and I will be down in a few minutes."

"You must be so upset about everything," Lurleen said after the others left.

"I miss Quinn so much. I can't sleep and even my dog, Saffron, is suffering. She wouldn't stay in the room with me last night. She whined until I opened the bedroom door. Then she roamed the halls looking for Quinn I'm sure."

As if on cue, or perhaps from hearing her name mentioned, a large yellow lab wandered in from Savannah's adjacent bedroom and settled at Savannah's feet.

"She's beautiful," I said.

Savannah nodded. "She's sweet and she's smart. If anyone tried to attack me when Saffron was around, she'd defend me with her life."

"Sounds like Ditie's dog, Hermione," Lurleen said.

"I thought I heard a dog last night," I said, "crying to get in or out of some place. Then the noise stopped abruptly, and I thought I must be dreaming."

"Saffron *was* behaving strangely last night." Savannah said. "I know she was bothered by all the lights and noise, and then when the noise finally stopped, she was still restless. She moaned to get out of my room and was gone for half an hour in the early morning."

"You let her outside?" I asked.

"No. I let her roam the halls, but when she came back, I didn't let her out again because I was afraid she'd disturb the other guests. I'm sorry she bothered you."

"She didn't bother me," I said. "I just wondered what made her upset."

Savannah nodded. "She's settled now, thank goodness. She's such a comfort to me when everything about the future looks so uncertain."

"Mason and Danny will find out what's going on," Lurleen said, "along with Buddy."

"Buddy?" I asked, looking at Lurleen.

"The chief insisted I call him that. He said I looked familiar to him, reminded him of an old girlfriend. No harm in that, is there?"

"I guess not. As long as Danny doesn't mind," I said.

"The chief isn't hitting on me," Lurleen said.

"Buddy is devoted to his wife," Savannah said. "Always has been, and that's after twenty years of marriage. She's pretty strait-laced, so he toes the line."

Savannah looked at us and smiled. "I'm so glad you're both here. Sometimes you need women around, and Anna is consumed with all the meals she has to prepare for the contestants."

She took Lurleen's hand and squeezed it. "I haven't had any time to grieve for Quinn. I suppose it's a good thing in a way—this contest keeps me from falling apart."

I moved an antique straight-backed chair closer to the couch where Savannah and Lurleen were sitting. "Do you have any idea when or how Quinn got the doxorubicin?"

"You mean the drug that killed him?"

"Yes. It's only given intravenously, " I said. "It's likely he got multiple doses—you mentioned that his hair started falling out several weeks before he died. There would be no way to predict when the drug would kill him or even if it would ever be fatal, but it is a drug that's hard on the heart."

"Did you know Quinn had had a second heart attack two weeks before the party?" Savannah asked.

"Yes," I said.

"Could the drug, the doxy—"

"Doxorubicin."

"Could that drug have caused his heart attacks?"

"It's possible," I said, "or it could have worsened his condition, brought on his congestive heart failure."

Savannah nodded slowly and dried her eyes.

"Quinn was always doing his own thing during the day, as I was. He had his main office in downtown Atlanta with a more informal one here. Even when the doctors told him to take it easy, he didn't do that. I got the feeling he'd started going in a New-Age direction about his health. He said he'd located a medical guru who helped men find their vigor again. I think it really bothered him that he couldn't—you know—perform the way he used to. He wouldn't tell me anymore than that."

"Do the police know about this?" I asked.

"I didn't tell them. It seemed so private."

"It could be important," I said.

"Yes, I can see that now. I'll talk to Buddy and look through Quinn's appointment book here—maybe he wrote something down about where he went for treatment. I'm sure the police have gone through his papers in Atlanta."

"Did he go to Atlanta often?" I asked.

"Not these days. It's a long drive, and Quinn tired easily."

"I'll let Mason and Danny know what you've told me," I said.

"Yes, yes, of course." Savannah glanced at her watch. "It's late. We need to get downstairs to lunch or everyone will worry about us."

We joined the others in the dining room. Anna served a lovely lunch of endive, apple and chicken salad with homemade rolls. Savannah assured us that once we completed the afternoon shoots the rest of the week would run smoothly. I wasn't sure I believed her.

Chapter Eight

Savannah sat with the contestants at lunch, but she claimed she wasn't hungry. Anna had prepared what looked like a green milkshake for her, and Savannah announced she was on a special detox diet.

I, for one, had heard her criticize those liquid detox diets, saying all they did was eliminate water and could be dangerous if they went on for more than forty-eight hours. I agreed with her. She'd always said what a person needed to do to slim down or stay healthy was simply eat natural foods in moderation. She was one of those cooks who recommended checking labels. If it had ingredients you couldn't pronounce, you shouldn't eat it, and the less processed food the better.

The only explanation was that Savannah was afraid of what someone might put in her food. She took one sip of what looked like frothy seaweed, tried not to grimace, and set it aside. She fidgeted with her napkin, until she noticed I was watching her. Then she put her hands under the table where I couldn't see them.

She wasn't the only one who seemed nervous. It might be that everyone knew about the rumor of a night time invader. I had overheard Frank and Izzy talking about it this morning after the second shoot ended.

"Do you think he actually got in the house?" Izzy asked.

"Maybe," Frank said.

"Should we be worried?"

I couldn't hear Frank's response. I tried to catch up with them, but they seemed to be avoiding me.

Savannah attempted to calm people's nerves. "You all did a fabulous job this morning," she said, "and I can see the competition is going to be tough. Do you have any questions before the afternoon taping?"

"Everything happens so fast," Rose said. "Do we ever get to do a second take?"

"Not usually, unless some problem with the equipment makes that necessary. The show's done in real time," Savannah said. "That's what makes it so exciting. Don't worry about small problems. Just carry on. That's what Julia Child would say. You've watched her old cooking shows I'm sure. She'd pick up a chicken she dropped on the floor and proceed as if nothing had happened. Sometimes a mistake or two is what makes a show charming."

Gertrude Flumm, seated at the end of the table, spoke up. "You do know Julia Child never dropped a chicken on TV, Savannah—that's a myth. You need to do some fact checking. It wouldn't hurt your recipes if you did that with them as well."

Savannah's warm complexion grew redder, but she didn't comment. Neither did anyone else, and for a few seconds we sat in silence. It was Lurleen who rescued the situation.

"I've watched all her shows," Lurleen said. "She may not have dropped a chicken, I can't recall, but she certainly dropped everything else."

Savannah gave her what looked like a grateful smile.

I couldn't remember Lurleen ever watching a complete Julia Child episode. That was something Lucie and I might do on a rainy Saturday afternoon. I had the shows archived.

The contestants in the room sipped a final cup of coffee.

The non-contestants were drinking wine, a French Sauvignon Blanc, and Lurleen was in heaven. "My favorite," she said to Savannah.

"You must come to one of my dinners, Lurleen. We have them a few times a year in my penthouse in Atlanta and feature a particular cuisine. I think French is on the agenda, isn't it, Anna?"

"In two months," Anna smiled. "In January."

"Everyone needs a little pick-me-up after the holiday season and what better way to do it than with a fine French meal," Savannah said. "You are obviously a person with French tastes."

"Shall I put you on the list, Ms. du Trois?" Anna asked.

"*Mais oui,*" Lurleen said.

"Does your family still live in France?" Savannah asked.

Lurleen blushed.

"No." She hesitated. "I have no family. My aunt died a few years ago."

"I'm so sorry to hear that. Where did she live in France?"

Again, Lurleen hesitated.

I stepped in. "She lived all over France including Provence. Lurleen has wonderful stories about her."

It was one of the few times I'd seen Lurleen look so vulnerable. I never knew when her stories were true or a figment of her lively imagination. Normally, I didn't worry about it, but it was obvious that something about this trip—maybe our proximity to Beaufort— had completely unnerved her.

"I see." Savannah smiled and changed the subject. She turned to George Kirkwood on her right. "You must be so proud of your wife."

"Always am."

George looked uncomfortable in his jacket, and his thinning gray hair was slicked down either with water or some kind of gel.

"What do you do for a living?" Savannah asked.

"Pig farmer, south Georgia."

Savannah made a few more gentle attempts to engage him in conversation and when she found it only seemed to make him more uncomfortable, she turned her attention elsewhere.

She looked relieved when lunch was over and she could excuse herself.

The non-contestants were free to do whatever they wanted for the afternoon. The rest of us were given twenty minutes to freshen up before returning to the kitchen set for our next assignment.

At five minutes to two, we were in our places. Precisely at two the lights came on and cameras began rolling. Savannah appeared in a new fall dress with earth tones. She wore a chunky amber necklace that reflected the tawny highlights in her hair—hair that was so straight and smooth, I felt a ping of jealousy. Hers fell just at her chin. My unruly dark curls always had to be short, so I didn't look like a wild woman and scare the small children in my practice.

Lurleen motioned to me from the audience, pantomiming a necklace and rubbing her fingers together. "Very expensive," she mouthed to me.

Savannah smiled at the camera and then at us as she announced the next technical challenge—beignets.

"These may not sound like Southern pastry, but beignets are the quintessential New Orleans breakfast. You should travel there if for no other reason than to have a truly perfect beignet with New Orleans' wonderful chicory coffee."

None of us had to fake the dismay on our faces.

I'd eaten one beignet in my life in a restaurant on Peachtree Street. To me it tasted like powdered sugar and air. I'd never tried to make it—something I seriously regretted at the moment.

The recipe indicated the mixture should be chilled for up to twenty-four hours.

Gertrude Flumm spoke up. "What do you want us to do, Savannah?" Her hands were on her hips, and she sounded as if she were talking to a recalcitrant child, not a celebrity chef. "Obviously, we can't complete this assignment in one shoot."

Savannah chopped across her neck to indicate cameras should stop rolling. They did. "There's no need to get huffy, Gertrude. You'll do the prep and then put the dough in the refrigerator. We'll move on to the next contest, Southern biscuits with a twist, and then come back and finish up the beignets tomorrow morning. It will all work out fine."

"You could have told us that in the beginning," Gertrude said.

"It's good to see how contestants deal with unanticipated events," Savannah said.

Gertrude took that as a personal dig. "I handle emergencies every day in my cafe. I just don't like running into problems that don't need to be problems in the first place."

Savannah motioned for Chris to start the cameras rolling once more. "As one of our oldest cooks pointed out—by that I mean one of our most experienced contestants—beignet dough must chill for up to twenty-four hours. We've built that into this technical challenge."

We all put the ingredients together and tried to determine how much flour to add and how long to beat the dough. I assumed it should stay sticky, so I went easy on the flour. Mine went into the refrigerator almost before anyone else's. When it was clear everyone had finished, Chris signaled the cameras to stop rolling.

"Take a ten-minute break," Chris said to us, "and then we'll start your next challenge."

Lurleen insisted I wear one of her scarves to look like I had on a new outfit.

When we were back on set at our respective stations, Savannah appeared, once again all smiles. She had changed into a soft brown skirt and sweater that accentuated the deep brown of her eyes. "Your challenge today will be Southern biscuits with a novel twist."

We could decide what that novel twist would be—savory or sweet, it didn't matter. Savannah exited, and Chris took over managing the production as he had in the morning.

Peter Young and George Kirkwood had left the audience before we started on the beignets. Lurleen exited now, either because she was tired of watching people cook or because she wanted to do some snooping.

Frank Moran stayed. Apparently, he wasn't willing to let Izzy out of his sight.

After half an hour, we were told to take a five-minute break to drink water and cool off. It was a relief to have the giant lights shut down. Lurleen ran up to me and urged me into a corner of the kitchen where she could speak freely.

"There's a serious problem," she said. "I mean serious! I heard George Kirkwood talking to Buddy and Mason just now."

I glanced at my watch. "I have to get back on set in a couple of minutes."

"I'll make this fast. George said he'd been restless and had walked the entire estate after lunch, a half mile in each direction. Said he just needed to be outside—that's how he normally spent his days. He found an overgrown path leading to the back gate. He saw signs that something big had been dragged along the path—perhaps a large sack. In a few areas he saw what looked like splatters of blood."

"What?" I asked. I wondered if Lurleen was embellishing the story, but I could see by the look on her face she was deadly serious.

"George said he'd slaughtered enough pigs to recognize blood when he saw it. What he didn't find was a dead animal. His search ended at the back gate, which was securely locked. He looked through the slatted wood. All he saw beyond the gate was a roadway and behind that more woods.

"Danny came up as George was talking and said the back gate was big enough to drive a truck through if it was wide open. Danny also said it had been padlocked when he examined it last night. It would have needed a key to open it."

"How did Chief Lewis and Mason react?" I asked.

"They looked worried. George said he wasn't sure it was any of his business, but after what happened to Izzy Moran and Quinn Nelson, he thought he needed to report it. He'd also heard the rumor that a stranger had been spotted near the gate last night."

"I hope it was a dead animal that accounted for the blood." That was all I had time to say. Chris motioned me back to my table and nodded to Lurleen to leave the kitchen.

"Buddy and Mason are going out with George to search for whatever it might be," Lurleen whispered to me as she left.

"Please stay put," I said to her.

"Danny already made me promise."

We had twenty minutes to finish our biscuits. I was making a variation on my Confederate biscuits, which were not quite as light as the more traditional ones. I made an almond butter and blueberry filling, which the kids loved.

Two minutes before time was up, Chris told us to plate three samples, as there would be three tasters today. Pepper Young was one of them and appeared on the set as if she were coming to a fashion shoot. She didn't seem pleased when Lurleen sat down beside her.

Over lunch I'd heard Savannah tell Lurleen how much the camera loved her. With Lurleen's striking bone structure, hazel eyes, and gleaming copper curls, how could that not be true?

Normally, this would have made Lurleen's day, but this afternoon when she came onto the kitchen set, she looked as if she were being dragged into a holding cell for questioning. No doubt she wanted to know what Mason and the chief discovered.

My hope was that they found nothing at all.

Gertrude Flumm, or Granny Flumm as she now insisted we call her, won the biscuit competition and James Bradshaw was eliminated. I fell in the middle—this time in the lower half. Savannah said that while my biscuits were tasty, they were not as original as she might have hoped.

.As we left the competition, I heard Chris tell Savannah that James seemed distracted during the afternoon contest. She responded that his biscuits were inedible.

Once the segment was finished, I ran up to my room to call the kids. I was concerned about what they might have seen in the papers—Lucie especially. It was Josh who picked up.

"Tommy, Eddie and the kids are busy getting dinner ready," he said.

"So they can't hear us?" I asked.

"No. You're worried about the newspapers and TV, aren't you?"

"Yes," I said. "Lucie has the nose of a reporter, so I'm wondering what news has made its way to Atlanta."

"We've heard bits and pieces about a woman having an allergic reaction to some food Savannah prepared. It only made the news because of what happened to Quinn Nelson, and we've kept the kids away from the newspapers and television."

"Good. Thank you. You'll need to keep that up—there may be more trouble brewing."

"Are you all right?"

"For now. Lucie hasn't seemed anxious about me?"

"No," Josh said. "Eddie is giving Lucie her own cooking school, so they're both happy as can be."

"That's a relief."

"Don't worry about us, Ditie. We're fine," Josh said. "Just take care of yourself. I'll get the kids so they can talk to you."

I could hear feet scampering in from the kitchen. Jason picked up first. "Mommy, hi. I miss you. When are you coming home?"

"I miss you, too. I'll be home at the end of the week."

"I'm a magician, Mommy. That's what Uncle Tommy says. He's going to get me a wand and a cape tomorrow. I will trick you when you come home."

"I can't wait." I smiled. It was impossible not to smile at Jason, my wonderful lively little boy. "I love you."

"I love you, Mommy."

Lucie hopped on the phone next. She sounded as happy as Jason did. "Eddie says I'm a wonderful cook. I'll make you the best dinner when you get home, Aunt Di—all by myself."

"That, dear heart, will be something to look forward to. Is everyone getting fat with Eddie's cooking and yours?"

"Uncle Tommy pats his stomach after every meal and says he has to stop eating like this. But, he never does, Aunt Di. Are you having fun?"

"I am, sweetheart." It was true, as long as I thought about what fun the kids were having. "I'm learning a lot." I told Lucie how much I loved her.

"I love you too, Mama Di." Lucie still wasn't quite sure what she wanted to call me. She'd sort it out over time.

As soon as I got off the phone, Lurleen entered my bedroom without knocking, took me by the arm, and marched me to her room. Then she dramatically closed the door. "I told Danny to find us here after the taping was over."

Danny showed up five minutes later.

"We don't know much more at the moment," Danny said, "but it isn't looking good. I'm only telling you, Lurleen, so you won't go around asking questions and putting yourself in danger."

Lurleen looked annoyed for a second and then nodded. "I understand. Now, tell us what you've found."

"Mason and Buddy went to see what was out there. Mason asked me to make sure no staff were missing."

"That means they think a dead body has been dragged off the premises?" I asked.

"It seems possible," Danny said.

"And?" Lurleen asked.

"All staff are accounted for. Buddy had a key to the back gate, so that's where he and Mason were headed."

"So," Lurleen said, "someone could have dragged a large sack, dripping with blood, containing a dead body to the back gate and then driven away with it."

"The only problem with that," Danny said, "is we haven't found a body, and no one appears to be missing."

Before Danny finished speaking, Mason knocked on the door and came in without waiting to be invited.

"We found him."

"Who?" I asked.

"The dead man," Mason said. "Chief Lewis knows the area, so he and I headed out to examine the road beyond the estate. I sent Danny back to keep an eye on things here. It looked from tracks as if a truck had backed onto the estate—gate must have been open—and then headed down the road. You didn't see any tracks last night, did you Danny?"

"No. This must have happened after we all went to bed around 3:00 am. I wonder if that's what woke you up, Lurleen? Some noise out back."

"Could have been. I left my window open to get a breeze. As I told you, all I saw was that officer sound asleep. I'll bet Buddy's going to have his hide."

"Already has," Danny said.

"We followed the tracks," Mason said. "They headed south on the road and then seemed to disappear. We walked for a quarter mile before we spotted them again."

Mason looked grim.

"It appeared that the truck had pulled over and stopped. It was a heavily wooded area with some paths running through it, maybe for hikers in the area. We searched and saw that something had been dragged along a path leading from the small parking area.

"The path dead ended into a leafy ravine. The chief said the ground was still damp from a rain they had a few days ago.

"He climbed into it, raked back some leaves and found what we were both afraid we might find. First a hand, then a face. A man, in his thirties, clean-shaven, was wearing bloody pajamas, probably shot through the side of his head while he was sleeping. No ID on him. A bloody potato sack was found near by—that's probably how someone got him off the estate."

I wondered why Mason was being so graphic. He answered my question before I could ask it.

"I want you both to know how dangerous this has become. A man has been murdered, apparently on the estate. I want you to go home as soon as you can."

It was after six when everyone heard the news. The chief gathered the contestants, spouses, and all the staff in the parlor to tell them what had been discovered outside the grounds. He didn't comment on the fact that the dead man was wearing pajamas or that the murder had most likely occurred on the estate, probably within the house. He passed around a picture of the dead man's face. It was taken so we couldn't see his shattered skull. No one in the room claimed to recognize him.

"I assume this means we all go home now," Peter Young said.

"No one can leave the estate, until I say so," Buddy responded. "And I ain't saying so right now."

The chief turned to Young, who had always seemed unflappable to me. This evening, he was clearly agitated, and his carefully groomed exterior couldn't hide his anxious expression.

"It's odd *you'd* be asking about that, Mr. Young," Buddy said. "You are one of the people we especially want to talk to. You were in Quinn Nelson's employ—so I can't help wondering what you're doing here—what with Quinn being dead and all."

Chapter Nine

Peter Young worked for Quinn Nelson? I looked at Lurleen to see if she knew about this. Her eyes were wide and she shook her head ever so slightly. The people who didn't look surprised were Savannah and Pepper.

Peter jumped up as if he might threaten the chief with physical violence.

Pepper also stood and put a hand on her husband's arm. "He's just asking questions, Peter, no harm in that."

The rest of us remained seated and silent.

Anna entered the parlor. Behind her stood two staff members with trays of champagne. Then she saw the expression on everyone's face and Savannah's wave to send them out of the room.

"Dinner will be served at seven thirty. There will be no cocktail hour preceding the meal," Anna announced and left. The staff followed her back to the kitchen.

Chief Lewis told us to go to our rooms and remain there until dinner.

"I'll be interviewing each of you privately, and I'll start with you, Mr. Young. You, Miss Pepper, can run along and I'll call on you when we need to talk."

She whispered something to Peter and then left. The rest of the contestants and spouses filed out.

I started to leave when Lurleen put a very strong hand on my arm. "We're not going anywhere. I convinced the chief we could be of use to him. Unofficial investigators. The way we were for the CWR murders."

"CWR?" I asked.

"The Civil War Reenactment murders. The chief was all over that."

I sighed and said nothing more.

Chief Lewis acknowledged us and closed the pocket doors to the parlor.

"I'm not talking with these people in the room," Peter said. "I want my lawyer."

"Okay, we can do this however you like," the chief said. "You can call your lawyer. We can go to my office in town past all the reporters at the gate who are hungry for news. Or we can talk here, casual like. It sure seems to me if you have nothing to hide, you'd want to get this interview over with as quietly as possible."

Peter looked at us.

"You must be kidding if you think I'll say anything in the presence of these two women."

"These women have worked undercover for the Atlanta police," Chief Lewis said.

I looked at Lurleen.

"We did work undercover," she whispered, "just not officially. Buddy doesn't care so much about credentials. He cares more about results."

"They'll stay because I say they'll stay."

Danny burst in and approached Chief Lewis.

The chief must have seen an urgency in Danny's face. "We'll need to delay this interview briefly. Young, go to your room and think about what I'm offering. I'll get back to you later."

Peter Young looked as if he'd just been given a 'get out of jail free' card.

Danny closed the pocket doors behind him.

"What you got for me, Danny?" the chief asked.

"I've got an ID on the dead man. Where's Mason?"

"Mason is interviewing the gardeners. Come with me," Chief Lewis said. He opened the doors and led Danny upstairs to a third floor room.

Lurleen and I followed them.

"This is Quinn's old office," he said to Danny. "He won't be needing it anymore. We'll use it as our headquarters for now."

It was a small office, about half the size of Savannah's suite, with a row of cabinets along the back wall and a large mahogany desk taking up most of the space in the room. The desk was cluttered with papers as if no one had disturbed it since Quinn's death. An opened door led to a half bath and to one side of the door stood a well-stocked bar on top of a mahogany credenza.

I couldn't escape the unsettled feeling that Quinn might lumber in and find us in his private space.

Chief Lewis saw us standing in the room, uncertain whether to go or stay.

"Lurleen, Dr. Brown, sit," the chief said.

Danny started to protest, and the chief raised one hand. "I like you, boy, but this is my investigation. I'll have the people I want here. Understood?"

Danny nodded.

Lewis pointed to the sleek gray sofa that lined the wall beside the door to the hall. Lurleen and I sank into its soft, deep cushions. I could imagine Quinn found this a comfortable place to rest.

"I know who you are, Dr. Brown," Chief Lewis said. "And I bet I know why Savannah was so eager to have you in the contest. It's the same reason I let you stay in the parlor downstairs."

Lurleen gave me a smug smile.

He took a seat in the chair behind Quinn's desk. "I have some friends big into Civil War reenactments, and of course everyone knows what you did with the Sandler case. You're establishing quite a reputation as an amateur detective, whether you like it or not."

"You're correct about Savannah, chief," I said. "She did invite me with the idea I might help figure out what's been going on."

"Call me Buddy. We're not strangers anymore."

He leaned back in what Lurleen whispered was a vintage Eames desk chair.

"That set them back a few thousand," she said. "And that's an antique Regency desk—meant to impress."

The chief looked as if he were in charge of the universe by the way he dominated the room. The sofa put us at a real disadvantage in that we were several inches lower than the chief. Was that how Quinn wanted it? Everyone who sat in that room had to look up to him, literally.

I began to wonder if Quinn was all smoke and mirrors. Did he really have the empire he'd claimed he possessed or was it all posturing—the way the chief was posturing now?

"You're saying we can stay and listen to what Danny has to tell you?" I said.

"I don't mind if you do," Chief Lewis said. "That boyfriend of yours, Dr. Brown, he won't like it. He's kind of a stickler for protocol. But, this ain't his investigation, and as long as you're here, I don't see why you can't help."

Danny, standing beside the desk, looked anything but pleased.

"Go on, Dan," the chief said. "Tell us what you know."

"The news media are all over this murder. Some have been camped outside the gate since the incident with Izzy Moran's peanut allergy, but now we have at least thirty news trucks—local and national."

"I know that, Dan. I got eyes," the chief said. "What'd you find out?"

"I passed around the photo, and a journalist from Charleston recognized the dead man. He made a sick joke about it. He said it was Nick Davis, a freelance reporter. Claimed Nick always wanted to make it big with a front-page story and now he had."

"I hate disrespect for the dead," the chief said. "You got the name of the journalist who mocked Davis' death?"

Danny nodded.

"No one claims to have seen Davis for the past two days," Danny continued. "They assumed he'd gone home when the allergy story ran out of steam."

Savannah entered the room without knocking. "What's this? You've taken over Quinn's office? You did this without asking me?"

"Most convenient place to meet, Savannah. Quinn won't be needing it anymore."

"Quinn hasn't been dead a month," she said with a catch in her voice, "and you act as if his death has no meaning."

"You know that ain't true, Miss Savannah. Quinn and I were friends, and I spent a lot of time in this room. Now, tell me why you're here."

"I need to know what's happening."

Chief Lewis stood and motioned to a place on the couch. Lurleen and I moved over, so she could sit between us.

"You do need to hear this, Savannah," the chief said. "We have an ID on the dead man—Nick Davis. That name mean anything to you?"

"No," she said. "Should it?"

"He's a reporter, local, been around for a while."

"I don't read the local press," Savannah said. "I don't have time when I'm here."

"Nick Davis won't stay local now. He was shot in the head while he was sleeping—looks like it anyway. He was in his pajamas. His body was dragged along a path in the back and dumped in the woods nearby."

"Oh God," Savannah said. "Are you suggesting he was killed on the estate, in the house?"

"Sure looks like it."

"What was he doing in my house?" Savannah asked.

"That's the million-dollar question, ain't it?" the chief said.

Savannah paled. "Do the contestants know?"

"Not yet," Buddy said, "but they will."

"All of them will want to leave," Savannah said.

"Sure they will, but that's not gonna happen until we know more," Buddy said. "A hell of a lot more. I guess that's it for now."

Savannah stood, clearly confused about what she needed to do next.

"Don't talk to anyone about this," the chief said. "Go to your room and stay there. I'll let you know what we're going to do next once I sort it out."

Savannah nodded and looked at Lurleen and me. "I don't want to be alone right now. Will you two come with me?"

Chief Lewis gave that idea his blessing, and Danny nodded his approval.

"Is there more you can tell us before we go, Chief?" I asked.

"Buddy, remember? We're practically family, might as well act like it."

He stared at Lurleen for a long moment. "Something about you, Miss Lurleen, just looks so familiar. You sure we didn't meet in another life?"

Lurleen shook her head. "I have that familiar face where people think I'm someone they know."

There was nothing familiar about Lurleen's face. It was stunning and unforgettable. I wondered what she could be talking about.

"Then that's all for now," Buddy said. "We're still figuring out how Nick Davis got himself killed on the estate and dragged to another location with no one noticing."

Savannah shivered.

."Don't you worry, Miss Savannah," he said. He gave her a bear hug. "I'll keep you safe. Now, why don't you go freshen up for dinner?"

Savannah walked us down the hall to her bedroom suite, carefully closed the door and locked it once we were inside.

She barely let us take a seat before she started talking. "This changes everything. Before I was trying to protect myself. Now, I have an estate full of people to worry about."

"Did you know Peter Young worked for your husband?" I asked.

Savannah sighed and slowly nodded her head. "I actually included Pepper as a contestant, so Peter could come along without anyone questioning why he was here. Pepper's a terrible cook, but she was thrilled she'd be on television. Peter was a bodyguard for Quinn and did other things for him as well. I wanted him here to keep me safe from whoever it is that wants to destroy me."

"You told the police about this?" I asked.

"No. I didn't want anyone to know. He wouldn't be much protection for me if everyone knew who he was."

"Why did you ask me to come to help solve a crime that hadn't happened yet?" I said. "I got my invitation before there was anything to worry about."

"I knew for a long time there was something to worry about," Savannah said. "There were threatening letters and items were disappearing—items of great value—even after Timothy's mother, Martha, died. It made me realize I might have misjudged her—perhaps she wasn't a thief. As for you, Ditie, Lurleen sold me on your qualifications, both as a cook and a detective."

I looked at Lurleen. She had the decency to blush.

"Perhaps I did say something about your investigative skills when Savannah mentioned the troubles she was having," Lurleen said. "We spoke over the phone after Chris tasted your tea cakes. I certainly had no idea the troubles would escalate to murder."

"Nor did I," Savannah said. "I thought you could find the person who was jealous of me and wanted to bring me down a notch."

As she talked, she paced back and forth in her crowded sitting room. "I think I need to speak to Buddy again."

We followed her to Quinn's office and joined the chief, Mason, and Danny in the small space. Mason and I exchanged a brief smile.

"We have to do something more," Savannah said. "All of you were here and a man was murdered on the estate. Under your very noses. No one is safe now."

"I've called for additional backup from Beaufort," Buddy said. "I can call on Charleston if I need to. I've helped them out in the past."

Mason nodded. "Good. We're going to need help just to control the press. They're forming a tent city outside the gate."

"This is big news around here," Buddy said. "Not much happens in Veracrue or Beaufort for that matter, not since the Civil War anyway. Everyone gets all excited about the movie stars, but this is something else. This is a small town with a murderer roaming around, and people will be scared."

"*I'm* scared," Savannah said.

"So far no one on your staff reported seeing or hearing anything unusual?" Mason asked.

Savannah shook her head. "No one has said anything to me."

"The gardeners denied noticing anything along that back path," Mason said. "I wonder how they could have missed it when George Kirkwood saw it so clearly."

"I told them to focus on the gardens at the front and back of the house and not to worry about the woods behind. I wanted everything to be as beautiful as possible for the shoot."

"It appears Anna is your only full-time female staff," Mason said.

"She hires additional help as needed for the kitchen and upkeep of the house, but they only come for the days when we have guests."

"So your staff are primarily men," Mason said. "Dorian Gray, the gardeners, your nephew Chris."

"Is that a problem?"

"Any of those men could have helped someone, a woman perhaps, dispose of an unwanted body on the estate," Mason said.

"I hope you're not suggesting *I* had anything to do with this murder," Savannah said.

"Calm down, Savannah," Buddy said. "Detective Garrett here is just doing his job. He don't have the manners of a true Southerner, but that's 'cause he grew up in a big city, ain't it, Garrett?"

Mason didn't take the bait. "Everyone on the estate is under suspicion, Ms. Evans. Even you. Someone managed to get Nick Davis into your house, gave him a place to sleep, and then shot him in the head. You're telling me no one noticed a thing. That's hard to believe."

"It's a large house with twelve bedrooms," Savannah said. "Two of those are in the basement for unexpected guests. They are rarely visited by any of my staff. Perhaps that's where the man stayed. Perhaps he found his way into the house through the basement door. Perhaps one of my staff forgot to lock it when they brought in supplies."

Mason didn't say anything. He was very good at waiting out a silence. He'd done that with me often enough.

After a few seconds, Savannah continued. "You said no one noticed, but I wonder if that's what upset my dog, Saffron. She couldn't sleep last night and insisted on wandering the halls."

"You went with her?" Mason asked.

"No. I waited until she returned and then I shut her in my bedroom, so she wouldn't disturb the guests."

"It's interesting," Mason said. "You have so many of the details correct without apparently knowing this man. Nick Davis was killed in a basement bedroom—as you suggested. One that isn't often used, as you say. We located it because your dog kept sniffing at the door when we were investigating this afternoon. It's quite possible she was restless last night because she knew something was going on—maybe she smelled the blood or heard the shot."

Savannah stood and then sat down on a small chair beside the desk. There was no place to run to.

Buddy put a hand on her arm and nodded towards Mason to continue.

"The bedroom is down the hall from the outside basement door. Nick Davis didn't just wander in. Someone let him in, and Davis had plans to stay for a while—brought a small backpack, a change of clothes. It looked

like he was working on something. The murderer took his laptop, if he had
one, but he missed Nick's handwritten notes, stuffed under the mattress.
I guess Nick knew someone might not be pleased he was there. Whoever
killed him didn't have time to go back and clean out the room. Left the
gun that killed him beside the bed and the sheets covered in blood. Looks
as if it was Nick's gun."

"So you have his notes?" Savannah asked. I couldn't tell if she was
worried or relieved to hear that.

"We can't talk about that," Buddy said, "even to you." He glanced at
his watch. "Dinner's at seven thirty, isn't it? I know you have things to
do, Savannah, so we'll let you do them."

When she left, Mason looked at the chief. "Did you find anything in
the notes?"

Buddy shook his head. "A single sheet. A few names. Nothing much,
but we can probably scare a few people by suggesting it was more than
that. He nodded to Danny. "Bring Young back in here, and we'll grill him
again before dinner."

Danny returned in five minutes. He had Peter enter the office ahead of
him. "He claims he's ready to talk."

"Good," the chief said, " 'cause we're ready to listen, and I'm gettin'
hungry. We'll keep this short and to the point, okay with you, Mr. Young?"

"I don't have anything to tell you that you don't already know. I was
Quinn's bodyguard, and Savannah asked me to protect her. It's good
money, and it meant my wife could get herself on national TV. She doesn't
so much want to be a star as to show her Atlanta friends that she's not just
some ditzy society wannabe. This show was going to help with her social
standing in Atlanta. The Junior League can only take you so far."

I looked at Buddy and he nodded at me.

"Savannah said you were more than a bodyguard for Quinn," I said,
"that you did other things for him as well."

"I did whatever Quinn wanted me to do, and that's the same arrangement
I have with Savannah. You pay me well enough, and I'll do anything you
ask." He must have registered what he was saying. "Short of anything
illegal."

"How about moving a body off the estate?" Mason asked.

"Don't be ridiculous!"

"It's almost seven thirty," the chief said, looking at his watch. "I need
some food. We'll finish this up later. You can go back to your room, get
your wife, and I'll expect to see both of you at the table in ten minutes."

Young headed back to his room. We were about to leave Quinn's office when James Bradshaw entered it without knocking. "So this is where you all hang out. A man dies and you take over his office."

"What can we do for you, Jim?" Buddy asked.

"I'm a busy man," Bradshaw said. "We're all busy people. You can't lock us up here while you look for a murderer who is probably long gone."

"We know the name of the dead man—Nick Davis—and we know he was killed on the premises." As the chief spoke, he stared at James. "I'm sorry for the inconvenience, Jim. You made a commitment to be here for five days. Hopefully, this will be cleared up by the time you would have left. Now, let's all go downstairs. I have a few announcements to make."

We met Savannah at the bottom of the stairs.

She grabbed Buddy's arm. "I've thought about this and spoken with Chris. I hope we can go on with the show. The ratings, you know. Chris says we have to finish this series or *we* might be finished."

The chief nodded his head and smiled. "Chris smells a great PR opportunity, don't he? Savannah Evans carries on despite the death of her husband and murder on the estate—reality TV at its wildest."

"You make him sound so crass," Savannah said. "I agree with him."

"I can see you do," the chief said. "As a matter of fact, it makes sense. It'll keep everyone occupied, and we'll know where our suspects are, in plain sight, so to speak—at least when the segments are being shot. Safer for them and easier for us."

Savannah nodded, and I noticed the tiniest smile. Then she straightened her face. "Buddy, you'll make sure there are additional police to guard us—on the grounds, in the kitchen and the house."

"Of course."

He followed Savannah into the dining room and asked for everyone's attention. "I've interviewed a few of you, and I'll get to the rest of you sometime tonight. I want y'all to stay inside the house. We'll need to know where you are at all times."

"How long are we talking about?" This was from Granny Flumm. "I have my cafe to run—it doesn't run itself, you know."

"With everyone's cooperation, we'll try to wrap this up before the end of the week," the chief said. "If you know anything or saw anything suspicious, you talk to me. For now, we're going on with the show, and I expect to see every one of you in the audience if you're not on stage when segments are shot."

"You're here for the contest anyway," Savannah said. "Buddy, Chief Lewis, has assured me security will be increased. A policeman will always be in sight."

"I'll go stir crazy," George Kirkwood said. "I can't sit around inside all day. I work outside."

"So you are essentially incarcerating us," James Bradshaw said. " with some crazy murderer on the loose, when we've done nothing wrong."

Chief Lewis responded first to George. "If I know where you are, Mr. Kirkwood, then I can let you go outside during the day. Perhaps you can work with the gardeners if you get bored and need something to do."

Kirkwood nodded, appeased.

"As for you Jim," the chief said. "I'd like to speak to you now before dinner. Anna, can you hold our meals for us?"

Anna nodded.

"The rest of you can go ahead and eat."

James turned to the chief. "Do you really have to do this? You know me."

"I do know you," the chief said. "And apparently so did the dead man."

Chapter Ten

Chief Lewis and James Bradshaw stood inches apart in the doorway leading from the dining room to the hall. If anyone else had tried to get into or out of the room, they'd never have succeeded. James was taller by half a head, but the chief had twenty pounds on him, mostly around his middle.

Bradshaw gave Buddy an icy look. "What the hell are you talking about?"

"You really wanna talk about it here?" Buddy asked, glancing at the faces turned in their direction.

"No, not here, not anywhere. I'm calling my lawyer."

"We aren't charging you with anything, just asking questions. Why get your lawyer involved—waste of good money if you ask me. If you had nothing to do with this man's death, then why don't you tell us what you do know?"

Bradshaw was silent as he apparently mulled this over. "I'll talk to you, but if it looks like you're trying to pin this murder on me, I'm calling my lawyer."

I stood at the doorway to the dining room and watched the men disappeared down the hallway toward the central stairs. Mason joined them and waved Danny away, so Danny sat back down beside Lurleen. I joined them and sat on the other side of Lurleen. Anna's helpers began bringing in large platters of pork chops smothered in gravy as she announced the menu. "Pan-seared pork chops with pear and Vidalia onion gravy, wild rice, green beans from the garden, and for dessert, Rose's banana pudding."

Rose blushed with surprise.

It was clear that Anna loved to cook and was a natural in terms of presentation. She wasn't Southern but she had a soft cadence to her voice that was very appealing. I had no trouble imagining her on television.

Lurleen obviously had the same thought. "When will you have your own cooking show?" she asked.

Anna frowned for an instant and then regained her composure. "You are so kind, Lurleen. Someday perhaps. For now, it's a pleasure to serve food enthusiasts like yourselves."

The words sounded rehearsed, as if she'd had to explain herself more than once. She was a lovely young woman with enormous poise and great skill as a chef. How could she be content to play second fiddle to Savannah? Could she really have so little ambition?

Half an hour later, Mason and Buddy returned to the table.

"Anything left for us boys?" Buddy asked. "James said he wasn't hungry. Could you send up something later to his room?"

"Of course." Anna brought in two plates for Mason and Buddy. "I kept your dinners in a warming drawer in the kitchen," she said. "I gave you a double helping, chief. I know your appetite." She looked around the table and sideboard. "There's a lot left anyway. People aren't eating much tonight."

I looked at the table, curious to see whose appetites had been affected by the recent news. George Kirkwood's plate was clean, and he was reaching for another pork chop. Unlike her husband, Rose ate very little. Was it my imagination or did she seem uncomfortable when Buddy returned to the table? She looked repeatedly in his direction.

Peter and Pepper Young barely touched their servings. I'm sure Peter anticipated further interviews with the chief after dinner about his role as an employee of Quinn Nelson. Pepper probably never ate much, not with her concern about how she looked. She verified that by leaning over to Lurleen. "How in the world can you eat all that gravy and rice and keep your figure? I look at gravy and gain five pounds."

Lurleen couldn't resist. "It wouldn't hurt you to gain five pounds, Pepper, if you don't mind my saying so."

Pepper clearly did mind. She turned away from Lurleen and began a stilted conversation with Rose about how delicious her banana pudding was.

Lurleen gave me a wink. It was obvious Pepper was annoyed that anyone might think she was too skinny. Particularly someone like Lurleen, who was also thin but with curves in all the right places.

"I hope I didn't hurt your feelings," Lurleen said when she caught Pepper's eye.

"Of course not." Pepper frowned and turned away to join a conversation between her husband and Savannah. I was sitting across the table from them and could hear only bits of what was being said. Savannah seemed to be reassuring Peter, something along the lines of—he had nothing to worry about, he'd done nothing wrong. He didn't appear to be all that reassured and excused himself without eating his dessert.

"All delicious, Anna. I'm just not very hungry tonight," he said.

Pepper stood when he did, and the chief caught both of them on the way out. "Don't go to bed early, Mr. Young. I'll need to talk to you some more this evening."

The party, if that's what it could be called, broke up promptly after people finished dessert. Lurleen and I stayed put with our coffee while we waited for Mason and Buddy to finish eating.

Danny stopped after his third helping of banana pudding.

"Man, that was good!" he said to Lurleen.

She smiled sweetly. "I could tell you liked it."

The dining room was empty except for the six of us. Savannah stood saying she was exhausted and needed to go to bed. Buddy told her there would be an officer outside her bedroom door.

"I'm not too worried. Saffron will protect me."

"Labs are so loyal," Lurleen said. "The ones I've known wouldn't leave their master's side at night."

"I'm sure it was Saffron I heard crying last evening," I said.

"It was Saffron who led us to the bedroom where the man was killed," Buddy said. "Do you know what time you heard her crying, Dr. Brown?"

"Sometime around two, I think. I always have a little trouble sleeping in a new bed, so I'd been reading. I heard the crying for maybe a minute, and then it stopped as abruptly as it started."

"It's odd she would have left your side," Lurleen said, "if she was worried about something, Labs stick with their owners when they sense trouble. You didn't go with her to see what was wrong? That's the only way I can imagine she would have explored the house or suddenly stopped whining."

"I said I stayed in my room!" Savannah sounded angry, said nothing more, and left the table.

I leaned over to Lurleen. "Is that true about labs, Lurleen?"

Lurleen shook her head. "Not as far as I know, but it certainly got a rise out of Savannah."

She looked at me intently for a moment. "I do know that a lab would do anything for its owner."

"How do you know so much about them?" I asked.

I thought she might lay her knowledge at the foot of another boyfriend, a dog trainer or breeder perhaps, but she didn't do that.

"I worked for a vet in middle school," she said, "and I had a lab—a dog the vet treated and no one claimed. That dog saved my life."

It was a strange sensation—I knew she was telling me the absolute truth, and I knew I wouldn't hear another detail at the moment.

Danny hadn't been listening. He remained focused on current events. "Can you fill me in on the interview with Bradshaw?" he asked Mason.

"I'd like to do that in private," Mason said. He didn't look at me or Lurleen, but his message was clear.

Chief Lewis nodded at me. "I told you he was a stickler. Look, Garrett, this is not your jurisdiction. In the South, the real South, we do things a little differently. We're not so uptight, and we let people help. This little woman of yours is a damned good detective. I want her working with us. Got that?"

I flinched at 'little woman of yours' and waited to see how Mason would react.

"It's your investigation here, Chief, but it's mine in Atlanta. I think we both know the murder of Quinn Nelson and the murder of Nick Davis are likely to be connected."

"Yes, we do know that, so let's get all the help we can. You don't mind sharing the limelight, do you, Garrett?"

Mason frowned in my direction and said nothing more.

Lurleen was clearly delighted. "You know Ditie and I come as a package, Buddy. I see and hear things and Ditie helps sort out what they mean."

The chief smiled at Lurleen. "I can imagine a man would tell you anything you wanted to know. I'm not sure most women would feel that way."

Lurleen laughed. "All right then, can we hear what happened in the interview with Mr. Bradshaw and what you know about the dead man?"

The chief nodded at Mason to start talking.

"As it turns out Nick Davis was a meticulous note taker," Mason said. "We have his day planner from work. He believed in putting things in writing and left the planner in his home office. That included three phone calls and two meetings with Bradshaw."

"That information upset James," Buddy said. "Bradshaw called Davis a damn fool for writing everything down."

"At that point Bradshaw decided to tell us what was going on," Mason said, "or at least that's what he claimed. 'You two have me over a barrel,' was the way he put it, and 'you'll have me up for murder.' He said he called Davis when he heard Quinn hadn't died of natural causes."

"Look, Garrett, this will take all night," Buddy said, "and we don't have all night. We'll listen to the recording. It's in Quinn's office. He had a lot of elaborate recording devices. We used one of them to interview James."

Buddy led us upstairs and locked the door once we were all inside Quinn's office. "For some reason, this office is sound-proofed. Perfect for our investigation, but I can't imagine why Quinn needed that. He was an odd fellow, paranoid about everything."

Buddy waited until we'd all found a seat, leaving the desk chair for him. "Everyone comfortable? Here we go."

He turned on the recording.

It was Bradshaw's voice we heard.

"I knew this whole organization of Savannah's was a scam. She's a lousy cook if you've ever tried to eat anything she's prepared. Anna can make a decent meal, but there is no way Savannah deserves the reputation or money she seems to have. And Quinn? He was a buffoon. He never sold real estate. He just talked about selling it.

"I brought in Davis because he was always wanting to make a name for himself by breaking the big story. I thought if he could poke through the house, go through Quinn's office he might find something important. Quinn was sloppy about his affairs, and no one had cleaned up after his death as far as I could tell."

"What exactly was Nick Davis supposed to find out?" Mason asked.

"He was supposed to find out where they got their money, where they really got it, and what Quinn Nelson was up to when he was supposedly selling real estate. I wanted Davis to expose them and maybe catch a murderer in the process. Not get himself killed, damned idiot."

"I've known you a long time, Jim." It was the chief's voice. "I've known your family, your daddy."

"Don't bring my family into this."

"Can't avoid it," Buddy went on. "Your daddy was the town drunk. Savannah's daddy was the mayor. You couldn't stand that. You got something against her because she didn't live the life you did. She lived in the big house that your family used to own."

"This isn't about revenge if that's where you're headed."

"Sure sounds like it, boy. Don't it sound that way to you, Garrett?"

Mason didn't comment.

"Where were you between the hours of one and four am two nights ago?" the chief asked.

"I was in bed, asleep, like any damn fool would be."

"That's not what Dorian Gray says. He says he saw you wandering the house about that time. Making enough noise to wake him."

"Then he's a liar. You want your murderer—maybe you should look at Gray and his past. He's always simpering around Savannah, and he hated Quinn."

That was the end of the recording.

"It's going to be a late night." Chief Lewis said as he heaved himself up from the chair. "I ain't used to this kind of excitement unless it's on TV, and the Georgia Bulldogs are playing. I'll take a break and get my men working on what Bradshaw said, starting with this mess of a desk. Who knows what's in here? Good thing Bradshaw bought the stuff about the notes under the mattress—he thought we knew a hell of a lot more than we did."

"Could you get anything else from the page Davis left behind—other than Bradshaw's name?" Mason asked.

"No."

"Mind if I take a look at it?" Mason said.

"Why? You think I can't read?" The chief caught himself. "Maybe later. It's scratched notes—things to investigate, nothing useful. Right now, I want you to interview Peter Young once more—keep him off balance.

"And you, Danny, you should interview the women—they'll take to you as a handsome Southern boy. See if you can find out where everyone was when Davis was killed. No offense, Garrett, but you have big city cop written all over you—no one will talk to you without their lawyer present. Let's meet back here in two hours. Better yet, let's meet in the kitchen for a beer."

Buddy seemed to remember there were ladies present. "I hope the tape didn't offend you with its rough language—our interview got under Bradshaw's skin. You two should go get your beauty rest."

Lurleen led me out of the room. "We've been dismissed. What shall we do next?"

"Sleep isn't a bad idea," I said.

"Nonsense. We can't go to bed yet—it's not even ten. We'll talk to Savannah."

Savannah seemed happy to see us, as did Saffron, once she'd sniffed us thoroughly and convinced herself we were friends and not foes.

"I'm sorry I left so abruptly," Savannah said. "I thought for a moment you were accusing me of something, Lurleen, but I suspect I was simply tired like everyone else."

Savannah did look exhausted, and I didn't have the heart to push her on anything. Besides, that would be Danny's job later.

We talked about other things. Savannah reminisced about how she'd started the business. She'd gotten some old Southern recipes from her grandmother, and they'd inspired her to create a cookbook. That led to a local show in Beaufort that went national.

Savannah said Quinn was enthusiastic about anything that made her happy, and he encouraged her every step of the way.

That's as far as we got. Mason knocked on her door. "I was in search of Ditie. Mind if I borrow her?"

"Not at all," Savannah said. "You'll stay with me, Lurleen?"

"Yes," she said, but I could see she was desperate to know what Mason might want from me.

He took me to Quinn's office, poured himself a cup of coffee from the Keurig machine that was sitting on the credenza. He offered me one, and I declined. One cup of coffee at this hour, and I'd be awake all night.

"What do you make of Savannah?" he asked.

"That's a big question," I said.

"Let's start with what you think of her as a chef."

"I think she's a bit like Madonna, like a lot of famous people, self-made, self-promoted. It's not her talent as a cook that's made her famous—not from what people have told me. It's more her personality, her drive. Some people are determined to be famous. I think Savannah is like that. It didn't hurt that she had her grandmother's recipes and Quinn's money to get her started."

"Interesting you should say that. You heard what James Bradshaw said—that Quinn didn't actually make a lot of real estate deals, so where did he get *his* money?"

"I can't help you with that, Mason. I don't run in those circles, but Lurleen might know someone who does. All her work at Sandler's Sodas—she probably knows some folks who could fill you in."

At that moment Lurleen breezed into the room. "Hope I'm not disturbing anything, *chéris.* Savannah wanted to go to bed and insisted I get some rest as well."

"Perfect timing. We have some questions for you," I said, patting a place on the sofa. "It seems Mason wants to know more about Savannah's skills as a chef and Quinn's work in real estate."

"Ooh, la la, the plot thickens. I like Savannah, I really do, but she doesn't know her way around a kitchen. Izzy Moran asked for an ingredient that Savannah had never heard of. Anna stepped in and pointed her in the right direction."

"It's true," I said. "On her shows, she never does anything that requires finesse. Everything is pre-chopped, pre-measured, pre-sifted. Your mother pointed that out to me, Mason, but then it's a thirty-minute show."

"What about Quinn and his real estate deals?" Mason asked. "Know anything about that, Lurleen?"

"When I worked at Sandler's Sodas, there were always real estate deals going on, not my department. I was an accountant with central administration, but I had a friend who worked in that area. It seems to me

Quinn Nelson's company was often involved. Funny thing, now that I think about it, my friend who worked there said it was Quinn's company but she never met the man. She assumed he was too busy. There was something else she said. What was it?"

Lurleen paused to push back a strand of wavy hair and stare into space.

"I know. She said the deals often weren't well executed. Sandler's lawyers grumbled about the way Quinn's company handled things. They wondered if they even had legitimate closing attorneys on staff. In the end they stopped using his company. That was ten years ago, something like that, right when Savannah was getting started with her local show."

Mason nodded. "Thanks, Lurleen."

I turned to her. "You got a chance to talk to Quinn before he died. Did you get an impression of him?"

Lurleen was good as sizing people up in a hurry.

"He wasn't feeling well, so it's a little hard to say." Lurleen closed her eyes briefly. "He was slick, that's how I would describe him, slick in a charming way. He told me how much he enjoyed my company, and he wanted me to stay beside him—a smooth talker in between his need to catch his breath."

"I got the impression that Quinn and Savannah really did care for each other," I said.

"*D'accord,*" Lurleen said. "I thought so too, at least from Quinn's perspective. He talked about how beautiful she was, how the fine clothes and jewels set off her loveliness, how she deserved to be surrounded by the best. If I'm not mistaken, that's when he appeared to get a little morose. He started telling me how much effort it took to keep up appearances. Then he laughed it off, but I think he meant it."

"And Savannah?" I asked. "She keeps talking about how he was the love of her life."

Lurleen nodded. "She says all the right words, but when I've seen people in mourning, they take to the bed—they don't plan how to take advantage of a terrible situation to improve their ratings."

"You make a good point," I said. "When I've worked with parents who've lost a child, they can barely function. Sometimes they're angry and look for a person to blame, but beneath all that they are hopelessly sad. We've never seen any of that with Savannah. When it was appropriate she'd cry, but otherwise she's been full of energy."

"You've both given me a lot to think about," Mason said. "It seems as if Chief Lewis knows Savannah well. He's talked about her being theatrical. Maybe he knows more about Savannah and Quinn's relationship."

Mason looked at his watch. "It's after eleven. You need your sleep."

"I haven't seen you all day," I said. "I suspect we're both too wired to sleep."

Lurleen nodded and glanced at me. "I'll see if I can find us some hot chocolate, and you two can have a moment."

I nodded gratefully. When Lurleen left, I gave Mason a quick kiss.

"I know you're on duty, but I've missed you," I said. "I spoke to Lucie and Jason this afternoon. They're having the time of their lives."

"I'm glad to hear it. I've missed you too," he said. He stood up and pulled me up beside him. One very long kiss and then another made us both feel better. "I don't want you or Lurleen anywhere alone, got that? I'd like you to share a bedroom for the rest of the week."

"I think we can manage that. I'll go check on her right now."

"We'll go together," Mason said. "You two need to get to bed, and I need to get back to work."

We found Lurleen in the family kitchen, not the one used as a set, chatting it up with Anna as Anna stirred cocoa on the stove. The family kitchen was a far more intimate affair with a double stove, refrigerator, dishwasher, and stools surrounding a modest island. A walk-through pantry separated it from the grander kitchen where demonstrations were held and cooking episodes were shot.

Anna smiled at us when we entered. "This is really my home base," she said. "This is where I experiment with new recipes."

"Anna insisted on making the hot chocolate for us," Lurleen said, "a secret recipe but without the liqueur. I told her you had to work, Mason."

Anna poured cups for the three of us.

"Won't you join us?" Mason asked.

She smiled, poured herself a cup, and perched on a fourth stool around the island. "Is this part of your investigation?" she asked.

"More part of getting ready for bed," Lurleen jumped in.

"However, if you know something, I need to hear it," Mason said.

Anna lowered her voice and lost her smile. "I do know something. I'm afraid to talk about it, but I'm more afraid not to."

Chapter Eleven

Mason remained silent, waiting for Anna to say more. She looked at all of us seated at the island and then glanced around the darker corners of the kitchen.

"We're alone in here," Mason reassured her.

"You don't realize how wired this whole house is. It was Mr. Nelson's idea. He always needed to know what was going on, and he was a lot less trusting than Savannah."

Anna stood, walked to the butler's pantry and punched numbers into a keypad. "That's better. I've turned off the system in here."

"Every room is wired?" Mason asked.

Anna shook her head. "No, only those that most worried him."

"Are they linked to a monitor or a computer somewhere?"

"Yes, but Mr. Nelson was very old fashioned. He actually made DVDs to preserve them."

"Where are the recordings?"

"In his study, the office you're using as your interview room. I can show you if you like."

"I need to see that," Mason said, "but first I want to hear what you're afraid of."

Anna sighed. "Something is wrong with Savannah's company, and it's been wrong for a while. I run the kitchen. It's all I'm supposed to do, but I see things. And Savannah confides in me. When she's here, which is almost every weekend lately, she talks to me constantly. I've seen the change in her. Before, she was always excited about some new project, some idea she had that would expand her popularity."

Anna stood up and offered us more hot chocolate. We declined, and she sat once more.

"In the past few months, she's started to worry about everything—last week's ratings, some negative review, a picture of her that made her look old. Two years ago, she was on the cover of every cooking magazine, and you could read about her life in *Cosmopolitan*. This past year, nothing. She started to believe it was all over, and like Quinn, she became paranoid that someone was out to ruin her. Lately, I've begun to think she might be right. With Quinn's death, I'm certain of it."

Anna hesitated again.

"I feel so disloyal, but I'm afraid she won't tell you what's going on."

She took off her apron and threw it in a hamper in the butler's pantry. It seemed to be a statement that she was now off duty and could speak freely.

She took a deep breath. "Savannah's empire is coming apart at the seams, and someone is masterminding its destruction."

"Tell me exactly what you're talking about," Mason said.

"Television is a ruthless business. You can be a star one moment and over-the hill the next. Savannah has always known that. She's inventive, looking for the next twist that will capture new viewers. A year ago she and I were discussing a culinary school, maybe for children, parts of which could be televised."

"You'd finally get your own show," Lurleen said. "You deserve that."

"Thanks, Lurleen. We planned to use land on the estate, but Savannah told me recently that she doesn't have the money to build anything. Then I found out she can barely pay her current bills."

"How did you discover that?" Mason asked.

"She asked me to clean out Quinn's office after he died. She said she couldn't bear to do it herself. Quinn handled the finances for his business and hers. You can imagine that was complicated. Frank Moran is the accountant for both of them. He kept things on track, or at least I thought that was what he was doing."

"Wait, wait a minute," Lurleen said. "Frank is a CPA?"

"Their personal CPA and their lawyer. I'm not sure he has other clients, but he might need some soon. I found a pile of unpaid bills, many of them for large amounts of money and long overdue."

"I should have recognized a fellow accountant," Lurleen said. "How could I have missed that?"

Mason tried to get us back on track. "Did Savannah know about the overdue bills?"

"I told her. She didn't seem all that surprised. She told me Quinn hadn't been able to keep up with things lately due to his health and tried to reassure me that everything would be okay. Then she asked me to stop looking into financial matters or any other papers on Quinn's desk. She assured me that Frank would handle it."

Mason sipped the last of his hot chocolate, stood up, and carried it to the sink.

Anna jumped up. "I'll take care of that." She collected the rest of our cups and took her time placing them in the dishwasher.

"Shall we go someplace more comfortable?" she asked when she was finished. "My office perhaps?"

"Is it also wired?" Mason asked.

"I convinced Quinn I needed a private place, unwired, and he agreed. I was one of a very few people he continued to trust. I do have a monitor that allows me to see what's going on in most of the rooms in the house, but nothing is recorded."

We moved to her office—the same space the other contestants and I had used while Savannah made her judgments about our entries. It was a cheerful room with a large window facing the back deck and the gardens beyond. Lurleen and I settled into a buttercup yellow loveseat. Mason took an upholstered chair with sunflowers on it. He looked distinctly out of place.

Anna saw me eyeing several filing cabinets standing beside the window. "I do most of my recipe research online—as you do, I'm sure, Ditie. But, I also collect old recipes and plan to publish a book on South Carolina recipes from the time of the Civil War—maybe called *Cooking in Black and White*."

"What a great idea," I said. "I did a little research into old recipes for a party I gave over the summer."

Mason looked at both of us and then he looked at his watch. I knew that look, and I stopped talking.

Lurleen, however, didn't catch his expression.

"You called Quinn 'Mr. Nelson' earlier and now it's 'Quinn,'" she said. "Were you and he close?"

Anna didn't respond right away.

"He was my employer, and I always tried to respect that. But, he was also my friend."

"Did he confide in you?" Mason asked.

"Not about money problems. Savannah made sure I was paid on time, and I earn a comfortable salary—that hasn't changed. It's only when I saw the bills that I got worried."

"So you didn't know about objects being stolen from the house?" Mason asked.

Anna colored slightly. "Yes, I did. Savannah blamed Martha Hill for that initially, but I always thought Martha was honest. I wondered if her son was responsible. He spent a lot of time at the house and got involved with drugs when he was fourteen or fifteen. Martha didn't want to see what her son was up to, and then she got sick with cancer."

"What year was that?" Mason asked.

"Six or seven years ago. Savannah fired her when she was too sick to work. She died shortly after that, and Tim never got over it."

"Do you think he killed Quinn?" I asked.

"I don't know. He wrote threatening letters, and then those stopped."

"And the stealing—did that stop?" Mason asked.

She shook her head slowly. "No. In fact, it got worse—objects of more and more value were taken. I would tell Savannah every time I noticed something missing, but she didn't seem to care. I wondered if she knew what was happening."

"You think she might have been involved with the stealing?" I asked.

"No. I thought she either knew who was taking things or that she had more important issues on her mind."

"Like what?" Mason asked.

"In the last year the threatening letters started again, along with vicious pranks."

"What pranks?" Mason asked.

"Salt in the sugar canister," Anna said, "and a few much worse."

"You think Tim was behind the recent threats and pranks?" Mason asked.

"No. He never came to the house after his mother's death. Most of the recent threats were directed only at Savannah. The pranks were meant to unnerve her. That's when I started to think someone wanted to destroy her or her empire."

"Do you have ideas about who that might be?" Mason asked.

Anna shook her head. "For a while I worried it might be Quinn. I know that sounds unbelievable, but he began to act so secretive and paranoid—you know, keeping track of what everyone was doing, including Savannah."

"Why in the world would he do that?" I said. "I thought they were close."

"They were at first. Then I heard more and more accusations about what Savannah was up to, more arguments on both sides really. When Quinn wound up dead, I realized it couldn't have been him."

"Do you have suspicions about who murdered him?" Mason asked.

"No," Anna said. "I assume it's the same person that's been stirring up trouble around here."

"When did the serious arguments begin between Savannah and Quinn?" Mason asked.

"I know the day they got bad. It was just over a year ago, on their anniversary—their fifteenth. They planned a quiet weekend for themselves here on the estate. They'd let most of the staff go, so it was just me and Dorian. All they wanted was peace and time to themselves. I heard the doorbell ring, and then I heard Savannah scream. On the doormat was a dead rat, its throat cut, and a note that said, 'Try this in your stew, Savannah. It might improve it.'

"Quinn called it a malicious prank, nothing more. He didn't want Savannah to notify the police. At the time I thought that was strange. Savannah and Buddy go way back. She's known the chief since childhood. Of course, Chief Lewis likes to gossip, especially when he's had a drink or two. Maybe Quinn didn't want that."

"I hear my name called?" Buddy ambled into the room. "So this is where y'all got to. I came in looking for a beer, but you all look mighty somber. And mighty quiet. Something I shouldn't hear?"

Anna turned bright red. She got up from her chair, went to the beer fridge in the butler's pantry and brought back a Bud Light for the chief.

"What? You think I need to watch my weight, Miss Annie?" He patted his generous belly and laughed. "I'll rummage through and find what I want. Don't let me interrupt. Act like I'm not even here."

Anna gave a helpless glance in Mason's direction.

I spoke up. "I'm exhausted. I need to get some sleep. Anna, I wonder if you could help me move into Lurleen's room. Mason wants us to stay together." I spoke more loudly than necessary so Buddy could hear as he rummaged through the beer and wine refrigerator. "I imagine you don't want anyone to stay alone for the rest of the week, is that right, Chief?"

"Damn straight," Buddy yelled from the pantry. He came back into the office. "That includes you Miss Anna, and the rest of the staff. I got a man on the servants' quarters, but you have your own room on the third floor, don't you?"

"Yes," Anna said.

"Then I want you bunking with someone."

"You can stay with us," I said. "I saw a daybed in Lurleen's room."

Anna nodded her agreement.

"It's late," Mason said. "You can get settled after you show me where the recordings are in Quinn's office."

"Recordings?" Buddy asked. "What the hell are you talking about, Garrett?"

Mason explained.

"Well, I'll be damned. I knew Quinn was getting a little squirrelly over the past few years, but I thought it was just old age. Every room in this house is bugged?" Buddy sounded genuinely surprised and something else—nervous maybe.

"A lot of them it seems," Mason said.

"I'm gonna have a late night," the chief said.

"We all are," Mason corrected. "I'll see if Danny can help."

"Hmmm," the chief said. He threw the rest of his beer in the trash.

Mason called Danny on his cell, and then announced that Danny had just finished a sweep of the perimeter with two officers, now stationed at the back gate.

Danny appeared in Anna's office two minutes later.

"It's all quiet out there," he said.

"You interview all the women?" Buddy asked.

"Everyone except you, Anna," he said.

"We took care of that," Mason said. "Come with us to Quinn's office."

We trooped upstairs. Anna showed us where the recordings were stored. Hundreds of DVDs and the machine to record and play them. Anna had a set of master keys including the one to the closet. Each DVD was carefully marked as to time and location. The earliest ones were dated one year ago, a week after the anniversary Anna had started to tell us about. The latest were two days before Quinn died.

Danny whistled when he saw the discs. "This is old technology, DVDs are dinosaurs now."

"Quinn was an old guy," Buddy said. "I'm amazed these aren't cassettes." Then he guffawed for a good five seconds. He was a man who enjoyed his own sense of humor.

Lurleen and Danny checked the surveillance monitor.

"He wasn't so old-fashioned," Danny said. "This is simple but up-to date equipment—the cameras are movement-and light-sensitive. If someone entered the room or turned on a light, the recording started with the date, time, and room printed—see here."

Lurleen backed up and fast forwarded the recording for a few seconds. She was as much a techie as Danny was. "It looks as if his focus was on the basement rooms, basement door, the billiard room and the kitchen—the big and little one—as well as the front and back door on the main floor. I guess that's where he expected trouble to come from. The cameras seem to run on a thirty-day loop."

"Meaning?" I asked.

"Meaning that after thirty days, the cameras record over earlier data," Danny said, "so if Quinn didn't transfer them to a disc that data would be gone."

"Nothing recorded from the hallways or the grounds?" the chief asked.

"Doesn't look like it," Lurleen said.

I swear Buddy looked relieved about that.

"Does the billiard room have an outside entrance?" Mason asked.

"No," Danny said.

"So, why the billiard room?" Mason didn't really expect an answer.

Lurleen and I offered to stay and help sort through DVDs, but the chief shook his head. "We'll handle this. You girls get some sleep."

Lurleen smiled. "We'll have a sleep-over in my room."

The chief took charge. "I'll look over the monitor. Danny, you and Mason can sort through the DVDs."

While the men started reviewing recordings, Lurleen and I got Anna settled in the bedroom and then began our own interrogation.

"It's clear you didn't want Chief Lewis to hear what you had to say," I said. "Why not?"

"I don't know who to trust," Anna said. "At the beginning of that terrible weekend a year ago, Savannah had asked the chief to visit while Quinn was out. Buddy stormed out of the house half an hour later. The pranks started the next morning."

"You're implying the chief was involved with them?" I asked.

"Buddy has an odd sense of humor and a bad temper, so I can't really say. The dead rat was just the beginning. No matter what meal I was preparing, something went wrong with it. The milk was sour. Rancid butter was in the butter dish. I found a baby frog in a salad I was preparing.

"After two days, Quinn called in the chief. Buddy and Quinn went through every room and found nothing. It was after that weekend that the threatening letters started again, and Quinn decided to put in a surveillance system."

"And you are sure the letters didn't come from Tim White," I said.

"Tim always signed his name, and they were short. He talked about wanting Savannah and Quinn to suffer like his mother had, but he never threatened direct violence. Poor Tim."

"*Poor* Tim?" I asked.

"He was probably sixteen when his mother died with no other relatives. It was all terribly sad. He blamed Savannah and Quinn for everything."

"Savannah made it sound as if she'd ensured his mother got good care," I said.

Anna hesitated. "Sometimes Savannah paints a picture that she can live with. The truth is she did let his mother go. She promised to continue to pay for her health insurance, but I'm not sure she did that. Tim found an experimental treatment that Quinn and Savannah refused to underwrite. It wouldn't have helped anyway—the treatment turned out to be ineffective."

"How do you know so much about this?" I asked.

"Ten years ago I was working as a cook in a local restaurant at night, to pay for my first year in nursing school," she said. "I dropped out of school when Savannah offered me a much better career as a sous chef—my first love has always been nurturing people through healthy food, but my second love is caring for those who are sick or suffering. Savannah hired Mrs. Hill at about the same time she hired me. She took care of the house, and I did the cooking. We became friends, and I took over some of her tasks when she was too sick to do them."

"What happened to Timothy White after his mother died?" Lurleen asked.

"I believe his mother's death drove him to get a BA as a registered nurse. We were all amazed he could make it through school. He never seemed that bright."

"As a nurse, White would know how to kill Quinn," I said.

"I never thought Tim was capable of hurting anyone until I heard how Quinn died, and then I wondered."

Anna stopped, as if she were in the middle of a thought.

Lurleen and I looked at her expectantly. "I suppose this room is bugged as well," I said when Anna was silent.

Anna shook her head. "Quinn didn't tape the bedrooms upstairs."

She loosened her bun and let her shiny black hair fall to her shoulders. The transition was remarkable. She went from an attractive woman to a stunning beauty. Both Lurleen and I noted the transformation. Her black hair framed her face, and her dark eyes and eyebrows made her face riveting.

Anna sat on the edge of the bed.

"What is it you're reluctant to tell us?" I asked.

"It's about the objects that have been stolen recently, objects worth thousands of dollars that have been in the house for a hundred years or more. Lurleen, did you notice anything odd about the centerpiece for our first night's dinner?"

"The epergne?" Lurleen asked, and Anna nodded.

"How do you know that name?" I asked.

"My mother worked in one of these grand houses," Lurleen said, "until she was let go. I helped clean sometimes, and she told me the history of all the more important pieces. The epergne was the pride of the woman she worked for."

Lurleen closed her eyes. "The lighting was lowered that first night, but I recall the centerpiece seemed remarkably bright. I wondered how such an old piece could be that shiny—where was the patina that came with age." She turned to Anna. "Are you suggesting it's a fake? The original would be worth thousands of dollars!"

Anna nodded. "Probably much more. The silversmith who worked on it was Addison from the early 1800s. When I told Savannah about my concerns, she refused to have it examined by an expert. She said she had too many other things to worry about. It was at that point I assumed Savannah knew what was happening to her valuable objects."

"How sure are you she wasn't the one selling them off?" I asked.

"I suppose I'm not positive. She never really seemed to care about her antiques very much, but she certainly cared about her heritage. I just can't see her doing that. Quinn was more likely to be the one. He didn't really value old things."

"You told us you liked Quinn, that he was a friend," I said.

"I understood him. I knew that sometimes people needed to have a cover story for their lives, and I accepted that. Quinn was a con artist in many ways. He could put on an act. I'd seen him do it a dozen times. I think he genuinely loved Savannah, but perhaps he became desperate for money and chose to sell off objects bit by bit to keep up their life style."

"Weren't Savannah's shows a big hit initially?" Lurleen asked. "The tabloids claimed she was making a million dollars a year."

"That was probably PR—Quinn style. She did make money at first, but this place demands a lot of upkeep, and Quinn loved the lavish life style. In the last year, Savannah's sponsors were starting to dry up."

"Even so, why would Quinn try to hurt Savannah or her work?" I asked.

Anna paused. "Quinn could be vindictive. If someone crossed him, he'd make them pay. As I said, Quinn and Savannah had a huge argument before their last anniversary, yelling, the works."

"About what?" I asked.

"About children," Anna said. "About *her* child to be more specific."

"But, Savannah doesn't have a child," Lurleen said. "I read all the magazines. They always say she's so devoted to her work, she never had time for kids."

"You can't believe what you read in those magazines," Anna said. "Savannah had a child when she was twenty, long before Quinn. It's a complicated story and it's part of the problem. Maybe a big part."

Chapter Twelve

"A child?" Lurleen asked. "How could she possibly have kept that quiet?"

"You never met her father, Wade Evans," Anna said, "but I did. He served two terms as mayor of Veracrue, but he had higher aspirations. Everyone said he was bound to be governor of South Carolina one day."

Anna walked to the window and stared into the blackness outside. We watched as she slowly cranked the casement window shut. "Sometimes, you can hear what's being said on another floor if these windows are left open. Besides, it's getting cold."

She shivered and returned to the two flowered armchairs near the hearth. She curled up in one, feet beneath her, as if she might have a long story to tell.

"Savannah's father died ten years ago from a stroke, but I still feel he may be lurking in a corner, trying to overhear what people are saying about him."

"You make him sound as paranoid as Quinn," Lurleen said.

"I did wonder if Savannah had married her father," Anna said, "but Wade Evans was more powerful than Quinn could ever hope to be. Mr. Evans wanted to manipulate the political scene. I'm not sure he planned to stop at governor, which meant that any stain on his reputation was unacceptable."

"Including any stain on his family," Lurleen said.

"Yes. He was a man with a lot of money and therefore a lot of influence," Anna said. "He could make problems go away and scandals disappear. When Savannah got pregnant, she was in her second year at an exclusive women's college nearby."

"Honey Rose College for Women," Lurleen said.

"You know the school," Anna said. "No one knows that school outside of South Carolina. You must be from around here. It's very small, probably five hundred girls."

"My mother worked there for a while," Lurleen said, "until she got fired."

I stared at Lurleen. She'd never told me one thing about her mother, and now in the space of a few hours, she'd mentioned her twice. She saw my look, shrugged her shoulders, and said no more.

"It's a few miles from Veracrue," Anna said, "in the country. I think her father hoped to protect her from the riffraff. By that he meant the poorer folks who lived on the wrong side of town. It didn't work, and he should have known better. Those girls may have stayed cooped up during the week, but they went wild on the weekend. There were plenty of bars in the low country that were happy to serve underage girls and plenty of boys willing to take them there."

"So she got knocked up by a local boy?" Lurleen asked.

"Not the expression Savannah would use, but yes, she got knocked up by someone from around here. Her parents were furious. I should say her father was furious. Her mother never had much to say about anything, according to Savannah. Her father whisked her away to a 'boarding school' as soon as they discovered she was pregnant."

"Why didn't she get an abortion?" I asked.

"Savannah told me it was something she wasn't willing to consider under any circumstances. That's what her father wanted of course, but by the time Savannah told him she was pregnant, she was too far along. I think it was also an act of rebellion. She swore she'd never let a man dominate *her* the way her father controlled her mother."

"But, she went where he told her to go!" Lurleen said.

"Savannah was a poor little rich girl," Anna said. "She knew she couldn't really survive on her own, so she went. I think she hoped her parents might reconsider, let her keep the child, if they had time to think about it."

"Who was the father of the child?" I asked.

"Savannah never said, and her parents didn't care anyway. No local boy would have been good enough for her in their eyes, certainly not one who would get her pregnant. They just wanted the whole thing to go away."

"And they succeeded in that?" Lurleen said.

"They did. There was a finishing school in the south of France, run by Americans, that handled 'delicate problems.' Savannah loved being in France away from her parents. She didn't love giving up her baby, but her parents made it clear she had no choice."

"They never came around?" Lurleen asked.

"Never. Wade Evans never backed down and always got what he wanted. Savannah was hoping for the impossible."

"Who adopted her child?" I asked.

"A French couple. It was an open adoption. Highly unusual at the time."

"Savannah kept in touch with the parents and the baby?" I asked.

Anna nodded. "She visited France twice a year claiming she had old school friends she wanted to see." Anna turned to Lurleen. "It's one reason she was so taken with you. She loved your French accent and your wonderful stories."

"My French accent?" Lurleen looked over at me and grinned.

I smiled back. Lurleen's accent clearly wasn't Parisian French. It was a blend of southern charm and something uniquely Lurleen.

Anna saw the exchange. "Savannah realized you weren't really French. She assumed you also had a secret past, and it made you all the more charming to her."

Lurleen looked slightly deflated and then rallied. She never liked to interrupt a good *histoire* as Lurleen would have put it. "Please, go on."

Anna wrapped a blanket around her. "I love this house, but it does get drafty."

I insisted we all get ready for bed and continue the story later. Anna took a long bath while Lurleen and I made up the day bed. As the shortest person, I would be the most comfortable on it.

When we were all settled under the covers—Lurleen and Anna in the king size bed and me across the room in my cozy corner—Anna picked up where she'd left off. She propped herself up with pillows, so I could see her clearly.

"Savannah got used to the arrangement and was content with it for years. She had her own life to live. Her son, Olivier, was more like a nephew, and she could see his French parents were devoted to him. Savannah made sure they and the boy wanted for nothing. She used money from a personal trust her parents had provided for her, something Quinn knew nothing about."

"Her parents never saw the child?" Lurleen asked.

Anna shook her head. "The boy was an inconvenience to them, nothing more. Her mother died shortly after Savannah's father, in an Alzheimer's unit for early onset dementia patients."

"No change of heart before either of them died?" I asked.

"No. Her father was a hard man, and by the time he died, her mother was too far gone—she didn't recognize Savannah except as a nice young woman when she came to visit. I think that may be what sparked Savannah's greater involvement in her son's life. She felt free to do what she wanted once they were both dead, and I think she began to realize how tenuous life could be. I know every time she forgot something, she worried it might be a sign of a more ominous problem."

"So, she wanted Olivier to be a bigger part of her life, but she never told you who the biological father was?" I asked again.

"No."

"You have your suspicions?" I asked.

Anna shook her head a little too quickly and vehemently. "I don't know, and I never pressed her to find out. She was twenty. It could have been anyone, a college date, a townie. Honey Rose was known for having smart girls who liked to have a good time away from school. Savannah loved to tell me colorful stories about her classmates."

"Did Quinn know Savannah had a son when he married her?" I asked.

"No, not for a long time. I guess she thought it was water under the bridge, and when she told *me* she swore me to secrecy."

"Why did she tell you?" I asked.

"She sometimes needed help with Olivier. She'd ask me to visit when she was too busy to go herself. She always wanted to make sure he was doing well."

"When did she tell Quinn?" I asked.

"That was part of the big argument around their anniversary last year. She'd talked to me about bringing Olivier over as a talented young chef, which meant she had to tell Quinn. He exploded. He was furious she'd never told him of Olivier's existence, but more than that he said he wasn't about to care for anyone else's child."

"It's a terrible secret to keep from someone," Lurleen said.

"Yes," Anna said. "Savannah has trouble understanding the impact her actions have on other people. Later, Quinn settled down. He wanted to keep Savannah happy and suggested they try to have their own child."

"They were both old to try for that," I said.

"They were. However, her own parents were older when they had her. I think Savannah was ambivalent, but she saw it as a way to boost her ratings and perhaps to bring a new spark to her relationship with Quinn. She also knew I was available to help care for the child. It never happened because it turned out Quinn's sperm count was too low."

"Savannah told you this?" I asked.

"It was Quinn who confided in me about his sperm count. I think he needed someone to talk to—someone he could trust to be discreet."

"That was the end of it?" I asked.

"No. Savannah doesn't give up on things. She's as stubborn as her father. When it was clear she and Quinn couldn't have their own child, she talked again about bringing Olivier to Veracrue, making him part of their life. Quinn wasn't about to have Olivier become the long lost son."

"So there were more arguments?" Lurleen asked.

"Yes. Quinn liked to see himself as a strong, virile man. He promised to do what he could about his sperm count—I guess he thought if he could give Savannah a child, she'd forget about the one she already had."

"And Savannah was satisfied with that?" I asked.

"Not at all," Anna said. "She wanted to send Olivier more money to help pay for his tuition in a culinary institute, and that was too much for Quinn. He asked where they were supposed to get the money for that. That's when I knew finances were a real problem. I think that's the first time Savannah knew it as well."

Anna fluffed up the pillows behind her and leaned back on one elbow.

"You look tired," Lurleen said.

"I know you need your sleep," I said, "and we'll stop in a minute. You seem to think this son, Olivier, is somehow linked to the murders. Why?"

"Because Olivier was scheduled for a visit here as soon as the taping for this show ended. He'd just turned twenty-one, and he was to come as a young French chef interested in working for Savannah. I don't think she'd made a decision about whether or not she would acknowledge him as her son. Curiously, he actually is a talented chef in Aix-en-Provence."

"And," I asked, "is he still coming?"

"That's the worrisome part. After Quinn died, Savannah couldn't reach Olivier or his French parents. Not one word. She had no explanation for that. She even sent Dorian over to investigate."

"So he too knew about Olivier?" I said.

"Yes. I don't know when Savannah told him. Anyway, he found out that the family had moved out of their house and left no forwarding address. Savannah got scared that someone else knew about Olivier and must have been threatening him. She was worried something might have happened to him. First Quinn and then her child. She thought it was the only explanation."

"And you've heard nothing more about him?" I asked.

"Nothing."

At that moment, someone knocked, and we all jumped. I got out of bed, grabbed a bathrobe and stood next to the door.

"Who is it?"

"It's me, Mason. I saw your lights still on. I need to speak to you."

I unlocked the door and felt relieved—until I opened it and saw the look on his face.

Chapter Thirteen

Mason entered Lurleen's room, checked to make sure we were all present, and locked the door behind him.

"What's wrong?" I asked.

"I needed to make sure you were all safe." He looked at his watch. "I'm sorry it's so late."

"Has something happened?" I asked.

Mason shook his head. "It's Anna I'm concerned about. Another threatening letter arrived today—postmarked from New York. Dorian brought it to me after he'd sorted the mail this evening. It's addressed to Ms. Evans, but it's intended for you, Anna."

Mason held out a sheet of paper in a plastic sheath, and Anna took it.

Lurleen and I peered over her shoulder as she read the letter. There wasn't much to read. "Tell Annie she's next."

The letter was typed and signed, "A Disgruntled Fan."

"Do many people call you Annie?" Mason asked.

"Everyone here on the estate."

I looked at Anna. Her expression didn't change. There was no look of fear or horror, nothing.

Mason took back the sheet. "Do you have any idea who sent this or why they would be targeting you?"

Anna didn't say anything for a moment and then shook her head.

"You don't seem surprised or particularly frightened," Mason said.

"I'm not surprised. I'm the person closest to Savannah. I would be the obvious next target if the goal was to torment her."

"I take this threat seriously. Perhaps more seriously than you do."

"I take it seriously," Anna said, "but it won't help anyone if I get hysterical about it."

I turned to Mason. "Have a seat. We need to fill you in on a few things."

Mason sat in one of the armchairs by the unlit fireplace. Lurleen and I settled onto the day bed, blankets wrapped around us to fight the chill in the air.

Anna saw us shivering and lit a match to the well-laid logs in the fireplace. I was certain this was Dorian's work. He seemed to pride himself on taking care of everyone's needs—usually before anyone had a chance to recognize what they were.

Soon a robust fire was burning. The room heated up and a warm glow added color to Mason's dour expression. Lurleen and I moved closer to the warmth and settled on the rug near Mason's chair. We left the other chair for Anna, but she remained standing.

Try as I might, I couldn't quite get warm. These old houses were drafty as Anna said, but I think the chill was more about the danger surrounding us.

Anna stood near the hearth, her back to the fire, and recounted the story of Olivier to Mason. She drew a timeline of recent events that ended with Olivier's disappearance shortly after Quinn died.

"How did Savannah manage to keep her son a secret for twenty-one years?" Mason asked when it was clear Anna had finished.

"Savannah has always told people only what they needed to know," Anna said. "That was something Quinn and Savannah had in common—they appeared to be open and outgoing, but in reality they were very secretive. Savannah told me about her son so I could handle discreet communications with his French family. She probably told Dorian about Olivier only when she needed him to find out where the family was. She couldn't spare me to make the trip, and she didn't want to put me in danger."

"Dorian found no trace of the family?" Mason asked.

"None," Anna said. "He suspects neighbors may have known where the family went and were protecting them. Savannah's suspicion was that someone threatened Olivier—perhaps the same person who wrote the hate mail to her—and that had prompted the family to disappear."

Mason looked at Anna. "What other people knew about Olivier?"

"Peter Young worked for Quinn for five years and now works for Savannah—he might have known. Frank must have known, since Savannah sent a monthly check to the family. Both Peter and Frank probably know other secrets I don't."

"They do," Mason said.

Before he could say more, someone pounded on the door and rattled the door knob. Then we heard the person fumbling with a key in the lock.

Mason pulled out a revolver and waved his free hand to get us on the other side of the door. He turned off the light, but the glow from the fire made everything in the room visible.

The door finally opened, and Buddy Lewis charged in—freezing when he saw Mason.

"What the hell is going on?" Buddy yelled. "You gonna shoot me, Garrett?"

Mason put his gun back in its holster.

"What are you doing here?" Buddy snarled. "It's midnight. I hear all this noise in here and you turn up chatting with the girls."

"Not chatting," Mason said. He handed him the letter.

"You should have brought this to me first," the chief said. "I'm in charge here. Don't forget that."

"I looked for you," Mason said. "You weren't in Quinn's office. I tried to call you and it went to voice mail. Where were you?"

"Taking a break in my room, if it's any of your business."

"Your room is on the other corridor," Mason said. "How did you end up here?"

"I don't answer to you, Garrett. You answer to me. What are *you* doing here?"

"When I couldn't find you, I came here to make sure Anna was okay."

Buddy simmered down. "She looks okay to me. You were telling them what we found out?"

"I thought you might want to keep that private," Mason said.

"Why? You think Miss Annie's involved with this? She ain't—this letter proves she's not involved—and she might be able to fill in some of our holes."

"It's your case," Mason said. "I'll do what you tell me to do."

"I'm tired of talking. You catch 'em up on what we know, and I'll listen," the chief said. "I'd like to hear how you're putting this case together, Garrett."

Lurleen, Anna, and I looked at Mason expectantly. He sat back down in the chair. The chief remained standing by the door.

Poor Mason. He was an Atlanta cop stuck in an antebellum mansion in South Carolina where he had no authority. He seemed to give in to that realization.

"We know about Quinn Nelson's money," Mason said. "Frank Moran told us about the legitimate side of the business. Young provided information about the rest."

"I wondered about Quinn's business," Lurleen said. "I told you how Sandler's Sodas stopped using the company for real estate deals in Atlanta." She edged closer to the fire. "It became a joke really. When someone screwed up badly at Sandler's, people suggested they must be working for Quinn

Nelson. That's pretty much the reputation he had all over town—as a has-been or a never-was. I read about him in the society pages, and I wondered how he continued to make money since no one I knew took his real estate business seriously."

"They must have taken something about Quinn seriously," I said. "Every dignitary in town showed up for his funeral."

"Quinn always was a big spender," Buddy said. "Donated to everyone's political campaign."

"It seems Quinn started out as a legitimate real estate broker," Mason said. "When he couldn't get the big commission deals, he found a better way to make money. He could provide unsold real estate, actual housing, for meetings that were meant to stay private. He apparently arranged gatherings where people could get together without being noticed. Some were legitimate events with a back room for people who didn't want to be seen together—or seen at all."

"What are you talking about?" I asked. "A place for illegal activity like drug deals, gambling? Was he part of some Southern mafia?"

"Frank Moran denies it," Mason said. "He said his accounting for Nelson was all legitimate, and Moran has a good reputation in Atlanta. He said Quinn's revenue stream fell dramatically in the last year, and it was Savannah's business that essentially kept things afloat."

I'm sure I looked skeptical. "If Frank's as good as you say, how could he not know what was really going on?"

"It's a fair question," Mason said. "He claims he was trying to extricate himself from Quinn's business and Savannah's as well."

"What about the objects that were disappearing from the house?" Lurleen asked. "Have you traced them?"

"Some of them," Mason said. "Usually they went to a few pawn shops around here where they were quickly purchased—part of a small money laundering scheme perhaps. We even found a few items on eBay. It appears the money went back to Quinn, based on bank records. Young and Moran both deny any knowledge of the stolen goods."

"Savannah trusts them both, for what that's worth," Anna said.

"It was Peter Young who told us about the meetings," Mason said. "According to Young, that revenue stream dried up suddenly."

"Why?" I asked.

"Young claims he didn't know at first. He says he was primarily a bodyguard, never did anything illegal, and thought the meetings were all legitimate."

"You believe that?" I asked.

"No," Mason said. "His story is that Savannah recently asked him to look into what Quinn was doing, so he did. He gave her the full story a few months before Quinn died. Quinn was close to bankruptcy and might have been facing a criminal investigation."

"She must have been so angry," I said. "Savannah was building an empire, and Quinn was destroying it."

"You're suggesting she could have a motive for murder?" Mason said.

"I guess I am."

"How sure are you that Savannah didn't know what was going on?" Anna asked. "If you still believe she's naive about money, you have that wrong. She's a very savvy business woman."

"Do you think she was involved with this scheme?" Mason asked.

"I don't know," Anna said. "It may be more that she didn't care where the money came from as long as it kept coming, and as long as it didn't hurt her reputation."

"It would have been lucrative to set up meetings the way he did," Lurleen said. "Dangerous but lucrative."

"It *was* lucrative until the police found out about one of Quinn's meetings ahead of time," Mason said. "This one involved half a dozen Georgia drug dealers intent on getting their territories straight. They were arrested. That's when Quinn's revenue stream dried up apparently, and he began to fear for his life. The drug raid was a year ago."

"It seems as if everything started to crumble a year ago," I said, "and that's around the time the big argument occurred. Maybe it was about a lot more than children."

"It's possible," Anna said. "I didn't hear all of it."

"I'm about to have a long interview with Savannah," Mason said, "but the note is my immediate concern. I'm putting Danny on overnight duty with you, Anna."

Anna nodded.

"I also need to know more about Dorian Gray. He claims that's his birth name." Mason stared at Anna. When she didn't respond, he continued. "All we can find out about him so far is that he suddenly appeared in New York twenty years ago when he began working as a butler. He tells his own story of where he was and what he was doing before that, but none of it has been corroborated. Savannah seems to put a lot of faith in him. She sends him off to France on a very important mission, and he comes back with nothing."

"He told me Olivier and his family had simply disappeared," Anna said. "Savannah has been heartsick about that."

"Dorian has an apartment in Manhattan, left to him by his previous employer," Mason said. "Could he have sent you that letter?"

"Dorian? Why would Dorian want to harm me?"

Mason waited a moment to see if Anna would say more. She didn't.

"I understand that you and Dorian were involved with one another."

Anna's face flushed. "Who told you that?"

"The surveillance information. It seems one time you and he forgot to turn off the recording device for a few seconds. You were seated on a bed side by side in one of the basement bedrooms. Dorian took your hand and then appeared to remember the camera. He shut it off at that point. When I confronted him, he told me you two had been romantically involved. He said the affair ended three months ago, but he didn't give much explanation for why that happened."

Anna looked puzzled. "He said that?"

Mason nodded. "Are you willing to provide the details?"

Anna didn't respond immediately. She turned her back to stoke the fire. When she faced us again, she spoke directly to Mason. "I'm sure Quinn told Savannah about us after he saw what the camera had picked up. She demanded the relationship stop or she would fire both of us. I'm not sure why she was so upset about it, but I think Savannah believes all loyalty should be to her alone."

"You broke it off to save your career?" Mason asked.

"This job is my life. I know it sounds ridiculous—a job over a relationship, but I have a future here. Someday I might have my own cooking school. That's what Savannah offered in exchange for ending the relationship, so that's the choice I made."

"Was Dorian angry about your decision—angry enough to want to harm you?" Mason asked.

"Dorian is not a violent man," she said.

"You didn't answer my question. Do you think he might be the one who wrote the note?"

"I don't know."

With that Anna turned her attention once more to the fire, which was slowly dying.

"We'll stop for now," Mason said. "Danny will be outside the door."

Mason left, and Anna didn't say another word. She went into the bathroom and ran a bath—her second of the evening.

Chapter Fourteen

I put another small log on the fire. It wouldn't hurt us to stay warm.

"What's she doing in the bathroom?" Lurleen asked. She stood beside me and rubbed her hands together to get some heat.

"Probably calling Dorian, to give him a heads up, or to find out if he's involved in some way. She took her phone with her."

Lurleen put her ear to the bathroom door. "All I can hear is water running." She returned to the fire. "One more log?"

I nodded.

Lurleen positioned a log so that the flames danced around it and set it ablaze. We were in our own little universe, faces aglow, bodies warm. Just beyond the circle of light from the fire, the room was dark and cold.

I shivered despite the warmth.

As she often did, Lurleen understood my feelings with no words spoken. "There's something evil in this house. I can tell you feel it too." She wrapped an arm around me like a good protective mother.

"Something or someone," I said. "Evil enough to commit two murders and make Savannah's life a living hell. It's as if real-life Halloween has settled into this place—maybe it's the haint Savannah talked about, evil under the guise of Southern charm and the comfort of old Southern ways."

"We do like our Southern traditions and politeness," Lurleen said. "I always have to put on my heaviest armor when I travel north to stave off what New Englanders call being frank."

"I find that honesty refreshing," I said, "but I know it can be jarring. In the Midwest, we tell you the truth, but we also make sure you have what you need to get through the winter. It's every man for his neighbor."

"I like that," Lurleen said. "Maybe we'll take a road trip to Iowa. Your kids should see where you grew up."

"You're right, Lurleen. Like you, I've kept a lot of my past to myself." This was all it took to make Lurleen change the subject.

"You realize Savannah could be the mastermind behind all of these disasters," she said. "Look at the sympathy she's generated for herself. I'll bet her ratings are soaring, and that is, after all, what every star wants."

"You may be right. I like her so it's hard for me to see her in that light."

"I love you dearly, Ditie, you know I do—"

"But?"

"You like to put people in boxes. All good, all bad. That isn't how people come. Believe me, I know." She studied my face. "Did I hurt your feelings?"

"No, it's true. My father was the best father in the world, and after he died he just got more saint-like."

"I wish I'd known him. From what you say, he was close to perfect, but surely, even he had his flaws. He never stood up to your mother, did he? He didn't keep her from sending your brother off to boarding school."

"No, he didn't. Dad didn't like a fight, and my mother could never resist one."

"That's all I'm saying, *cherie*. People don't fit in those neat little packages you make for them."

I sighed. "I know they don't. That's why I read cozy mysteries where good people catch the bad guys and put them away."

Lurleen laughed. "Sometimes, you tell me those stories get a little boring. Real life is never boring, sweetie."

She turned her back to the fire.

"It's a beautiful home," she said, "but can you imagine the money it takes to heat it, let alone keep it up? There's no doubt it's a money pit."

Lurleen wrapped a throw around her shoulders and threw me a blanket from the daybed. I curled up with it in one of the armchairs. Lurleen poked again at the fire and then settled into the other chair.

"I for one, won't mind returning to my bungalow," Lurleen said. "Why would anyone need 18,000 square feet when 1800 is plenty?"

This was coming from a woman who could have either.

"Fame demands a face doesn't it?" I said. "A facade that says I've made it. You can imagine Savannah's feelings if she sees her wealth disappearing."

"And what's behind the facade?" Lurleen said. "Decay perhaps? What do you think of Anna's story?"

"I think there might be a lot we don't know about Anna," I said. "She told us she was frightened, but she didn't look scared to me."

"I agree, *chérie,*" Lurleen said. "Mason says her life is being threatened, and she barely bats an eye."

"She doesn't seem to be troubled that we know about her affair with Dorian Gray," I said.

"They're an unlikely pair, don't you think?" Lurleen asked. "I know opposites attract, but here's Anna, full of life, a beautiful woman. Then there's Dorian, as gray as his name. Someone who's content to live in the shadows."

"He's an odd duck all right," I said, "putting on the airs of a British butler circa 1900. It feels like he's an actor in a play. Has he ever dropped his guard with you, Lurleen?"

"Never, and you know I've tried to get him to open up. Who better than a butler to know what's going on?"

"Unless the butler is the one causing the trouble," I said. "I wonder what his real name is. I'm sure Mason is trying to trace that."

The water was no longer running, so we spoke more quietly.

"I swear Anna almost smiled when Mason showed her the new threat," Lurleen said, "as if she expected it or it was part of some plan."

"A plan to make her look like a potential victim, you mean?" I asked. "What would she have to gain? She needs Savannah's empire to succeed," I said, "unless of course, she thought she might take it over. Perhaps in the midst of a scandal, she could become the new Savannah Evans. Dorian Gray conveniently found the threatening letter. Perhaps he and Anna never really broke off their relationship. Perhaps together they know enough about the organization to make it work for themselves."

I shook my head. "It's a lot of 'if's'. Would they really resort to murder to get what they want?"

Lurleen shrugged her shoulders. "Anna and Dorian could certainly have pulled off all the pranks, the warnings."

"And kill the poor reporter? Drag his body off the estate?" I said.

"It's possible," Lurleen said. "Perhaps the reporter discovered what they were up to. People do all kinds of things when they're desperate enough."

We heard the water draining out of the tub, and we remained silent, waiting for Anna to reappear.

When she did, she looked as if she'd been crying. Lurleen jumped up and offered her the chair beside me. Anna settled into it. "I haven't been entirely honest with you," she said softly.

Neither Lurleen nor I spoke.

Anna wrapped her bathrobe tightly around her. "I didn't break off the relationship with Dorian for my career."

"We wondered about that," Lurleen said. "So you two are still involved?" She sat on the rug next to Anna's chair as if she were a small child waiting for a favorite bedtime story.

"No, Lurleen, you misunderstand me. Dorian and I are not an item. I did break off our relationship, but it wasn't because of Savannah's threat. It was because I was involved with another man."

I tried not to let my mouth fall open. I'd grown up in a rural community in Iowa, but I wasn't naive about affairs. They turned up there from time to time and usually hurt or destroyed the families involved. It was more that Anna was tossing out information on her love life like Mardi Gras beads.

"You seem disturbed, Ditie," Anna said, as she finished drying her hair with a towel. "I hope I haven't shocked you. I'm not a bad woman simply because I fell in love with someone. I never meant it to happen. Neither one of us did."

"Is that the person you were talking to in the bathroom?" Lurleen asked.

"What do you mean?" Anna said. "You were listening at the door?"

"I couldn't hear anything," Lurleen said, "but why else would you take a phone in the bathroom if what you wanted was a bath?"

"Your second bath," I added.

"You both act as if you don't trust me. I'm the one being threatened."

I stood and moved to the daybed. I wanted to see Anna clearly and from a little distance. "You were saying you broke off your relationship with Dorian for someone else. Naturally, we assumed you were calling that person just now."

Anna gave a short, bitter laugh.

"If only. I wasn't calling anyone. I was flustered and needed to calm down. I guess I grabbed the phone by mistake. My whole life is being exposed here." Anna pulled her dark hair back into a ponytail. "You won't understand what I'm about to tell you. I don't understand it myself."

"Try us," I said.

"We've liked you from the start," Lurleen said, "and we don't make judgments."

I looked at Lurleen. She smiled innocently back at me.

"We just want to know the truth," I said.

Anna got tearful again. Was it genuine or a play for sympathy?

"Quinn and I loved Savannah," she said. "We'd have done anything for her. But, she constantly threw us together, almost as if she wanted something to happen, and it finally did."

"You had a relationship with Quinn Nelson?" I asked.

She nodded. "It's like a bad movie, isn't it?"

"Yes," I said under my breath. I couldn't fathom why a beautiful thirty-year-old woman would be attracted to Quinn Nelson.

"You didn't talk to Quinn, did you, Ditie?" Lurleen said.

"Only at the end of the party when he was clearly in distress."

"I did," she said. "If you'd had a conversation with him earlier in the evening, you would have realized how charismatic he was. He could have been eighty years old and still gotten any woman he wanted. When he turned his attention on you, it was like a beacon of light, like you were the only woman in the room. Certainly the most desirable."

"I want you to understand," Anna said, "I couldn't help myself. And it wasn't what you're imagining, some kind of sordid affair. Quinn couldn't really have the physical relationship with me or Savannah that he might have liked, and that really bothered him. Ours was emotional more than anything else, a deepening friendship that turned into love. I hated what we were doing to Savannah, but I swear Savannah wanted it to happen. Why else did she throw us together all the time?"

"Maybe she trusted the two of you," I said. "You were the two people closest to her."

"I've told you Savannah isn't naive. If you still think that, then you have her all wrong. She knew what Quinn was capable of. She didn't always like it, and when she didn't like it, she turned a blind eye." Anna grabbed a tissue and twisted it. "I think Savannah knew about us. I think she wanted it to happen."

"Why?" I asked.

"I think she was getting tired of Quinn, especially when it was clear he was no longer a wealthy man. Maybe she was ready to move on. I even wondered if *she* had someone waiting in the wings. Perhaps she wanted to make it easy for everyone involved. She could get Quinn settled with a new woman—me—and then have a quiet divorce—or a noisy one. I'm not sure she cared. She could look like the wronged woman. It would do wonders for her image and get her back on the talk show circuits."

Lurleen and I stared at each other.

"Do you know who Savannah's new interest might be?" I asked.

Anna shook her head. "It's only been since Quinn's death I've had time to think about how it all started. She'd ask me to look out for him while she was away. And then she'd be gone for a day or a weekend. Peter Young often went with her. I remember wondering about their relationship, but Peter denied there was anything between them. He claimed he was acting as her bodyguard, something Quinn asked him to do."

A gentle knocking on the door silenced us.

Lurleen whispered before she opened the door, "Who is it?"

"It's me, Danny."

Lurleen unlocked the door and opened it a crack.

"It's late," he said. "After two. Y'all okay in there?"

"Yes," she said. "We'll fill you in tomorrow."

"I'll be right outside in the hall," he said. "You keep this door locked."

"Will do." Lurleen gave him a quick kiss, closed and locked the door, and switched off the overhead light. The dying embers from the fire gave us enough light to let us get settled in bed.

"You know you'll have to tell Mason and the chief everything you've told us."

"I know," Anna said. "I'm relieved to tell you the truth."

"Speaking of the truth," I said. "You must know Dorian's real name. What is it?"

Anna was slow to answer. "Dorian told me his past was over and done with, and in this new life he was Dorian Gray. I didn't push that. You have to believe me."

I wasn't sure I did, but what I needed was a good night's sleep. Things were always clearer in the morning. I settled into the cozy daybed and pulled the warm quilt over me. I tried to watch the last flickering light from the fire, but I was asleep before the embers died.

Something roused me in the middle of the night—a dog whining? I listened and then got up. I wrapped a bathrobe around me and opened the door cautiously. Danny was standing by his chair.

"You heard it too?" I asked.

"It's not so much what I heard as what I saw," he said. "I saw a figure in a flowing white gown come upstairs and cross to the other hallway. I followed and saw the person…, " here he hesitated. "I'm not nuts, and I haven't been drinking. I saw the person disappear into a wall. I swear they walked right into a wall."

Danny locked the door to the bedroom, and together, we headed to the other hallway.

"Just about here," Danny said. He poked on the wall and nothing happened.

"Maybe there really is a ghost," I said.

"You don't believe in that stuff, and I don't either," Danny said.

Saffron appeared as if from nowhere and stood beside us whining.

"This is what I heard. What's wrong, girl?" I asked.

She let me pet her but kept her nose to the wall where we were standing.

"Let's take her back to Savannah and make sure everything's okay."

An officer sat outside the door to her suite. He stood when we approached and rubbed his eyes as if we'd caught him napping.

Savannah met us inside her suite. "There you are," she said to Saffron. It was nearly three am., and Savannah was fully dressed.

"Just couldn't sleep," she said, when we both stared at her clothes. "I haven't been anywhere. The guard outside my door can tell you that."

We hadn't asked her that question, so I wondered why she needed to answer it. Danny and I went back to Lurleen's room. He unlocked the door for me and waited while I checked inside. Both Lurleen and Anna were asleep. I nodded to Danny and slipped back into my cold bed.

Chapter Fifteen

Everyone was up early the next day for a seven thirty breakfast. Anna was out of our room by six. Lurleen and I found her in the small kitchen a little after seven. How Anna had time to make Eggs Benedict for twenty people along with Banana Foster French Toast, I will never know. And how she did it on six burners and two stoves made it more amazing. She moved through the kitchen like a professional chef, but without the shouting. I heard her speak quietly to three staff as they cooked and plated the breakfasts.

Two shows were to be taped that day after we first completed the beignet challenge. By the end of the day, two more contestants would be eliminated. Still in the running were Rose Kirkwood, Gertrude "Granny" Flumm, Izzy Moran, and me.

I wondered if James Bradshaw would be allowed to join the tasting table. When I entered the breakfast room I saw him seated once again beside Granny Flumm.

I sat down at a table next to them. I was very curious to know what these two had in common. Lurleen joined me. She had dressed with particular care in hopes she would once more be included at the tasting table to comment on the entries. She wore a yellow wool sheath that suited her coloring and her curves. "I wouldn't want to outshine Savannah," she told me. She gave me a wicked smile when she saw Pepper Young enter the dining room. "Her, I don't mind outshining."

It wouldn't be hard to do on this particular morning. Pepper looked as if she'd had a sleepless night. Her face was drawn, and while her long skirt and sweater belonged in *Vogue,* the rest of her did not. I wondered if she was coming down with something. When I tried to say hello, she acted as if she hadn't heard me.

Sarah Osborne

I put one finger to my lips when Lurleen started talking again. She saw me straining to hear the conversation between Bradshaw and Granny Flumm, and she was silent.

"This must disgust you, James," Flumm said. "All this pretend civility. I know it disgusts me. Savannah, to the manor born, to the manor stolen more like it."

James grunted and continued eating.

"It won't be for much longer, James," Flumm said. "She will be royally exposed when this is over."

"Damn reporter," James said.

"That's over and done with," Flumm replied. "What I need from you is a little sobriety—just until the end of the week."

"Don't order me around," he said. "No one orders me around."

"You want to get this mansion back? If so, you need to keep your wits about you."

Anna was making the rounds to see if anyone wanted seconds. That silenced the two of them. I looked over at Lurleen, and she gave me a bewildered look. She hadn't been able to hear the conversation. Izzy and Frank Moran asked if they could join our table before I could say anything.

"I can't thank you enough, Dr. Brown, for what you did that first night," Izzy said.

"Please, it's Ditie. I'm glad I was there, but there were at least two other EpiPens in the house—you had one and so did Savannah."

"It's such a frightening experience. It makes one lose one's bearings."

"Are you fine now?"

"More than fine—ready for the next challenge."

"Do you have any idea where the peanuts came from?" I asked.

"No. Do you?"

I shook my head.

"You can bet I have my EpiPen right here beside me." She patted her small purse.

Izzy struck me as remarkably calm about the whole incident. Maybe that's what happens when you have a lethal allergy with a quick way to reverse it. Still, I wasn't sure I'd be so calm.

"Do you know any more about the investigation?" Frank asked. "Any more about that reporter?"

He hadn't touched his breakfast, and I wondered if this was why he'd chosen to sit at our table. He certainly couldn't get the information from the police. We undoubtedly seemed like a more likely source.

"No one's telling us anything," I lied. "You probably know more about what's going on than I do."

"What do you mean?"

"You work for Savannah. You know all the players."

"I think it's an outside job," Frank said. "A drug dealer, perhaps."

"You knew about that?"

Frank sat back. "Like everyone else, I read the details in the paper. My work with Quinn and Savannah has always been legitimate. I don't like your insinuation."

"No insinuation," I said. "Curiosity."

"Curiosity can be dangerous." Frank stood and left his full plate behind. Izzy silently followed.

"That struck a nerve," Lurleen said. "You think innocent Frank might not be quite so innocent?"

"I wonder." I told Lurleen about the conversation between Granny Flumm and Bradshaw—the one she hadn't been able to overhear. My acute hearing seemed to be the one super power I possessed. The same one my dad possessed. It used to drive us crazy when Dad would hear Tommy and me planning a dangerous tube trip down our raging creek after a rainstorm. Now, I clearly saw its value.

I sent Lurleen off to tell Mason and Danny about both conversations, and I headed for the set.

The first taping started at 8:30. We each got our beignet dough from the refrigerator. When Chris signaled action, we set to work. I knew Lurleen would carry out her mission, and I could focus on cooking.

Each of us had a deep cast iron skillet and plenty of vegetable oil in which to fry the beignets. I, for one, had no idea how large they should be or how long they should fry. I assumed like a doughnut, they'd float to the top of the oil when they were ready to be flipped. It was amusing really—for me anyway. I was creating something I'd tasted once in my life, and I tried to remember the right size and shape as I rolled out the dough. A couple of inches square I thought. My beignets cooked quickly, and I hoped they were cooked through when I put them on the rack to drain and sprinkled them with powdered sugar.

We all finished within half an hour, the time allotted, and put them on a plate with our name beside it on a card turned face down. I heard Granny Flumm muttering as she put her sample next to mine. "Why does Savannah want these fancy recipes? No Southerner outside of New Orleans cares about beignets, and they're really not Southern anyway."

Savannah entered alone. In the technical challenge we did not have to leave the room. She tasted and discussed each sample one by one, calling us up once she'd had a bite of beignet and turned over the card beside it.

"A bit soggy," she said to Izzy. "Not quite cooked through. I think your oil wasn't hot enough."

"Acceptable," she said to Granny Flumm. "Could have been a bit lighter. I think perhaps you overworked your dough."

Granny Flumm barely managed to keep her face composed. "I've been making biscuits for fifty years, Savannah. I know how to keep from overworking my dough."

I was sure this comment would be edited out.

Rose was next. "I've never eaten a beignet, and I had no idea how they were supposed to look."

"Well, you did very well with it," Savannah said. "They're bigger than I might like, but people differ on how large they should be."

Rose smiled and returned to her station looking relieved.

"These are the right size and the right texture," Savannah said to me. "Slightly undercooked, perhaps, but very edible."

I also breathed a sigh of relief.

We had a fifteen-minute break before our next episode. That gave me just enough time to find Mason.

He started talking before I could. "Lurleen told me about the conversations. Bradshaw and Flumm are up to something together, and it's highly likely Frank Moran knows more than he's telling us. Thanks, Ditie."

"There's more," I said. I told him about our conversation with Anna from the night before.

Mason looked as disbelieving as I felt. "Anna told you that she and Quinn had an affair?"

"She said it was more emotional than physical."

"Why would Anna be interested in a man like Quinn? Did she think he could be a sugar daddy for her?"

"Lurleen says there was something about the man that was irresistible— something I never saw. Anna also said she thought Savannah wanted it to happen—that she might have had a new love interest herself. Lurleen wondered if it might be Peter Young."

That's all there was time for. I had five minutes to get back on set.

Savannah entered the room and smiled at the camera as she described the next challenge. It was to make a unique pecan dessert. Anything was acceptable except for pecan pie. The other contestants groaned with that announcement. I was secretly pleased. I'd never mastered the art of pecan pie, but I did know a thing or two about pecans. I used them in cookies, bars, granola. Everything tasted better with Southern pecans.

We had one hour with our usual five-minute break. During the break, Lurleen caught up with me to fix my make-up. She used the time to whisper that she was sticking close to Savannah and might have information later.

Chris got us back to our stations promptly, and one minute before time was up, we served up plates or bowls of something pecan. As usual each dish had a code number beside it, and we were sent to the viewing area in Anna's office.

Savannah, Pepper, and Lurleen sat at the tasting table. A seat had been left for James Bradshaw, but he was a no-show. With a nod from Savannah, Chris had the unclaimed chair removed.

"This is a very close contest," Savannah announced after sampling each selection and conferring with her tasting partners. "However the winner is the pecan bread pudding."

She opened the card. "Rose, you win again. A master of puddings I would say."

Rose was delighted. Granny Flumm took second, and she was not a happy loser. Savannah said her pecan almond tart was too close to a pecan pie to be a first-place contender.

"How could you eliminate pecan pies from the contest when they are the mainstay of the South?" Flumm growled at Savannah.

Undoubtedly, that comment would also be left on the cutting room floor. Savannah never lost her smile, but if looks could kill, Granny Flumm might also be left inert on the cutting room floor.

I came in third with my pecan nutfest cookie cake.

Izzy Moran took fourth place and was eliminated. She was gracious. "I'm happy to have made it this far."

I thought she might be happy just to be alive—no peanuts got mixed in with the pecans.

We had a two-hour break before the afternoon session, and I was determined to put it to good use. First, I tracked down Mason. He was in a huddle with the chief.

"I can take a break," Mason said. "What's up?"

"I just need to touch base with you," I said. That was often our code for 'I need some private time with you,' if the kids were around. It took Lucie a good five minutes to figure out what that meant. "If you want to be alone, Aunt Di, just say so. Jason and I can go play or watch TV."

Mason stood up, and Chief Lewis gave him a nod. "Take your time. I got plenty to do here."

Mason and I walked outside through the formal gardens at the back of the house. "Did you get a chance to interview Anna?" I asked.

"I did while you were working with your pecan dessert. Did you save any for me?"

"Yes, unless the crew found what I set aside. I can always make more."

Mason smiled in that way that made his whole face light up and mine as well—the smile that made me feel loved and special.

"Back to Anna," I said to help us both stay focused.

"Anna confirmed what you said. I also talked to Savannah during the break between shoots. She acknowledged that her finances were in disarray and that she had a son in France who had disappeared. She looked genuinely worried about that. The place she would not go was to a lover. That she claimed was absurd. When would she have time for a lover? She adored Quinn. Why would she do that to him?"

"Can I do anything to help with the investigation?" I asked.

"I wonder if you and Lurleen might get something more out of Savannah than I did."

I smiled. "Lurleen is already working on that. It seems Savannah thinks they have a special bond. I'll be around Anna a lot. Perhaps I can see what else she knows and isn't saying."

"You don't think she's being entirely honest?" Mason said.

"I don't think anyone in this house is being completely honest, do you?" Mason shook his head. "No."

That was all he had time for. "I've got to get back. Be careful."

"Always," I said.

He left me just inside the back door with a quick kiss.

It was nearly time for lunch. I went in search of Anna and found her in the kitchen supervising the staff.

"Can I do something to help," I asked, "or should I stay out of your way?"

"Neither one. I think my staff have things under control. I can visit for a few minutes." She left the women to their tasks and walked with me to the back deck.

"It's such a beautiful day. Why don't we sit out here for a while?" She settled herself around a wrought-iron table. I sat across from her. For a moment we both enjoyed the cool breeze. "It's such a relief to have told you and Lurleen the truth."

"Did you tell us all of it?" I asked.

"What do you mean?"

"I mean—is there more you haven't said? You didn't seem upset by the threat. Most people would have been terrified, especially after what happened to Quinn."

Anna started to protest and then seemed to think better of it. "All right. It's true I wasn't frightened."

"And why was that?" I asked.

"Because I think I know who sent that note."

Chapter Sixteen

I drew my chair closer to the table. The cool breeze had turned into something less pleasant, and I wished I'd brought a jacket with me. November afternoons in the South were unpredictable and getting more so. One minute I'd need my coat and the next I'd be happy in a sleeveless blouse. Anna saw me shivering and asked if we should go inside. I shook my head. We had far more privacy where we were, and that meant it was more likely Anna would be candid with me.

"You know who sent the letter? Why didn't you tell us?"

Anna sat up a little straighter and ran a hand through her black hair to put back in place what the wind had tousled. "I wasn't sure, and I'm still not positive. I didn't want to get someone in trouble if they weren't involved."

I leaned forward. "What kind of cat-and-mouse game are you playing? Everyone here is a suspect or a potential victim, including you. Who do you think wrote the note?"

"I'm not playing games with you." Anna looked down at her hands. "I think Dorian may have sent it. He was very angry when I broke off the affair and even more hurt when he discovered my relationship with Quinn."

"You think he sent all the threatening letters?" I asked.

"No, just mine. You remember how he wrote Annie, not Anna. Only two people call me that—the chief and Dorian. The chief likes me, so I assume it was Dorian."

"You told us that was a common nickname for you on the estate. You lied about that."

"Yes. I didn't want to get anyone in trouble. I think perhaps Dorian used the nickname so I wouldn't be too frightened."

"How did you two get together in the first place?"

"We were two lonely people. I suppose that's how."

"Why didn't you tell Mason you thought he might be behind the threat to you?"

Anna sighed. "I didn't want Detective Garrett to go after him. It's as simple as that."

"It doesn't sound simple to me. And why should we believe anything you say when all you've done is lied to us?"

Anna shrugged.

"Maybe you sent that note to yourself so we wouldn't get suspicious of you. You admitted to a year of nursing school. You'd certainly know how to start an IV."

"I loved Quinn. How could you even suggest that?"

"What I can't figure out is how his death might have benefited you?"

The sun came out, and I realized I was no longer shivering. I was focused on Anna, desperate to hear the truth from her no matter where that led.

"Maybe your loyalty was to Savannah and not Quinn. He'd become an albatross for her. Without him, perhaps the two of you could reenergize her empire, and you could get your cooking school."

"If you actually think I'm a murderer, aren't you being foolish to tell me that?"

I couldn't argue with her. I often talked when it would be better for me to keep my mouth shut. But, I also didn't want to believe Anna could be a killer.

"I know you and Savannah are close. Is your relationship more than a friendship?"

Anna laughed. "I suppose we're a lot like sisters. We get on each other's nerves at times, get jealous of one another, that sort of thing. But, if you're talking about a love relationship, no. We are both heterosexual women, and believe it or not, I think we both loved Quinn. She wanted someone like me to take him off her hands before she saw everything she'd worked for destroyed."

"Was Quinn willing to get a divorce to be with you?"

"No. We would be two penniless people. Quinn couldn't stand the idea of being poor. He cared about me a great deal, but he needed Savannah. He'd do anything it took to make her happy."

"That's where the virility treatments came in?"

"He thought if he could give her a child, she'd leave Olivier in France and never ask again for a divorce."

"Savannah asked for a divorce?"

"Yes, in the midst of one of their worst arguments. He said he'd never agree to that—they would stay together on paper at least because he knew where all the bodies were buried."

"You've just given Savannah a perfect motive for murder," I said.

"Have I?"

My head was starting to hurt. Anna had a way of presenting her story and then twisting it until I didn't know which end was up.

I turned back to the mysterious Dorian Gray.

"You think Dorian's anger at you would be enough to make him send you a death threat?" I tugged on my short unruly curls, something I only did when I was annoyed and trying hard not to show it.

"Dorian likes to stir the pot, but if he did send it, he wouldn't carry through on anything. Dorian's afraid of his own shadow and certainly doesn't want to lose his job."

"How did he get his job with Savannah?" I asked.

Anna stopped talking for a moment. I couldn't tell if she was actually trying to recall the history of his employment or perhaps making up a story.

"He started working for Savannah shortly after I did. She'd call him in for parties and liked what a perfect butler he was. I think he made her feel she'd regained some of the old Southern splendor that had flourished in this house before the Civil War. She couldn't hire a black butler these days, but one with British airs—she thought that was perfect."

"You didn't really answer my question. How did she find out about him if he was in New York?"

"I had something to do with that. I lived in New York when I was young and came south after my parents died. They lived in Manhattan and loved their parties. I met Dorian at the home of a friend of theirs—the man who employed him for twenty years. I suggested Savannah use him for a big gathering. She did and loved him. She used him for all her formal parties."

"You claim he only wrote the note to you, not the other letters. You say he wouldn't hurt a fly. Why are you working so hard to protect him?"

"I feel sorry for Dorian. He leads a miserable life. I don't want to get him in trouble for a stupid, childish note. As a young man, he had far greater hopes than to be a butler. He was going to be an actor. You can see how talented he is—his British accent and airs. No one would believe he isn't English."

"What happened?"

Again Anna paused as if she'd told me more than she intended. "He was at NYU in his second year and actually performing off-Broadway. He never told me the details—just said he ran out of money and had family obligations. He had to give up on his dream."

I shook my head. "I like you, Anna, but getting the truth out of you is like pulling teeth. You denied knowing his real name, but I don't believe you. What is it?"

Anna hesitated and then looked me in the eye. "Dorian reinvents himself to suit the occasion. For now, he's Dorian Gray. He thought that was very clever. He claims he can be reborn any time he wants. He never has to age. He's harmless, really, a harmless, unhappy man."

"I hope you're right. I have to tell Mason about this. Is there anything else you're hiding?"

Anna shook her head slowly. "I'm trying to be open and honest with you, but I don't know any more than I've told you. Someone wants to destroy Savannah, and they're doing a pretty good job of it. It isn't me, and it isn't Dorian. We depend on Savannah for our livelihood."

I was never particularly good at telling when someone was lying to me. My psychiatrist friend said no one was really good at it, even those who claimed to be.

I'd give Anna one more try. "Do you know where Quinn was going to get his virility treatments?"

"He was very secretive about that, embarrassed, I think. He let me know he was doing it as a way to explain why he couldn't perform sometimes. It wasn't the sexual part that mattered to me. It was something much deeper. I lost my father when I was young, and I suppose it was something about the way in which Quinn wanted to protect me—I'm sure that's part of the reason I loved him as much as I did."

"He drove himself to the appointments?" I asked.

"No. Quinn didn't drive—felt it was beneath him. Peter Young might have taken him or one of the gardeners. They took care of his vintage automobiles. Now that I think about it, I believe Quinn called a service when he had an appointment somewhere. Wait, I might be able to find a card."

Anna left me to the sun and cool wind that had picked up again. I moved to a comfortable outdoor sofa protected from the weather by the overhanging roof. It was tucked in a corner, the back of the sofa lined up with the back of the house. Apparently, no one knew I was there. Inside the hallway, I heard murmuring and then what sounded like an argument. Anna had left the back door open slightly.

I heard a deep voice and then a soft one. "You stupid fool. You got no more sense than a chicken without a head." I recognized the chief's voice. I couldn't make out the mumbled response. "I'm doing the best I can to keep you out of this," Buddy continued, "but I'm a police officer. I got the law to contend with and I got one smart detective breathing down my neck. Get your act together."

I rose as quietly as I could and stood near the open door. In the hallway I saw Buddy with his back to me. The woman he was shouting at was Rose Kirkwood. Rose made eye contact with me and her eyes grew wide. She jumped when I announced my presence by closing the outside door.

"Such a breeze out there," I said. "I'm sorry. I didn't mean to slam the door."

"No harm done," Buddy said. "These doors have lasted two hundred years. They'll last a few more. I think I heard the dinner bell. I'll leave you two ladies to it."

Rose and I walked down the long hallway toward the dining room. "I couldn't help overhearing," I said. "I didn't realize you and the chief knew one another."

"We don't," Rose said. "I don't know what you thought you overheard. Buddy wanted my recipe for pecan pudding for his wife. I guess he got upset when I said I didn't give out my recipes."

She spoke quietly, but her hands were shaking.

I nodded. Rose was scared, and I wished I knew why. I couldn't ask any more questions because Anna caught up with me, breathless.

"The card you wanted, here it is," she said.

Rose looked at me curiously.

"It's nothing important," I said. "I wanted a new mixer, and Anna was giving me the name of the manufacturer."

Rose looked as if she no more believed *me* than I believed *her* explanation of the argument with the chief.

Chapter Seventeen

Anna urged us to come to lunch, as they were already serving.

I found Lurleen in the dining room seated next to Izzy Moran. She'd saved a seat for me.

Izzy was cheerful. "I'm happy to be done with the competition. It's so much pressure."

Her husband, Frank, was less pleased to see me, but he sat down beside his wife. He turned to Savannah who was seated on his other side. "I won't be sorry to see this contest end. No offense, Savannah."

"None taken," Savannah said. She leaned across him to speak to Izzy. "I'm pleased you were willing to stay, Izzy, after the peanut crisis."

"Did you find out what happened?" Frank asked.

"No, but I can assure you we were very careful with the pecans we ordered from a Georgia grower. He has his own processing plant and deals with nothing but pecans. It can be a real problem in the South with so many small peanut and pecan farmers who must share processing plants. I'm convinced it was a terrible accident, nothing more."

I wondered if Savannah could actually believe that, considering everything else that had happened. At the very least it was another prank. At the worst it was attempted murder.

The rest of lunch was uneventful. I didn't see Mason or Danny or the chief and wondered what had kept them from a hearty meal of shrimp and grits with fried green tomatoes.

Rose, Granny Flumm, and I left before dessert in order to get ready for the semi-finals. Savannah joined us on set a few minutes before the next segment.

"You have been wonderful contestants," she said. "Any one of you could join my staff, just say the word."

I glanced at my two fellow contestants. Flumm looked perfectly comfortable in that reserved way of hers. Rose looked distracted. She glanced over at her husband, George, who sat on the front row. He gave her a thumbs up and then put two fingers at the corner of his mouth. She got the message and smiled—a stiff anxious smile in my opinion.

Savannah took her place in front of the camera, welcoming viewers and contestants back to the semifinals. She announced that one could not live on desserts and side dishes alone. A good Southern cook needed to know how to prepare a wonderful main dish, and what could be more Southern than fried chicken. Therefore, today's cooking challenge would be Southern fried chicken with a modern-day twist. We would have two hours.

Not much time for a marinade, I thought. My twist would be baked chicken that tasted fried but was a lot healthier. I watched the other two contestants frantically grabbing up ingredients. Rose ran back and forth, a bit like a chicken with her head cut off. Wasn't that how the chief had described her? What could those two have in common?

Once the time started, we all settled down. Savannah had left the room. Most of the eliminated contestants and their husbands were present as Buddy had ordered. A policeman was stationed at each door leading into or out of the kitchen. Lurleen was in the front row next to George. There was no sign of James Bradshaw.

The crisis didn't start until halfway through the episode. Rose had just started frying her chicken when we all heard a pop. A short burst of flames leapt up around her frying pan. The flames stopped almost as soon as they started. She jumped back and screamed.

"Yikes!" Chris yelled and then waited a second before he swooped in with a fire extinguisher. I noticed he didn't nix the cameras.

I ran to Rose. "Let me see your hands," I said. "Did you burn yourself?"

"I don't think so."

I examined her hands carefully, along with her arms to see if grease had splattered anywhere on her body.

"I'm okay," Rose insisted. She didn't sound like it. She was gasping for air and appeared to be looking around for her husband. An officer was keeping him away while I ministered to her.

I led her to the prep sink and held her arms and hands under cold water. "I don't see any burns. Do you know what happened?"

She shook her head. "One moment the chicken was sizzling the way it should, and the next moment I thought the pan was on fire."

Lurleen ran up to us. "I saw what happened. The flames came out from around the pan, not *in* the pan. It was a malfunction of the stove top. Or something else."

"Someone wanted to hurt me or get me out of the competition," Rose said.

"You and I need to talk," I said. "I heard everything the chief said to you. What was that all about?"

"I don't want George to hear. Do you understand? If I can talk to you privately, I'll do that, but he can't know about this."

"We may be talking about your life. Do *you* understand *that*?"

"Yes."

Chris announced there would be an hour break during which a new stove top would be substituted for the one Rose had been using. They would reshoot the entire episode and splice and dice the film as needed.

I wondered briefly if Chris had orchestrated the whole thing to make the episode a little more thrilling. The burner had worked fine for the beignets. Had someone doctored it for the fried chicken episode?

Why weren't Mason, the chief, and Danny on the set? Chris saw me searching for them. He said the chief had left with Danny and Mason seconds before the segment began—to follow up on some lead the chief said he had. Chris would try to reach them.

Rose spoke briefly to her husband, and then Lurleen, Rose, and I went to my room to talk. I'd moved most of my things to Lurleen's bedroom. That meant no one was likely to find us in mine. Rose didn't want Lurleen present, but I insisted. Lurleen promised to keep the conversation private.

At that point, Rose broke down, big gulping sobs. "I've made a mess of it," she mumbled between a storm of tears. "George is such a good man."

Lurleen handed her tissues. I gave her a glass of water from the bathroom sink. "Breathe slowly and tell us what you're so upset about."

"It's Buddy Lewis," she said between sniffles. "I knew him years ago, or rather he knew me. Thirty years ago I didn't look the way I look now. And I didn't have George."

"You did something before you married George?" I asked.

Rose nodded and blew her nose. "I was a pretty girl in those days. My family didn't have any money. Someone told me a producer was in town looking for beautiful girls to act in his films. When I met him, he told me I was just the kind of girl he was looking for. I jumped at the chance. I was in my twenties, working in a drugstore. He offered me more money than my dad made in a year." She paused. "He said I had to keep it a secret from my folks. Later, I understood why."

"Porn films," Lurleen said.

Rose nodded. "Me, the only girl in my high school who had never been kissed. Someone promised me fame, and I jumped at it. One thing led to another. By the time I realized what I was doing, it was too late, and the money was so important for my family. The producer kept saying how the movies weren't real—it was all pretend. They never made me get totally naked, but it looked that way on screen. When I saw one of my movies, I died of shame. I finally quit, but those films were distributed, and Buddy saw them over and over."

"No offense, but they must be ancient," Lurleen said.

"Buddy was a teenager at the time. He was at least twelve years younger than me and had this adolescent crush, I guess. He must have thought I was an exciting older woman who could teach him what he needed to know about life. Me of all people!

"We'd gone to the same high school, and it didn't take him long to figure out who I was and where I lived. At first, he just wrote me fan mail. Then he said how much he wanted to meet me. He'd come over to my house with candy or flowers. I never responded, and my dad would shoo him away. I was still living at home. My mom had died, and I was taking care of my dad until he got back on his feet. I don't think Buddy liked to be rejected, but the funny thing was he never told my dad what I'd done."

"Why not?" Lurleen asked.

"I don't think Buddy is ruthless like that. At least, I didn't think he was ruthless until now. He wanted to take me out on a date back then, and maybe when he saw that was impossible, he moved on. I think he married a local girl soon after he graduated from high school.

"George and I came early to Veracrue for a little vacation. While George was in the hardware store, I saw Buddy walk by. He paused when he saw me, and I told him how grateful I was that he'd never told my dad what I was doing years ago. It took him a minute to recognize who I was. Then he did something I couldn't believe. He threatened to tell George about my past if I didn't help him out."

"What did he want you to do?" I asked.

Chapter Eighteen

Rose frowned. She tried to do something with her thin, dry hair, sticking out in all directions—as if it were as frightened as she appeared to be. Her lower lip quivered. Age spots on her face stood out against her pale complexion.

She was sitting on the bed beside me, looking straight ahead. When I asked her again what the chief wanted her to do, she stood and turned her back to me. She wrapped her arms around herself and didn't face me when she said, "Buddy wanted me to sabotage the contest or at least help him sabotage it."

"Why?" I asked.

Rose turned around slowly.

"He said he needed to bring Savannah down a peg or two. That's all he told me."

"Were you involved with the peanuts in the hors d'oeuvres?

Rose hung her head and nodded. "I didn't mean for anyone to get hurt."

Rose started crying again. She looked years older than her sixty years.

"Buddy took me into his office at the police station and gave me an EpiPen. He said he'd handle getting peanuts into something Savannah would eat. I was to pull it out if she actually stopped breathing. He said he just wanted to scare her. Then the wrong person got sick and I panicked. Thank goodness you were there, Dr. Brown."

"This is really serious," I said.

"I know. I know I'll probably go to jail. My life is ruined. Buddy said he'd deny everything if I spoke up."

Lurleen walked over to Rose and put her hand on her shoulder. "Your life isn't ruined. I've seen far worse, *chérie.*"

"You don't know George. He's a simple man. He'll never forgive me for this."

"Did Chief Lewis ask you to do anything else?" I said.

Rose turned red. "Whoever made it to the finals was going to run into trouble. He said it wouldn't be me but the other person—if I made it that far. I told him that wasn't how I wanted to win anything, and he said no one would win that contest. He also promised no one would get seriously hurt. He told me to put a big dose of pepper in what Savannah sampled to make her sick with a coughing fit on screen. The food would be inedible. He wanted to ruin the climax. I told him I wouldn't do that. That's the argument you heard when he told me to settle down. That's probably why he made my burner catch fire—to teach me a lesson."

"Why does Buddy hate Savannah?" Lurleen asked. "With us he acts as if he only wants to protect her."

Rose shook her head. "I don't know, but you have to believe me. I'm telling you the truth."

Mason entered the room without knocking. Rose and I both jumped.

"The chief took us on some wild goose chase in town, and I got back a few minutes ago. What's going on here?"

Rose looked at me. "You promised this conversation would be confidential."

"Nothing's confidential during a murder investigation," Mason said.

Rose sniffled.

"It's important, Rose," I said. "You have to tell him."

"I just want this to go away," she said, putting her head in her hands.

Mason read her her rights and asked if she wanted a lawyer present. She shook her head and started talking. Buddy burst into the room midway through Rose's confession.

"I've been looking for you everywhere," the chief said to Rose. "I thought I'd find you talking to the wrong people. What lies has this woman been feeding you?"

He turned to Mason and puffed himself up, straightened his belt buckle and his badge. He looked like a caricature of a county sheriff. It would have been comical if everything hadn't been so serious. "You do know you have no jurisdiction here in South Carolina, Detective Garrett."

"I know that I have to intervene if I see a police officer doing something illegal."

That seemed to take the wind out of the chief's sails.

"You want to know the true story?" Buddy asked. "Rose came after me—I was just a dumb high school kid on the football team. I looked good in those days." He patted his generous belly. "Not an ounce of fat on me, all muscle. I was a prize back then. Rose introduced herself after one of our games. She was the older woman you always hear about. She was at least thirty, and I was what—eighteen."

Rose shook her head and then hid her face as Buddy continued talking. She sobbed quietly.

"Rose wouldn't leave me alone. She was pretty, I'll admit that, but I could have had my pick of any girl in town. I rejected her. She went off the deep end. She said she'd show me what I was missing. She sent me some of her porn movies. Seemed real proud of them to be honest. It was Savannah who told me to steer clear of Rose. Savannah and I had grown up together—she came to my games at Veracrue High."

Lurleen couldn't contain herself. "You both went to Veracrue High? You and Savannah are close to the same age? You look years older than Savannah."

"Hey," said Buddy. "Don't rub it in. I'm a few years older than she is, but Savannah also kept her looks with a lot of plastic surgery. I didn't have that luxury. Veracrue High was the only school in town, so yeah, we both graduated from there." The chief stopped talking and stared at Lurleen. "Why'd you mention the school? Did you grow up around here? You do look damned familiar."

Lurleen turned away and vigorously shook her head.

That only made the chief stare harder at her. "You go to that school? You're what—thirty-five, thirty-six? You're a lot younger than me, but I never forget a pretty face. Just can't quite place you."

Lurleen looked more and more distressed.

I intervened. "How well did Savannah know Rose?" I asked. "Did she include Rose in the contest because she knew her?"

"No. Rose was way before her time and mine. I remember I told Savannah in high school that some older woman wanted my body, but I didn't say her name or how I knew her. Savannah told me I should watch that movie—you know the one."

"*The Graduate,*" I supplied.

"Yeah, that's the one. It did sober me up a little."

"So, how did Rose get on the show?" I asked.

"Don't know. When I saw her in town, I decided it was time to let bygones be bygones."

All this time Rose looked away, tears streaming down her face.

"Let me get this straight," Mason said. "You're saying you never set her up to sabotage the contest. You never threatened to tell her husband about the movies she made if she didn't help you out."

"That's what I'm telling you. Hurt Savannah? I'd hurt my firstborn before I'd hurt Savannah."

"Someone's lying," Mason said.

"Well, it ain't me, and I resent the implication," Buddy said. "I'm a police officer. You take the word of some bimbo over me?"

Apparently, Lurleen had heard enough. "Who do you think you are, calling Rose a bimbo? Where do you get off?" She put her face in front of the chief's, as if she were begging him to react.

"Easy," Mason said. He stepped between the two of them.

"I heard the argument you had with Rose," I said.

"What argument?" Buddy blustered.

"The one in which you told her to settle down. The one in which you sounded as if you were directing things and afraid Rose might crack."

Buddy Lewis tensed and turned toward me.

Before Mason could react, Lurleen had already swung into action. She stood behind the chief, and with a single kick to the back of one of Buddy's knees, she made him crumble in agony and land unceremoniously on the floor.

"I learned that in self-defense," Lurleen said. "My teacher, Wendy, will be so proud of me."

Being flattened by a female took the stuffing out of Buddy.

"I want my lawyer," was all he'd say.

Chris knocked on the door and then opened it. Savannah peered over his shoulder.

"There you are," he said to Rose and me. "Everyone all right in here? I thought I heard a scuffle."

Chief Lewis got himself off the floor and stood, rubbing the back of his knee. "I'm not as young as I used to be, tripped over the carpet."

"We've been looking everywhere for you two," Savannah said. She glanced at her watch.

"Cartier," Lurleen whispered to me, nodding at the watch.

"We're already late," Savannah said. Then she took a good look at Rose's red eyes. "I'm sorry, Rose. Chris told me it was a ghastly explosion. Can you go on with the show?"

Rose nodded.

"She'll be fine," Lurleen said, placing an arm around her shoulders.

"Good, good," Chris said. "Nothing seemed to be wrong with the stove top, but we got you a new one anyway. It looked as if someone dropped a small firecracker in the burner plate—we found the remnants."

"I'm just so sorry, Ms. Evans," Rose said.

"You have nothing to apologize for. In fact, we should be apologizing to you."

Savannah left the room and walked rapidly down the hall with Chris, as if to distance herself from the rest of us. I could hear them discussing how best to save some of the footage. "This will make a spectacular episode," she said.

"It will be the best series we've ever done." Chris agreed. "Of course, no one will believe it's for real."

I studied Chris. The invisible Chris Evans. He was so young and had a frat boy look that was easily forgettable. Preppy, his brown hair stylishly long, his khakis appropriately casual with a ribbon belt. He didn't wear a blazer or a ribbed sweater. Instead it was an Oxford blue button-down shirt, conservative. And on his feet, he wore tasseled brown loafers.

Chris was every wealthy young man in the South. He had impeccable manners, there to save the day when needed but never really seen. What was his story? A nephew of Savannah's who made good with a little nepotism? He was cool and efficient, and I'd never seen him unnerved.

I wondered how much he knew about events on the estate. He certainly knew about Quinn's death being ruled a homicide. He seemed to know how everything ran on the estate. He'd easily know how to get a reporter into the house without being noticed—or to get one out who might cause trouble. Did he know about the threatening letters, the pranks? There was no reason Savannah would keep him in the dark about that.

Lurleen waved at me and veered away as I entered the set. I couldn't take my mind off Chris, now directing the stage crew to get the next segment started.

On the surface, he seemed to care only about the show and how to make it more engaging. The more drama that could be added to it the better. He'd have had easy access to the burner, and he'd have known how to make it flare at the right moment. I had trouble imagining the chief capable of that much finesse.

On Chris's orders, the show did go on. Rose, Granny Flumm, and I were at our places by five minutes to four. Rose had a stage presence even at sixty. Her hysterics were over, and she smiled at the camera as if she had nothing on her mind beyond finishing her current challenge.

I imagined she could have had a good acting career if some unscrupulous producer hadn't scooped her up first. Was she acting when she spoke to us, pretending to be frightened and befuddled?

No. I'd heard the argument between them. I'd seen how scared Rose was after the fire. No one was that good an actress, except possibly Lurleen.

Where was Lurleen? I glanced around the kitchen stage. Normally, Lurleen was seated in the first row, eyes glued on what everyone was doing. This afternoon she was nowhere to be seen. On the front seats were Izzy Moran, George Kirkwood, and Pepper Young. Where were Peter, Frank, and James Bradshaw? And why wasn't Lurleen there to cheer me on? The chief demanded that everyone be present on the set, so where were they?

Chris announced the restart of this episode, and we got busy with fresh ingredients as if nothing had happened an hour earlier. Our portions were smaller. A lot of good chicken had gone to waste, but that only meant our task of frying and baking went more quickly.

"You have twenty minutes," Chris announced after an hour during which we remade our entrées.

If I didn't pay attention, my chicken would be dry as leather. I checked it in the oven—a nice golden brown crust was forming. It was time to start on the sides. I whipped up my sweet potato mash and pan roasted some green beans with fresh tomatoes.

"Ten minutes."

I was just about to take the chicken out of the oven when James Bradshaw stumbled into the room. Crashed might be a better description. It was like a nightmare in slow motion. He knocked down a row of chairs before falling onto the stage at my feet. He looked drunk. His shirt was open, and at first I didn't notice what looked like blood oozing from his side.

"You have to help me," he yelled before he fell unconscious.

"Cut," Chris shouted.

Chapter Nineteen

I knelt beside James Bradshaw and looked at his wound. I made sure it was the only one he had. The bleeding had almost stopped, and from the look of it, it was a shallow cut across his upper abdomen, three or four inches long, more like a swipe than deep penetration. I grabbed a clean hand towel from my station and applied pressure while I checked his pulse.

"His pulse is fast but strong," I said. "Can you talk to me, Mr. Bradshaw?"

He gave a garbled response, but he was conscious. I could smell alcohol on his breath.

"Someone call 911," I said.

"I got it," muttered Chris, as he dialed the number. "Are you sure this is necessary? You sure he isn't just drunk?"

I looked up at Chris. "Yes."

Chris was standing five feet away, trying to keep others from getting too close. He obviously hadn't seen the blood.

"Okay, okay," he said. "It's just that he has the same reputation his daddy had before him, town drunk if you know what I mean. He's lived here forever and always acts like the victim of some great injustice. Even when Savannah gave him a chance on this show, he didn't act grateful. I warned her he'd probably show up drunk if he came at all."

"Not this time," I said. "He may be drunk, but Mr. Bradshaw's been stabbed."

"Oh, God," Chris said when he saw the blood on the dish towel as I removed it from the wound. I asked for a clean towel as I examined the extent of his injury. The cut had stopped bleeding. "I need some warm water and soap."

"Of course," Anna said. She was at my side in five seconds and watched as I washed the thin line that was now oozing blood at only one site.

"The wound looks superficial," I said, "but I can't rule out internal injuries. He needs to be checked out at the hospital."

The paramedics arrived in record time. "Stand aside, Miss," they said to me. "We've got it."

I stood up. My hands were covered with blood.

Savannah had arrived on the set, and she led me to a prep sink at the back of the room while Anna calmed the other contestants.

Savannah stood beside me as I scrubbed my hands. "I'm glad to have you alone," she said. "What do you think happened?"

"I was going to ask you the same question," I said.

"Me? You think I know something about this? My whole world is collapsing, and you think I might be involved?"

I took the towel she was holding and dried my hands. "There is a lot you haven't told us, like what Bradshaw was doing in a contest for cooks. Chris said he told you not to take on James as a contestant, and you did it anyway."

"Stop torturing me," she said.

"I'm not torturing you, but someone is. You say you want my help and then you tell me almost nothing. If you don't tell us what you know, then someone else may get killed. And it just might be you."

Mason had come up behind us. Savannah jumped at the sound of his voice.

He put a comforting hand on my back. "Ditie's right, and you know it."

Savannah nodded slowly. Before she had time to speak, Chris shouted to everyone within hearing.

" Mr. Bradshaw's been taken to the hospital—looks like he'll be fine. It was all an accident. Please get back to your stations. We have to wrap up this episode, so let's get it done."

I seemed to be living in some alternate universe. A man is stabbed, and we're back smiling and cooking our chicken. But, what would be the point of stopping now? Mason and the police on site would be looking into the stabbing. We'd only be in the way and make things more complicated if we were cut loose. We might as well get this episode wrapped up, as Chris said.

I finished wiping my hands and slipped on clear plastic gloves. "I'll wear these for the rest of the segment. I scrubbed my hands, but everyone will feel more comfortable, including me, that I'm not contaminating the food with some bit of blood I missed."

Savannah shivered. "Such a terrible image," she said. "I could never stand blood and gore."

I couldn't help but think whoever killed the reporter Nick Davis and disposed of his body saw a lot of blood and gore. Savannah was acting the part of a good Southern damsel in distress, but maybe she was more like a steel magnolia—looking fragile when she was anything but.

I stared at the big clock on the wall at the front of the room. It was well designed to be seen clearly from every corner of the kitchen set, so we always knew how much time we had left. The delay caused by Bradshaw's dramatic entrance had lasted half an hour, and I realized my chicken had been in the oven all that time.

"I can't imagine our food will be edible now."

"I'll wing it," Savannah said, "and we'll talk after the taping. I'll tell you everything, I promise."

We all took our places and pretended to pick up where we'd left off. I pulled my chicken out of the oven. The golden-brown crust had turned black. It flaked off like the charred remains of an animal thrown into a fire. I searched for a piece that was less than charcoal and scraped off what I could. Granny Flumm and Rose were doing the same.

I ended up with three small pieces of chicken, all of them hard and dry. From a distance the viewers probably couldn't see that. The cameras began to roll, and we plated our food. The sides were cold but still looked decent. As instructed by Chris the cameras focused on our faces rather than our creations. We were told to look pleased with our plates and as if we were rushing to get the food out on time. We did the best we could.

When time was called, Savannah announced that since this was the semi-finals, she'd be making the judgments on her own with no help from other tasters. That got no dispute from Izzy or Pepper who seemed relieved not to be asked to participate. Again, I searched the room for Lurleen, but she was nowhere to be found.

Savannah took her time. She sampled each plate and pretended to savor the now cold, dry, and overcooked food. Chris cut the cameras after each tasting, so she could spit the inedible food delicately into a jar beside her chair.

The final break in filming allowed her to deposit the last bit of food into the scrap jar.

Then she smiled at the camera. I could see it was the smile that made her win so many converts. The smile said I'll tell only the truth, but I'll do it kindly.

Instead, she lied through her teeth. "This has never happened before," she said, "but I can't declare a winner. The food of all three contestants is simply too delicious."

"Too horrible to eat," I murmured under my breath. Fortunately my mic was off.

"So," Savannah continued, "all three contestants will go on to the finals and have a chance to win a Savannah Evans's Dream Vacation—a trip to France and a week-long baking class with Charles Vignon, the renowned pastry chef from Provence. The winner and her guest will stay in a lovely chateau, and I will be the winner's sous-chef for the week."

Murmurs and gasps came from the small audience, followed by polite applause. I was quite sure Chris would find a way to amplify the sound and make the reaction seem more enthusiastic.

Lurleen, now ensconced in the audience as if she had never been missing in action, was especially excited. "Provence," she murmured loudly enough for everyone to hear, "my home away from home."

It was close to seven when Chris declared it was a wrap. That was after a series of close-ups of each contestant looking worried about her entry and then beaming at the results.

I had no idea how tired I was until Chris announced we were done. I wasn't sure I could do anything but go straight to bed.

I looked at Rose and Granny Flumm. George stood beside Rose giving her support—literally—with one arm under hers. Granny stood alone, straight-backed and stern, but even she looked the worse for wear. When she saw me staring at her, she gave me a wan smile, as if to say we'd been through the trenches together. That was the warmest expression I'd ever seen from her, and it heartened me a bit.

Chris made a quick announcement that James Bradshaw was recovering at a near-by hospital. He said Bradshaw's wounds were superficial and accidentally self-inflicted.

Mason entered the room as I was getting ready to leave. He hurried to my side. "You look worn out," he said.

"I am, but tell me what you've found out. You think the wound was an accident?"

"That's the story for public consumption," he said. "We're telling reporters Bradshaw slipped and fell on his pocket knife."

"Which just happened to be open for some reason?" I said.

Mason shrugged. "Best we could do."

"What did happen?" I asked.

"We're still trying to figure that out. James clammed up. He's the one who says it was an accident."

I nodded and looked around for Lurleen. I would have expected her to be hovering near me, trying to make sure I was okay. Instead, she walked slowly in our direction.

"Where were you?" I asked.

"What do you mean, *chérie?*" Lurleen looked as if she'd swallowed a canary or maybe something larger.

"I mean where were you during the shoot when Bradshaw stumbled onto the set?"

Lurleen clasped her hands in front of her and gave me her Mona Lisa smile. "*Eh bien, chérie. I have a petite histoire to tell you. You'll like it.*"

"I'm listening," I said.

"Me too," Mason said.

Danny approached us before Lurleen could begin. "Savannah Evans has disappeared. No one seems to know where she is. Have any of you seen her?"

I shook my head. "I watched her impressive acting job, but when Chris called it over, all I could think of was how much I needed to sit down. I didn't see her leave the room. Did you, Lurleen?"

Lurleen shook her head slowly. She had something to say, and I assumed she didn't like Savannah or anyone else stealing her thunder.

The contestants had exited the stage. The camera crew was getting ready to leave. Chris was directing traffic.

"Where's Savannah?" Mason asked him.

Chris shook his head. "She said she had some urgent business. Maybe you should try her office."

Mason and Danny took off for the third floor with Lurleen and me close behind.

"Where's the chief?" Mason asked as he bolted up the stairs.

"Chief Lewis has become the strong silent type," Danny said, "so, we're waiting for his lawyer to arrive. He's in Quinn's office."

"Someone with him?" Mason asked.

"I was until I heard Savannah was missing. Then I came to find you. I left his deputy with him and told them both not to leave the office."

"Stay with them, Danny, for now."

Danny split from us on the third floor to head to Quinn's office where Buddy was under house arrest apparently.

We didn't find Savannah in her suite.

"Now what?" I asked.

"She couldn't have left the property," Mason said. "An officer is stationed at every door."

"Don't you want to hear what I know?" Lurleen asked. "It may make finding Savannah easier."

Mason motioned to the couch opposite Savannah's elegant plantation desk. He sat in the desk chair and listened.

"I decided to do a little investigating on my own," Lurleen said. "You two had your hands full, and when I called Danny, he was busy with Buddy. I thought I'd just see what everyone else was up to."

Lurleen was relishing her tale.

Mason motioned her to speed it up.

"Of course, *Monsieur Mason.* I will cut to the chase as you request. I decided to check on the spouses of the contestants. You never know who might be involved in murder. Do you know there is a lovely billiard room on the first floor—at the end of a long hallway off the west wing?"

Mason nodded.

"Well, that's where the missing spouses hang out. It has a full bar. Since I'm pretty good at billiards from my brief affair with Alphonse, the men were very tolerant of me. I became one of the boys."

Again Mason moved his hand in a circle urging Lurleen to get to the point.

"If I didn't adore you, I would find you a bit impatient," Lurleen said. "Very well. James Bradshaw was there. Peter and Frank showed up later."

"So, that's where they went," I said. "I wondered why they weren't in the audience."

"I was there a minute or two before Peter and Frank arrived. James was making use of a well-stocked bar, and I thought I might find out a little more about his relationship with Savannah. I didn't get the chance. As soon as Frank and Peter came in, James pointed a finger at Frank. 'I know you,' he said. Then he pointed at Young. 'You too. I know both of you. So, what are you up to and why are you here?' "

Lurleen fluffed her hair and then saw the expression on Mason's face.

"All right, I'll hurry. The men seemed to forget I was even present. I pretended to be intent on practice shots at the table. Then things heated up. 'We could ask you the same question,' Young shouted. 'Why the hell are you here? You're no cook, just a bad food critic.'

"That really got a rise out of Mr. Bradshaw. I think he was well on his way to getting drunk. He pulled a knife out—one of those knives that snap open."

"A switch blade," Mason said.

"*Exactement.* He said he was going to bring Savannah down if it was the last thing he did. He'd show the world what kind of woman she was. When Frank tried to talk sense into him James lunged at him. Peter came from behind and grabbed the knife out of his hand. Then he motioned him out of the room. Peter told me to stay put in a very unfriendly tone, and at that point Savannah turned up. She came in through a door I'd never noticed. A secret door I think, by the fireplace. She told Frank and Peter to get Bradshaw and take him somewhere to dry out."

Lurleen paused to take a breath.

I gave her a serious look. "You aren't embellishing the story, are you Lurleen?"

Lurleen's hazel eyes narrowed. "Ditie, how could you doubt me? Savannah tried to tell me it was all a misunderstanding. Men will be men, that sort of thing. That's when I heard a stumbling around followed by an ungodly scream. That's when I'm sure James Bradshaw was stabbed."

"You're saying Bradshaw was stabbed by Moran or Young," Mason said.

Lurleen nodded.

"And what did Savannah do?" Mason asked.

"She didn't have time to do anything. Frank Moran stuck his head in the room. 'Everything's fine,' he said. Savannah asked if James was hurt. Frank shook his head. 'You know James, a little scratch, and he thinks he's been mortally wounded.'

" 'All right, then,' Savannah said, 'I'll talk to you and Peter after the show.' "

Lurleen flung back her curls and held her head up high. "So, if you want to find Savannah, I suspect she's in the billiard room talking with the husbands of two contestants. And I'll bet you money she got there through some secret passageway. It's just like Nancy Drew."

"Or Clue," said Mason drily.

Chapter Twenty

Lurleen and I followed Mason along a long curved hall on the main floor to the billiard room. The hallway looked like a newer addition to the house with a row of floor-to-ceiling windows. As we hurried down the wide corridor, we could see a Japanese garden unfold outside the windows—a small pond, a draping willow tree, and carefully placed rocks along a low-lying berm. A slightly different view revealed itself with each step we took. If I lived in this house, this would be my favorite spot.

Lurleen and Mason marched ahead. The brick flooring dulled the clacking of their feet.

Three cushy chairs were spaced out in front of the windows. Beside each one was a miniature Meyer lemon tree that filled the air with its enticing scent.

Lurleen glanced back at me. "Holly Swivel Armchairs, over $1,500 each. Sweet, huh?"

It was a quiet space for introspection that ironically led to the billiard room, which was bustling with noise and activity.

I could hear three people shouting over each other as we neared the entrance to the room.

"He had it coming." "It was lucky the damn fool wasn't killed."

From Savannah I heard, "I don't pay you boys to get me into trouble. I pay you to keep me out of it."

Mason strode through the open door with Lurleen and me at his heels. The room was a magnificent space with wood-paneled walls and a window seat stretching along one side of the room. A fireplace and bar took up most of the opposite wall. In the middle stood the pool table.

Peter Young and Frank Moran stopped talking as we entered. Savannah didn't seem surprised to see us there.

"I guess you filled them in on what you saw, Lurleen," she said, "about the fight. I'm glad you did—it saves me the trouble. I'm relieved to hear James will be all right. Peter, Frank, and I have been going over what happened. James was drunk and in a foul mood. He was waving around his knife as if he intended to use it. Frank and Peter did what they could to keep anyone from getting hurt."

"Where are the police?" Mason asked.

"I convinced Buddy to leave this corridor free," Savannah said, "so I could come and go as I pleased."

"Unbelievable," Mason said. "You should know Buddy is no longer in charge of this case. And police will be everywhere."

"You have no authority here," Savannah said. "That's what Buddy told me."

"When I find out who will take over the case locally, I'll let you know. For now, I'm it." Mason looked at her. "You're saying Bradshaw's injury was an accident, something done in self-defense."

"Yes, and I'm glad no one was badly hurt. When James drinks he gets belligerent. Usually, he doesn't remember what he's done when he sobers up."

She looked at Mason and the rest of us and directed us to sit on the upholstered window seat. "This is my favorite part of the house. I love the hallway, and Quinn always loved the billiard room. When he was well, he would play pool every day while I sat reading in the walkway, staring out at my Japanese garden.

"He said he made his best deals in this room." She mimicked Quinn's voice. " 'You can always size someone up by the way they play pool—braggadocio versus talent, timidity versus a determination to win at any cost.' I suppose he could also evaluate how a man held his liquor. As I've said, James was never good at that. Has he told you a different story, detective?"

"He also said it was an accident and refused to say more."

Savannah offered Mason a drink, but he shook his head.

"You act as if this incident has no connection with anything else going on in the house," Mason said.

"I don't see how it could. James and I are not close. We've always had a stormy relationship, but it's never amounted to more than words. We are cousins after all. I can't imagine any connection to the death of my husband or that poor reporter."

"Really?" Lurleen whispered to me. "Who is she kidding?"

"Tell me about your relationship with James Bradshaw," Mason said. "We can do this in private if you prefer."

"I have nothing to hide," Savannah said. "These men work for me. They know the whole story, and as for Lurleen and Ditie—I want them to hear the truth. James Bradshaw has always been a thorn in my side. He hated Quinn with a passion."

"And yet, you included him in your contest," Mason said, "when he's known to be a bad cook and a bad alcoholic. Explain that to me."

"Have a seat, detective. This may take a while." Savannah offered to freshen everyone's drink and poured herself a glass of orange juice.

"Stalling for time if you ask me," Lurleen whispered.

Lurleen and I sat together on the window seat. Mason remained standing as did Peter and Frank.

"Sit down you two," Savannah said to them, and they did as they were told. Savannah chose a seat on a barstool that put her at eye level with Mason and across the room from him— perhaps in an effort to maintain control of the space and her story.

"Let me try to explain the situation. James and I are cousins as I said. Our family and our disagreements go back two hundred years. This house was built in the 1820s for the Bradshaws—Calvin Bradshaw to be precise—as a summer home. He'd made a fortune off Sea Island cotton and the Gullah slaves he'd brought from West Africa to run his plantation.

"My family, the Evans family, lived in the North, on Nantucket. My ancestor Josiah Evans was the brother of Calvin's wife, Jane. Josiah was a sea captain, a Quaker, and a staunch abolitionist. The two sides of the family had little to do with each other until the Civil War began."

Savannah stopped talking to take another sip of juice. "Do you know the history of this area, detective?"

"Some, but I'd like to hear from you the part that is pertinent."

"Beaufort and the surrounding area, including Veracrue, was occupied early in the war by the Union forces."

"As a result of the Battle of Port Royal," Mason said.

"November 7, 1861. It is not a date Southerners forget," Savannah said. "It was the beginning of the end of the Old South. All the plantation owners fled. Many left their slaves behind. Calvin Bradshaw contacted his brother-in-law Josiah for help. He wanted someone in the house to protect his things and keep the place from being looted. He knew only a Northerner would be allowed to do that. I guess he was counting on the idea that blood was thicker than water.

"Josiah agreed to do what he could for the sake of his sister. He had recently retired, but he was still a Quaker and an abolitionist. He came as much to help the slaves as his relatives. While some slaves were freed and given the land they'd been working, many south of here remained in bondage.

"Josiah lived in the house, protected it from looters, and offered his services to the Union forces. For a while, the house was used as a hospital, but Josiah had grander ideas. He made it a safe house on the Underground Railroad. He constructed hiding places in the house and built a tunnel to the river. It remained a treacherous journey north by boat, but some made it."

"So, I was right when I said you had a secret way of getting to the billiard room," Lurleen said.

"You were right," Savannah nodded. "A door next to the fireplace leads to my office upstairs. And another door underneath the small carpet by the hearth leads to the tunnel and the river."

Danny entered the room as Savannah finished speaking.

"I'm glad I found you," Danny said. "The chief's lawyer just arrived. I agreed to give them half an hour alone."

"Savannah's giving us a history lesson related to the house," I said.

"I didn't think there was an Underground Railroad here," Lurleen said. "I knew some courageous people helped slaves escape, like Roberts Smalls and Harriet Tubman."

Danny couldn't stay quiet.

"You know about them?" he said, smiling at Lurleen. "Robert Smalls helped his family and friends escape slavery on a confederate ship in 1862—he doesn't get nearly the fame he deserves, and Harriet Tubman led a Union raid that freed 700 slaves."

Savannah nodded enthusiastically as Danny talked. She seemed delighted to move the conversation away from current events.

"Why did you keep the tunnel open?" Mason asked.

"That was Quinn's idea. I think he believed he might need a quick escape route at some point, and I liked the idea of preserving the history of the house."

"He knew he was in danger?" Mason asked.

"He thought he was," Savannah said. "It was always hard to sort out Quinn's paranoia from what might actually be happening."

"He and Bradshaw remained enemies?" Mason said.

"Yes. Quinn didn't approve of James and the feeling was mutual. Quinn thought James was a low life, no matter how he tried to dress himself up as a Southern gentleman. Still, he *was* part of my family, so I insisted we be civil. Then when James lost the questionable deed to the house in a poker game with Quinn, the gloves came off. "

"When was that?" Mason asked.

"A year or so ago. James had been trying to get some lawyer to take his case and finally did, I think. Then the poker game happened, and he lost any hope of getting back this house."

"Do you think Quinn cheated?" Lurleen asked.

At first Savannah looked shocked and then changed her expression as if she were removing a mask among friends. "Quinn knew how much I cared about this house, so I wouldn't put it past him. James was drunk as usual. Afterwards he claimed Quinn had cheated him out of his rightful heritage. No one at the table backed him up."

"You're giving Bradshaw a solid motive for Quinn's murder," Mason said.

"I suppose I am. I think James was determined to get the house back no matter what the cost."

"You still haven't explained why you included him in the contest," Mason said.

Savannah paused. "Frankly, detective, I felt sorry for him. He's lost everything he values—the house, his career. He was a lousy food critic, and I thought I might give him a new start."

I didn't buy that explanation. From the look on Lurleen's face, she didn't either.

"How is it the Evans's side of the family came to own the house the Bradshaws built," Mason asked.

"After the war, these houses were sold off for pennies to the dollar. That's when Josiah bought it. He agreed to let Calvin buy it back from him when he got on his feet, but that never happened. Calvin drank or gambled away whatever money he was able to make, just like James. James will tell you a different story," Savannah said, "but he knows the truth."

As Savannah finished speaking, Chris burst into the room.

"We have a situation," he said.

"Another one?" Savannah asked. "What now?"

Chris looked around and closed his mouth like a snapping turtle, so fast and sharp I wondered if it hurt.

He stood next to Savannah at the bar and whispered, "Olivier is here."

"You don't have to whisper," Savannah said to Chris. "They know I have a son. Olivier is here? As in waiting at the Charleston Airport to be picked up?"

"Here, as in sitting in your office," Chris said. "He just arrived."

Chapter Twenty-one

"Thank goodness," Savannah said. "I was so worried about him." She looked at us. "I can't answer any more questions right now. I have to go. I have to see Olivier."

"You don't go anywhere without us," Mason said.

Savannah rushed to the fireplace, depressed a brick and a door opened to an elevator. "Lurleen and Ditie, you may ride with me," she said. "The rest of you can hoof it."

Mason nodded at Danny and indicated that Peter and Frank were to come with them to the third floor.

Lurleen and I slipped into the elevator beside Savannah. It was a tight fit, but we all made it. We had a quick ride. The elevator opened into a closet of Savannah's office. She slid open the door to her room and called in French to the handsome young man who sat on the couch before us. The young man, undoubtedly Olivier, jumped up when he saw us. He was very good-looking with curly brown hair. He had Savannah's smile. He looked American, but more than that, he looked familiar. Not so much like Savannah, more like—-

"He's the spitting image of Buddy—without the gut," Lurleen whispered to me.

"My thoughts exactly," I said.

Savannah was all over him. "You are safe, my dearest." She ran her hands over his shoulders and face as if to make sure he was unharmed. "I was so frightened when I couldn't reach you. Why did you disappear and how did you get here?"

"So many questions, *maman,* but you can see I'm here, safe and sound."

At this point the men came thundering into the room.

"The cavalry, *maman*?" Olivier asked.

Mason spoke up. "I'm Mason Garrett, a homicide detective from Atlanta."

"Homicide?" Olivier asked. "Someone has been murdered?"

"Quinn," Savannah said.

"I knew he died, but murdered? He had a bad heart, and I know you worried about that. Are they sure it was murder?"

Savannah nodded and began to cry.

"I am sorry, *maman*." Olivier placed a protective arm around his mother's shoulder, and that seemed to make her cry harder.

"A reporter was also murdered," Mason said.

Olivier gave him a blank look.

"We suspect the reporter discovered something the killer didn't want anyone to know," Mason said. "How long have you been in the US and how did you get into the house?"

"I was met at the airport and brought here a half hour ago. As a surprise."

"Picked up by whom?" Savannah asked.

"Mr. Bradshaw was supposed to pick me up, but it was someone else, someone British who said that Mr. Bradshaw had had an accident and that he was sent instead."

"Dorian," Savannah, Lurleen and I said in one breath.

"You called, madam?" Dorian entered the room with a cup of coffee and a brioche for Olivier. He smiled.

"Dorian, you said you couldn't find him when you went to France. You didn't know where he was," Savannah said.

"That was the truth, madam. Later, Mr. Bradshaw informed me that he'd found out where Olivier was staying and that he'd made arrangements to bring him here as a surprise for you. Before Mr. Bradshaw left for the hospital, he asked me to pick up Olivier at the airport, and that's what I did. Mr. Bradshaw said I was to bring him to your office without anyone seeing."

"Thank you, Dorian." Savannah took Olivier's hand. "I was so worried about you, Olivier. Was it James Bradshaw who also told you to disappear with your family?"

"No, that was Chief Lewis. He came to visit me in France, and when it was obvious I really *was* his son, he told me to disappear with my family—that I could be in some danger. He said he'd notify me when everything was cleared up. He didn't say there had been a murder, only threats against you, *maman*, and me."

"I suppose you all see the resemblance," Savannah said to the rest of us. "Buddy Lewis is Olivier's father. He didn't know anything about Olivier until a year ago. I felt I had to tell him then because I had plans to bring Olivier to the US to work with me. Buddy was furious and worried about his reputation and his marriage. His wife believes in fidelity above all else. He didn't think she'd forgive a transgression, even one from years ago."

Lurleen's mouth was agape. "You had a relationship with Buddy Lewis? When and why?" She didn't do a good job of keeping the disbelief out of her voice. While she could imagine Savannah with Quinn, Buddy was a different story apparently.

"I'd rather not discuss this with Olivier present," Savannah said.

"What, *maman*? I'm not to know your history even when it relates to my biological father? I know you didn't love him enough to marry him, and I'm grateful for the life I've had."

I wondered if Olivier had gotten therapy to deal with the trauma of adoption. On the other hand, he'd had contact with Savannah throughout the years, so perhaps for him it wasn't a trauma.

"I can hear all of it, *maman*. It will not embarrass me or make me think less of you, but if you want me to leave I will."

Savannah looked torn. "I don't want you to leave."

She sat on the sofa beside Olivier and held his hand as she spoke. "It was a long time ago, Lurleen. I was different then. I was wild in those days, and Buddy was fun and very handsome. I was sick to death of toeing the line as the daughter of the mayor. I wanted adventure."

"You didn't tell Buddy you were pregnant?" Lurleen asked.

"No. Buddy was about to be married when we met at a bar. I think he was nervous about that. It was one night. We both had too much to drink. The usual story. I had no desire to interfere with Buddy's plans and certainly no wish to marry him myself. I never told anyone, including my parents, until it was necessary. I don't know how my cousin James found out—maybe Buddy told him."

Savannah took a deep breath. "James said he'd ruin me—tell the world I had a child out of wedlock and then deserted him. He demanded compensation for his silence."

"Bradshaw blackmailed you," Mason said.

"Not the term he used. He said he was having a hard time getting by. I owed him. I had to put him on my show, talk him up as a chef and food critic, get his career back on track."

"So, it wasn't altruism that got him on the show." Lurleen spoke softly to me. "Savannah never struck me as the altruistic type."

"And you agreed to that?" Mason said.

"What choice did I have?" Savannah held Olivier's hand more tightly as she spoke. "Quinn wasn't ready to accept Olivier into our lives. James knew enough people to ruin my reputation. I couldn't have that." She squeezed Olivier's hand and then released it. "More than that I couldn't have Olivier involved in a scandal, not at the start of his career, not ever."

"The French are used to this sort of thing," Lurleen said.

"The French may be, but South Carolina is not," Savannah said.

"Haven't you watched 'Real Housewives of South Carolina'?" Lurleen persisted.

I looked at Lurleen. "That show doesn't exist!"

"It should."

"Enough," Mason said. "Buddy confronted you about Olivier?"

Savannah nodded. "When I first told him he was Olivier's father, Buddy was enraged. He wanted me to promise I'd never bring Olivier here. I couldn't promise that.

"After Quinn died, when I told Buddy that Olivier was coming here possibly to stay for a while, he got angry again. Then he seemed to do an about face. He said he wanted to meet this person who claimed to be his son but that it needed to be a private meeting. The last thing he wanted was for his wife to find out, and I promised to do everything I could to keep that from happening.

"After that conversation, I never heard another word from Olivier. Buddy, of course, denied that he was responsible in any way for Olivier's disappearance. Obviously, that was a lie."

"Do you think he sabotaged the contest to keep Olivier away?" I asked.

"What exactly are you talking about?" Savannah asked.

"The peanuts in the hors d'oeuvres, the stove top blowing up," I said. "According to Rose, Buddy was behind the dangerous pranks on the set. I heard them arguing about it."

"It's the kind of thing Buddy would do," Savannah said. "I think he was responsible for the pranks a year ago. He wanted to unnerve me. He wanted to make it seem unsafe to bring Olivier here, but I was determined to have him come. I assume that left Buddy no choice but to pretend to be concerned about Olivier's welfare and urge him to go into hiding. Surely, he must have known Olivier would contact me eventually."

Olivier nodded. "I would have done that."

Mason turned to Olivier. "James Bradshaw told you the coast was clear?"

"The coast, it is clear?" Olivier said to his mother.

She translated and he nodded. "He did. He contacted my French mother. He said the danger was past, and I was to come immediately—as a surprise for you, *maman*."

"We know Bradshaw brought the reporter here," Mason said, "from the scribbled notes we found under the mattress in the room in which Nick Davis was killed. Davis was to dig up as much dirt as he could about you and Quinn. Olivier would be another pawn—providing lots of publicity about the son you abandoned."

"James hated Quinn and me so much," Savannah said. "He not only thought we cheated him out of this house but that we were responsible for his losing his license as a pharmacist."

"Losing his license?" I said. "That's a big deal. In the bios for the contest it said he'd retired."

"James got drunk one time too many at work," Savannah said. "He gave the wrong prescription to a patient, and she nearly died. We had nothing to do with that but if anything went wrong for James, we got blamed for it."

"We have two men, Bradshaw and the chief, who were furious with you," Mason said, "but with very different desires regarding Olivier. Bradshaw wanted Olivier here to discredit you, and the chief wanted him to stay away."

Mason continued to think out loud.

"The chief would not have been happy to know that Nick Davis was in the house digging up information about Olivier. That sets him up as an obvious murder suspect, but I wonder who else might have worried about what Davis could discover—someone with their own secrets."

Mason scanned the room as he spoke. I did the same. Dorian remained by the door with no emotion on his face. When he saw me looking at him, he nodded and smiled. Savannah stared straight ahead, but it seemed she held Olivier's hand more tightly. Peter remained cool, like a block of ice, while Frank fidgeted and looked at the floor.

"The murderer turned off the recording equipment before he killed Davis," Mason said. "Who knew about the system your husband had in place?"

Savannah shrugged. "I'm not sure."

"We all knew," Peter said. "It was a joke really, Quinn, thinking he could spy on us. We used it to spy on Quinn and everyone else."

"And what did you find out?" Mason asked.

"We knew when Bradshaw let the reporter into the house," Peter said. He realized immediately that he'd said the wrong thing. "Look, I have nothing to hide."

"There's a rumor you and Savannah are having a relationship," I said.

"It isn't true," Savannah said. "I was loyal to Quinn until the end."

Peter's complexion deepened. "Who said that?" He didn't wait for my reply. "You think I killed Quinn and then the reporter to keep some imaginary involvement with Savannah quiet?"

"People have killed for less," Mason said. "We've checked backgrounds. You're a medic in the Reserves. Do I have that right?"

"Yeah, so what?"

"So, you would know how to start an IV and use a syringe. You might even know where to get doxorubicin."

"That's ridiculous," Peter said.

Apparently, Mason was done asking questions. "No one is to leave the premises. Is that clear?"

He turned to Savannah. "I'm going to have an officer stay in the room with you and Olivier."

Savannah nodded. "I understand."

He looked at Frank and Peter. "I'll talk to you two individually this evening. Go to your rooms and stay there."

The men were only too eager to leave.

I followed Mason, Danny, and Lurleen into the hallway.

"Let's regroup," Mason said, "in Quinn's office. We seem to have more than enough suspects who might have wanted Quinn dead."

"Like *Murder on the Orient Express*," Lurleen said, "maybe they all did it."

Chapter Twenty-two

We found Buddy and his lawyer seated together on the low sofa in Quinn's office. Mason took the chair behind Quinn's desk and was about to usher me and Lurleen out the door when Buddy asked us to stay. His attorney shook his head.

"I pay you, right? So, we'll do it my way. There are enough snitches in the house, not to mention recording devices, that whatever I say here will be in the news tomorrow. I want the girls to hear my side of the story."

Danny left the room and returned moments later with chairs for us. He stood by the desk as Mason settled himself in the chair behind it.

Mason produced his own recording device, announced the date and time. He read Buddy his rights, and then began asking questions.

Buddy seemed eager to tell his story, at least some of it. "I never had any idea I had a son until a year ago when Savannah announced it to me as if she were giving me a birthday present. Some present. She wanted to bring the boy over to stay with her and expected me to welcome him!

"A son I knew nothing about, that I wasn't even sure was my son. Savannah and I had a one-night stand—that was it. She never thinks about anyone but herself. She's met my wife. Mary is as fine as they come, but she's not exactly tolerant of mistakes—even those made years ago."

"You left in a rage after Savannah told you," Mason said.

"Damn right I left in a rage. Savannah was about to destroy my life."

"The nasty pranks started the next day. Those were from you?"

Buddy conferred with his lawyer and then spoke over the lawyer's obvious protest.

"Yes," Buddy said. "Once Quinn heard about a son he knew nothing about, he agreed to help me. We had to convince Savannah that it wasn't safe to bring Olivier to Veracrue."

"The second batch of threatening letters began a week later," Mason said. "Was that you as well?"

"No, but you can bet I didn't mind them. I wondered if Quinn sent them— and then he went and got himself murdered."

"You're telling us you don't know who was sending the hate mail?" Mason asked.

"That's what I'm telling you."

Mason questioned Buddy for another ten minutes. Buddy said he went to France to get a DNA sample from Olivier, but once he saw his son, he didn't need one. No two people could look that much alike and not be related. He admitted he might have recommended Olivier and his family go into hiding for a while because of the death threats. After all, Quinn had been murdered, and no one was safe.

Buddy denied knowing anything about Quinn's virility treatments.

On the issue of the mishaps during the show, he came clean and verified everything Rose said. He still maintained he had nothing to do with her being on the show, and he had nothing to do with the reporter's death.

At the end of the interview, Mason stood and made it clear that Buddy could no longer supervise the investigation.

"I got that," Buddy said, "and I'm glad to be done with it. You should know the deputy chief, Matt Lewis, is my nephew, but he's a straight shooter."

Mason told Buddy he was to remain on the estate under house arrest for the time being. They'd sort out charges later. Danny brought Matt Lewis into the office. Mason told him they'd be working on the case together. Matt would be the officer in charge—on paper.

Buddy nodded at both men. "You'll make a good team."

Mason dismissed the chief and his nephew—they were to find an available room in which they could both stay. The lawyer also left, saying he'd contact Buddy later.

Lurleen and I moved to Quinn's more comfortable couch. Mason and Danny remained standing and offered us coffee.

"I wish we had some of your cookies to help us think," Mason added.

"I'm sure Anna could fix us something to eat," I said.

Mason shook his head. "The fewer people who know what we're up to, the better. What are your thoughts about the chief?"

Danny spoke first. "It's pretty convenient the hate mail started right after Buddy found out about a son. The letters would be a lot more frightening than a few crazy pranks."

"My thoughts exactly," Mason said, "and Buddy was one of two people to call Anna Annie. "

"According to *her*," I said. "You have to remember Anna's story changes every five minutes. First Annie is a nickname everyone used and then it was only Dorian and the chief who called her that. Maybe she's protecting someone else.

"I can give you my opinion of Buddy for what it's worth. It seems to me he was honest with you about a lot of things—things his lawyer might not have wanted him to reveal."

"Buddy has a nasty temper." Lurleen said. "You heard how vicious he was about Rose, and it was all lies."

"I agree," I said, "but he seems to go off half-cocked without thinking things through. He gets Olivier to go into hiding but with no thought about what happens next. The murder of Quinn took careful planning over time. I'm just not sure Buddy is capable of that. And Quinn wasn't the threat. Savannah was."

Mason was silent for a moment. "I was thinking about what you said, Lurleen. I hope it's nothing like *Murder on the Orient Express*, but I wonder if we're looking for two or more people working together to commit these murders. It would be hard for one person to manage either killing without help.

That opened up the field.

"Bradshaw and Granny Flumm were concocting some scheme when I overheard them talking," I said. "It's obvious they both hate Savannah."

Mason nodded. "But, Bradshaw brought Nick Davis into the house, so why would he kill him the same night he came?"

"Maybe he didn't," I said. "He's been drunk most of the time we've seen him—not a great way to commit murder. Besides, he wanted Davis here, as you say. Gertrude Flumm asked him to stay sober, but I don't think he's capable of that. Maybe she had her own secrets to protect and took matters into her own hands."

"She's a steely woman," Lurleen said. "Perfectly capable of murder in my opinion."

"I agree," I said, "but she'd have needed someone to drag his body off the estate. I imagine there are a lot of people in this house who might have been anxious to keep a nosy reporter from digging up information.

Frank Moran for one—he was desperate to know what you were finding out, Mason, and Peter Young has admitted he'd do anything for money."

"Savannah has Frank and Peter working for her," Danny said. "Maybe they're working for her or maybe she just thinks they are."

"That's assuming Savannah isn't at the heart of this," Lurleen said. "She was tired of Quinn and he wouldn't give her a divorce. I'll bet Frank or Peter could have helped her get him out of the way."

We heard the dinner bell. "That's enough for now," Mason said. "We'll take this up again after dinner, but this idea of a murdering partnership makes sense to me."

I gave Mason a quick kiss and told him I'd join him in the dining room once I called home. I went to my room and got Tommy on the line.

"Are you holding up okay?" I asked.

"I'm great. I'm even growing fond of your dog. Your cat liked me from the start—leave a cat alone and they're all over you. Josh loves your house, and he's pressuring me to buy a home with him. He's not as fond of condo living as I am.

"You continue to amaze me, Tommy," I said. "I didn't think you had all this domesticity in you."

"I'm glad I can still surprise you."

His tone changed and he became more serious.

"Are *you* okay? We've gotten wind of problems there. I try to keep the news away from the kids, but nothing gets by Lucie. She's worried and so am I."

"Don't be. We have more policemen here than potential victims. I'll be home in a few days. I made it to the finals, even though that doesn't mean much."

"I never doubted you," Tommy said.

"Are the kids around?"

"They're out to dinner with Josh. He wanted to become a proper uncle to them and not just my boyfriend."

"Tell them I love them. Tell Lucie not to worry and that I'll call them both tomorrow."

The dinner bell rang once more, and I said goodbye. I started to leave the room when I noticed opened drawers at the small desk. I hadn't left them that way. My suitcase was also unzipped. Someone had been in my room. They hadn't found anything because there was nothing to find. I hadn't brought anything valuable and I hadn't put any of my suspicions on paper.

I told Mason at dinner. He started to leave, and I urged him to sit back down. "It's better not to let anyone know about this by your sudden absence," I said.

He agreed, and he pretended to focus on the meal.

Dinner was delicious and uniquely local—low-country boil was a mainstay of the region. It was a simple dish of potatoes, sausage, corn on the cob and shrimp. Anna warned people that the dish contained beer and for anyone who might prefer a dish without that, she had one ready.

Anna left the room to servers who placed four platters of low-country boil on the table, which was covered with heavy brown paper. This tended to be a messy meal. For half an hour Mason and I ate our shrimp, corn, sausage, and potatoes in silence. We served ourselves from the non-alcoholic platter, as it seemed clear we had a long night ahead of us.

Chapter Twenty-three

After dinner, I met with Mason, Danny, and Lurleen in Quinn's office.

"We'll split up," Mason said, "but no one is to be without a police officer nearby—got it?"

This was directed at Lurleen and me, and we both nodded.

"Okay," he said to us. "You two can mingle. Danny and I will search your room for any evidence your intruder may have left behind. We'll meet back here in one hour."

Lurleen headed to the second floor in search of the elusive Granny Flumm who was most likely ensconced in her room for the night.

I planned to go to the main parlor and see who might be there, but Izzy Moran stopped me at the top of the stairs. She was wearing a coat.

"Do you think we could talk—outside? I know the house is bugged, and I'll feel better there."

"Of course."

I ran to my room. Mason was just finishing up. I told him where I was headed, and he reminded me about having an officer nearby—even if it was only Izzy I was talking to. I grabbed my jacket and met her downstairs.

We walked outside to the back deck and stood near the far railing. A police officer was stationed at the back door, close enough to help me if I needed it.

In front of us loomed the formal gardens looking ghostly in the deepening night. It made me think about Savannah's story of a haunted house. There was enough heartache in that house over the past century and a half to stir up a lot of ghosts—if one believed in that sort of thing.

"What are you up to, Dr. Brown?" Izzy asked. "You and Detective Garrett question my husband as if you think he's involved in something illegal. My husband is an honorable man."

"How long has your husband worked for Quinn and now Savannah?"

"For years, and he's never done anything wrong if that's what you're asking."

"Everyone here is under suspicion. Even Frank. Even you."

"I shouldn't have come to speak to you. Frank told me not to."

"I can't keep you here," I said, "but all I want to know is the truth. Why were *you* included in this competition?"

"Savannah knew I loved to cook, and she thought I'd do well on the show."

"I'm sure you're a fine cook, but that isn't why she included you."

Izzy turned toward me, and I assumed she was about to storm off. Instead, she put a hand on my arm.

"I know who you are," she said slowly. "I've read about you in the paper. Savannah brought you here so you could quietly play detective."

"And you? Why are you really here?"

"It's Frank that Savannah wanted, not me. We came as a package. Savannah wanted Frank to sort through what Quinn had been up to. She wanted to make sure she couldn't be prosecuted for Quinn's activities."

Izzy looked around to be certain we were alone. The police officer was staring at us, but he was too far away to hear our conversation.

"I've told Frank for years to get away from Quinn—that he was bad news. Frank kept telling me everything was all right. He promised he'd get out from under soon, but it was never the right time. Frank is a good man, a moral man, but I could see Quinn dragging him down, putting him in situations that might ruin his reputation—that might even land him in jail. I couldn't let that happen."

"Did you do something to stop Quinn?" I asked.

Izzy looked at me in the dim glow provided by the lighting under the rails.

"You mean did I kill Quinn? No. However, if I'd needed to do that, believe me, I would have. What I did instead was talk to Savannah about everything I knew or suspected. Frank was furious, but Savannah seemed grateful. She had a long talk with Frank, and that's the reason we're here. She wanted Frank to extricate himself from Quinn's affairs and do whatever he needed to do to protect her. He was to look through all of Quinn's books— including the ones Quinn didn't show Frank for accounting purposes."

"Does Frank know you're telling me this?"

"He tried to stop me, but I told him I trusted you, and he'd have to trust me."

"You realize I'll need to tell Mason everything you've said to me."

"I know that," Izzy said, "and Frank knows that as well."

Izzy didn't seem ready to leave.

"What is it?" I asked.

"I like Savannah, I really do, but she'd do anything to protect her empire. And she's shrewd, street smart. She got that from her father and a lifetime in politics. I wonder if she actually knew what was going on with Quinn and the money. As long as the money kept flowing, she could keep her status unchanged. Savannah loves the lights, and I don't think she likes the thought she could lose that."

"You said she was grateful when you told her about your suspicions," I said.

"Yes. Relieved perhaps that all the lies and corruption would finally end, and she could avoid a scandal."

"Do you believe she'd be ruthless enough to commit murder?"

Izzy didn't have time to answer. We both heard the heavy outside door open and shut with a force.

"There you are," Savannah said. "What are you doing out here? It's cold."

I'm sure I looked as guilty as I felt, my tell-all face as Lucie called it.

She took a good look at both of us. "I feel as if I've caught two small children with their hands in a cookie jar. Or perhaps something worse."

"I asked Izzy why she was included in the contest," I said, "and she told me it was so Frank could clean up any financial mess Quinn might have left behind."

"Nothing wrong with that," Savannah said. "Nothing to make the two of you look as guilty as you do. Izzy let me know Quinn's income might have come from dodgy sources. I didn't want any part of that. I asked Frank to investigate and keep me out of it.

"Now, what is it you were really discussing? From the look of you, you were talking about me, imagining I might have taken matters into my own hands. You were wondering if I might be a murderer."

Savannah didn't wait for an answer. She started to walk away and then turned back to us. I could see her hands shaking. I couldn't tell if it was anger or fear. "If you want to discuss this further, Ditie, I'll be in my office. If we do talk, I want Lurleen there. She seems to be the only one who has remained loyal to me. I want no police present, or I'll say nothing."

Savannah regained her composure, and her fine features hardened. "I am disappointed in you, Izzy. We've known each other for years, and now you turn on me. I wonder how far *you*'d go to protect Frank."

She walked back into the house.

Izzy followed and caught the heavy door before it slammed shut. "I have to talk to Frank."

I found Lurleen in Quinn's office staring at a computer screen. Danny was beside her.

"We're almost done here," she said when I entered.

I explained that Lurleen was to join me in Savannah's suite, and Danny was not to come.

"This isn't a good idea," he said.

"More information is always good, sweetie," Lurleen said, "and Ditie and I will be together."

She gave him a kiss.

"I'll tell Mason," Danny said. "We'll be nearby, and with luck, we can record the whole thing,"

"You seem to forget that Savannah is too smart for that," I said, "but we'll do our best, and there will be a policeman just outside the door."

Lurleen and I found Savannah seated at her desk. She seemed eager to talk and motioned us to sit down. I sat in a chair near the desk, but Lurleen remained standing at the door as Savannah walked to the keypad on the wall and punched in numbers. "No recordings," she said.

Savannah and Lurleen sat side by side on the sofa. "You seem to be the only one who understands me," Savannah said.

Lurleen smiled and said nothing. She and I had decided she'd play good cop and I'd be the bad one.

"What is it you wanted to tell us?" I asked.

"What is it you want to know?"

"Let's start with your financial situation," I said.

"I only recently understood there was a problem. Quinn handled our finances, and I was hands off. That was fine with me. I had a television show to run. After Quinn's death, Anna told me about the unpaid bills, and I called on Frank to sort things out."

I gave her what I hoped was a hard look. "You're saying you had no hint of anything wrong before this?"

"I heard the rumors, like everyone else, that Quinn was making money on the side through some questionable business meetings, but I know how jealous people can be. We are, after all, movers and shakers in Atlanta."

"Or were," Lurleen couldn't resist saying.

Savannah dropped Lurleen's hand. "Et tu, Brute?"

I stepped in. "We've heard from a number of sources that your financial situation might be desperate. You've said as much yourself. We just want to know what's going on."

Savannah stood and walked to the desk. It seemed her tête-à-tête with Lurleen was at an end.

"Yes, I was worried about our finances. I could see that Quinn was becoming less of a benefactor and more of a burden."

"Anna thought you hoped she'd take him off your hands," I said.

Savannah was quiet, and then she nodded.

"Yes. If you must know, it seemed like a perfect solution. Anna is by nature a caretaker. She was very willing to look after Quinn, even as his physical condition deteriorated. I could see they genuinely liked each other. If that turned to love, who was I to stand in the way?"

Once again, Lurleen could not remain silent. "Anna suggested *you* might have someone else waiting in the wings—someone like Peter Young perhaps."

Savannah's face grew hard. "That's absurd. Peter works for me. He has no money of his own. Why would I possibly want *him*?"

"Perhaps because he would do anything you asked him to do," Lurleen said. "Your entire empire was starting to crumble. You're not a chef. Anna is the real power behind the throne—the one who makes everything work. Your ratings were falling. Your show might be canceled for the next season. If a scandal arose about Quinn's money that would end everything. You might even go to jail."

So much for good cop, bad cop.

Savannah turned on Lurleen.

"I thought you were my friend. I thought you of all people might understand about inventing a new life. I know from stories you tell that's what you've done. They're amusing, and they are all lies. You're the one who's dishonest and a fraud."

Lurleen paled slightly, but she didn't lose her composure. "This isn't about me. This is about everything you hold dear. Quinn could no longer give you what you wanted or needed. If you could find a man who could do that for you, so much the better. If Quinn left you for another woman, you could look like the sympathetic victim. Then you, too, could take another lover, perhaps remarry."

"Never remarry," Savannah said. "You make me sound so calculating. That's not who I am. I loved Quinn."

"Perhaps you did love him, but I think you felt desperate," Lurleen said.

Once more, Savannah's demeanor changed. Instead of a warrior, she looked more like a wounded child. "I did feel desperate but not in the way you mean, not desperate for another man to take care of me. I felt desperate to take care of myself. I could see my world falling apart, the empire I'd spent so much time and effort creating. Bradshaw was like a yapping dog at my ankles, anxious to take a bite out of my Southern heritage and claim it as his own. Quinn was bleeding money—stealing from me to keep up appearances. He somehow believed I wouldn't notice, or if I did notice I wouldn't care. Love can take you only so far.

"When Quinn became so physically ill, I started to imagine life without him—what a simpler life that would be—either because he died or because someone else took him off my hands."

"Someone like Anna," I said.

"Yes, Anna was perfect. She was so pliable, so good for Quinn. And me. Whatever I suggested, she'd do."

"And I suppose if your scheme didn't work," Lurleen said, "and Anna and Quinn didn't decide to marry, there was always murder."

Savannah's anger returned. "I knew nothing about the medicine that killed Quinn or how to administer it. Make her stop badgering me," Savannah said, looking at me.

"She isn't doing that," I said. "She's asking you to tell us the truth."

"Get out," she said to Lurleen. "You're no friend of mine. At least Ditie doesn't hide who she is or what's she's about."

Lurleen stood, looked at me and walked to the door. I followed her and opened the door slowly as she punched in the numbers on the key pad that turned the recording device back on.

Chapter Twenty-four

Savannah remained seated at her desk, staring at the pile of letters in front of her.

"This can't be happening. Everything was going so well two years ago. I was on the cover of *Food and Wine* and *Southern Living*. Everyone loved me. I often wondered if Quinn couldn't bear my success. After all, he was beginning to fall apart as I was soaring."

I didn't say anything. Fame was like any other addiction. At first you thought you were in control, enjoying the high, and when you realized how desperately you needed it, you were lost.

"You think I'm vain and selfish," Savannah said.

I shook my head. "That wasn't what I was thinking."

Savannah examined papers on her desk, arranging them in piles—some for her inbox and some for the outbox. She sighed and began to open a small stack of mail while I remained silent.

"Lurleen makes me sound like a monster. I'm not a monster," she said. "See this pile of letters? These letters are from my fans."

Savannah straightened her back.

"I have allowed myself to care too much about what people think of me and my empire. And it was *my* empire, never Quinn's. Quinn wanted me to be a pretty object, wear lovely things, even when he couldn't afford those things. My fans wanted me to be as pure and perfect as my grandmother's pound cake." She paused and looked up at me. "Frankly, I was getting sick of all of it, and I was sick of people constantly telling me what I should and shouldn't do."

Once more, she focused on the letters, opening them one by one with a pearl-handled letter opener. She read each letter—smiled or frowned, depending on the content, and put it aside. "It's amazing people still write letters at all. Most of my fans use social media to reach me, but a few are more old-fashioned. They know the value of a handwritten note, true Southerners I call them.

Savannah grabbed a pile of letters.

"These are from people who love me and say I've changed their lives. There's nothing like it, realizing you're in everyone's heart. Once you have that, how can you live without it?"

"You must have worried that to keep their admiration, you could never tell them the truth about who you were."

"When things started to unravel, when it was clear Quinn was failing financially and physically, I felt trapped in a way I never had before. Fans don't want to see their heroes lose strength."

Savannah tapped the letter opener on the desk. "I had to keep up appearances!"

"What did that mean exactly?" I asked.

"I had to pretend everything was still perfect. When Anna asked about the culinary school, I had to pretend it was in the works. I had to give the same lavish parties I'd always given."

"Obviously, you couldn't keep that up," I said.

"No. At first I thought Quinn's problems were temporary, and I thought my falling ratings would improve. I went on every talk show that would have me. Then producers stopped returning my calls. I worried my show would be canceled. I didn't think I could stand that."

"So?"

"With the help of a very good man, I began to examine my options. I began to find my way. I'm a fighter, and I began to fight."

"Peter Young?"

"Of course not. Someone far more decent. My friend helped me realize I didn't have to be trapped. 'People reinvent themselves every day,' he said. 'That's how successful people maintain their success.' I thought about it and I realized he was right. He also said that Quinn wouldn't be around forever, and that I should think about how I would live without him. Somehow that freed me to see a world of possibilities."

"You were ready for that," I said, "life without Quinn."

Savannah shifted back in her cushioned desk chair. "Yes. Once I saw the possibilities, it opened my world. Anna and I could start a cooking school, here on the premises. I could change the format of my television show to use guest hosts like Olivier or even Granny Flumm. She's a very good cook, and she looks great on camera—like everyone's grandmother. Maybe out of the guest hosts I'd find one I could work with on a regular basis."

"You didn't mention Anna as a guest host. She looks beautiful on camera. I happened to see her as she was arranging the prep tables. I guess the cameras were running to test the lights."

"I love Anna, but she and I are too much alike. We wouldn't look good side-by-side on camera—there wouldn't be enough contrast between us. She'll do great as the head of a culinary institute, once we find the money for that. She's a wonderful teacher."

"I wonder if you were afraid she'd steal your success. She's a striking beauty, ten years younger than you, and a great chef."

"You too want to bring me down! Why? Because I have what you will never have?"

"I'm thankful I don't want what you have," I said. "I couldn't really live like that—waiting to see if I'd be renewed for another season, if my fans would continue to stick with me. It's a hard way to live."

"You're right, it is a hard way to live. Fame is such an overwhelming experience—you get a little and you want more. It's never quite enough. I'd look at the number of people who'd watched my last show or bought my latest cookbook, and I'd get frantic if the numbers weren't increasing."

"So, what did you do?" I asked.

"What are you talking about?"

"What did you do with all that frustration?"

Savannah said nothing for a moment. Instead she used the sharp point of her letter opener to violently slice through another envelope. She read what was inside and it seemed to calm her. She even smiled, and then she looked over at me.

"I turned for comfort to the one man who could provide it—provide it and keep his mouth shut, a man who had his own secrets."

"The man who gave you such good advice."

Savannah nodded.

"Who was it?" I asked and waited while Savannah seemed to be deciding whether or not she'd tell me.

"Dorian Gray," she said at last.

"What? According to Anna, he wanted to have an affair with her—now you say he actually wanted it with you?"

Savannah looked at me wide-eyed. "Anna said that? You don't know who Dorian actually is?"

"I don't know his real name if that's what you mean."

"He'd never have wanted an affair with Anna. Anna is his sister."

She stopped speaking and stared at me.

"You're shocked. I can see it on your face. Dorian would do anything for me, anything at all, and he knew how to keep his mouth shut—even from his sister."

"You found him attractive?" I asked, thinking of the obsequious man who had waited on me, the man who looked pasty and unwell.

"Yes, in a way that has nothing to do with physical appearance. We never had an affair unless you call our abiding friendship an affair. I knew Dorian always had my best interest at heart."

"Do you intend to marry him?"

Savannah laughed—a hard-edged laugh. "Don't be absurd. I will never let a man dictate my future again. Besides, it would be like marrying my uncle."

"You don't seem like a particularly patient woman," I said, "and the walls were closing in on you. What did you plan to do if Quinn didn't divorce you for Anna?"

"Quinn was a very sick man. He'd had two heart attacks," Savannah said.

"And survived them. You could be waiting a long time for that future you dreamed of."

The color rose on Savannah's neck and she clutched the pen knife until her knuckles grew white. "You think I killed Quinn? I loved Quinn to the end, and I never wanted to hurt him or see him suffer. Why would I make such a point of getting people to protect me if I'd done that?"

"It would be a good alibi," I said, "and when the reporter came, perhaps you felt you had to kill him before he found out what you were up to."

Even as I spoke, I could hear Mason's admonition—don't accuse anyone of anything. "I'm sorry I said that."

"Sorry perhaps, but it is what you meant." Savannah picked up a letter from the desk. Then she stood, holding the letter opener in her right hand and the letter in her left.

I couldn't read her expression, even as she walked toward me. Her face was blank.

Mason flung the door opened and wrestled the letter opener out of her hand. "I was watching this from Quinn's office."

Savannah stared at the letter opener on the floor. "I didn't kill Quinn, and I wasn't going to kill Ditie. What kind of a fool do you take me for? I wanted her to read this letter."

In her left hand she held a carefully folded piece of linen stationery, which she handed to Mason.

Chapter Twenty-five

Mason unfolded the letter. I read it over his shoulder. It was typed and signed "A Disgruntled Fan."

You know what you've stolen from me—the promises you've made and never kept. I will destroy everyone and everything you love. First your husband, then your son, and finally your reputation. Tell no one about this letter or I will reveal to the world what you have done.

There was no date on the letter.

"When did you receive this?" Mason asked.

"A month ago. A few days before Quinn died."

"You told the police about this?"

"No. People would think I'd done something horrible."

"Your pride may have caused the death of your husband and the reporter Nick Davis," Mason said.

Savannah teared slightly. "My image is everything. I couldn't have it tarnished."

"You know what the writer is talking about then." Mason made it a statement, not a question.

"Of course not," Savannah shrugged. "I have no idea what the letter refers to, but I'm aware I have enemies. James Bradshaw believes Quinn and I stole the house from him. Buddy believes I'm threatening his marriage and his reputation. Poor Timothy White believed I took his mother from him. Perhaps he's behind all of this."

"You don't really believe that," I said.

"No," she said. "Not Timothy."

"You are telling me you have absolutely no idea who wrote this letter or why," Mason said.

"That's what I'm telling you." Savannah said. "It was left with my other mail. No postage, no return address."

Mason waited, but Savannah was done talking.

"We're finished with you for now," Mason said. "You're to go nowhere. Do you understand? An officer will remain in your room to make sure you follow my orders."

Mason brought the officer at the door into the suite.

"She is to be in sight of you at all times. Understood? There are more secret passages in this house than there are rooms."

The officer nodded and folded his arms.

Mason left and took me with him.

We returned to Quinn's office where Lurleen and Danny were waiting.

Mason showed them the letter. "We need to talk this through," he said. "Get yourselves some coffee. We're going to be here a while."

Danny set up an easel with paper and a black marker.

Lurleen gave him a questioning look. "I've been working with Mason a long time," he said to her. "I know how he works."

"Pen and paper?" Lurleen asked.

"I want everyone to see this as we go," Mason said. "I don't want to be scrunched over a computer screen for the next hour. And I don't want anyone hacking our computer to see what we're thinking."

"Got it," Lurleen said.

"Let's go over what we know." Mason made himself another cup of coffee and stood beside Danny. "Let's get the time line straight. The dip in Savannah's ratings started two years ago in the fall?"

Lurleen checked her iPhone. "Savannah's last big magazine spread was in the September issue of *Southern Living* year before last. Her last television appearance was two weeks after that as a guest judge on *Clipped*. Nothing since then."

Mason nodded. "The drug bust at one of Quinn's gathering places happened the following summer. You got the date, Danny?"

"July fifteenth last year."

"Then everything blew up during their anniversary celebration a year ago according to Anna," Mason said. "When Savannah told Chief Lewis and Quinn about her son. Why did she do that?"

"I think she hoped to use Olivier to boost her ratings by bringing him to the US," I said. "He was young, talented, and French," Lurleen added. "What could be a better combination for Savannah?"

"We don't yet know who was responsible for the threatening letters," Mason said. "They started immediately after the anniversary and ended with Quinn's death."

"Anna said she thought Dorian might have written the one that threatened her," I said. "That was when she claimed she broke off an affair with him, before we knew they were brother and sister. Why would she implicate her brother in murder?"

"Relationships may be the key to these murders," Mason said, "particularly if we suspect two or more people worked together to kill Quinn and Nick Davis."

Mason took the marker from Danny. "We'll start with Dorian Gray and see what he has to say for himself. Shall we bring the deputy chief in as well? You think he can be trusted, Danny?"

Danny nodded. "Matt said Buddy helped get him on the force but never tried to influence how he did his work. If he thought he couldn't be objective, Matt promised he'd step aside. I believe him for what it's worth."

"Then get them both in," Mason said.

Danny left, and Mason started a new page. "Suspects," he wrote. "This could take a while."

Chapter Twenty-six

Five minutes later Danny entered the room with Matt Lewis and Dorian Gray. Mason had just enough time to turn the page on the easel to a blank sheet.

"Did you require something?" Dorian asked, his British accent slightly more pronounced than usual.

"Just the truth. Sit, Mr. Gray," Mason said. Matt and Danny stood with their backs to the closed door.

Dorian did as he was told.

"We know a lot about you," Mason said. "We know Anna is your sister. What we don't know is your real name."

Dorian appeared unruffled, but when he spoke again his British accent was gone. "My name is David Hayes, and I *am* Anna's brother. I've looked after her since our parents died when she was a young girl. I had the opportunity to work here as a butler, and I jumped at it. I'm very good at that work and enjoy it."

"Why the disguise?" Mason asked.

"Savannah was looking for a British butler, someone to bring sophistication to her elegant house—I couldn't very well be Anna's brother and British at the same time. Besides, I've always been an amateur actor, so here was an opportunity for an ongoing role. It all made sense."

"You planned to continue that role for the rest of your life?" Mason asked.

Dorian—or David as we now knew him—laughed softly. "Of course not. My employer in New York died last year and left me plenty of money. I thought I'd come for a while, make sure Anna was doing well, and then travel."

"You've been here how long?" Mason asked.

"Twelve months on staff. Before that I came when Savannah and Quinn were having a party and needed extra help."

"As you know we have surveillance footage with you and Anna. It looked like a private talk. You lied to us before about it. Why?"

"That was stupid. I knew Anna was involved with someone, and I thought it might be better if the police thought it was with me."

"So, what were you doing in the room with Anna?"

"She was upset about her work here. She couldn't seem to get ahead and wondered if she should leave. I told her not to go, that I thought Savannah valued her work and would give her a culinary school when she had the money. Savannah and I had become close by that time."

"You were having an affair with Savannah?" Mason asked.

David laughed. "Look at me. Savannah is a beautiful woman. She may have been having an affair, but it certainly wasn't with me."

"Savannah knew who you really were?"

"Eventually. She's a showman herself, so she didn't care that I was putting on an act. She really wanted the same thing from me that Anna did, someone to give her good advice. I like that role. I'm a religious man, and I might have been a minister if circumstances had been different."

"Circumstances?" Mason asked.

"If our parents hadn't died, if Anna hadn't needed me. I was twenty at the time, and Anna was ten. Their deaths shook my religious faith for a while, but I've found it again."

"That's all for now," Mason said. "You can go. I may have more questions for you later."

Once he left and Mason had locked the door, he turned to the rest of us. "Do you believe what David Hayes just told us?"

"I believe he loves Anna," I said. "I don't know about the rest. I'm not sure I buy his explanation of why he didn't initially admit they were siblings."

Matt spoke up. "I know Buddy likes him and trusts him. Savannah as well. Could he be that good an actor?"

"He had me fooled with his British accent," Lurleen said.

I wasn't sure Lurleen was an authority on the authenticity of accents.

"He's been kind to all of us," Lurleen added, "and he doesn't look strong enough to carry a dead body along a broken path. I saw him using an inhaler. He told me he'd had asthma since childhood."

"What would his motive be?" I asked. "Anna's future seems tied to Savannah's success, not her downfall."

"So it seems," Mason said. "Let's move on."

He turned back the sheet, and Danny took over writing.

"Rose Kirkwood had a colorful history as a porn star," Mason said. "The chief knew that and used it against her, but he claims he had no idea she was in the contest until he saw her here. If that's true, why were George and Rose Kirkwood included? As far as we know, George is what he seems—a pig farmer from South Georgia."

"It was George who found the bloody trail and later helped find the body," Danny said. "We can't be certain he's an innocent bystander. What if he knew about Rose's past and the fact a reporter was on the premises? What if he was afraid the reporter was there to dig up dirt on the participants?"

"Whoever murdered Nick Davis was aware of the recording devices in the house," Mason said. "They covered their head when they entered the room and turned it off. How would George Kirkwood have known about that, even if he did get wind of a reporter in the house?"

"If I may," Matt Lewis said, "the whole town knew how screwy Quinn was, meaning no disrespect for the dead. He'd question local people if they seemed to know too much about his business, and he was always calling us when a stranger turned up and stayed for more than a day or two in Veracrue. Those of us in the police department knew about the fact he'd wired his house. Savannah told us. Quinn told my uncle about the tunnel and secret rooms."

"That means Chief Lewis could have gotten himself anywhere he wanted without being seen," Mason said. "He could have disposed of Davis's body when he knew everyone was asleep, including the officer who was supposed to watch the back of the house. Maybe he even sedated that officer, so he wouldn't have to worry about him."

"I suppose that's possible," Matt said. He paused for a moment. "I love my uncle, and I don't believe he's involved in any serious wrongdoing, but I want the truth as much as you do. I'll go where the evidence takes us."

It was a noble speech, and hopefully it was an honest one.

"Back to George Kirkwood," Mason said. "Sometimes a murderer can't stand to leave his victim unfound, and whoever moved the body had to be strong. A woman couldn't have done it without help."

Lurleen jumped in. "You're suggesting George Kirkwood, who looks a bit on the scrawny side, would have to be strong enough as a pig farmer to move a dead body."

"I am," Mason said. "We need to find out if George has any connection to Quinn, any reason he might have wanted him dead."

"Of course, if we suspect two people were working together then it could have been anyone," I said.

"You mean like Rose and George?" Mason asked, looking at me.

"Or Savannah and Anna," I said. "She and Anna work closely together. I like them both, but I'm trying to think outside the box—Lurleen accuses me of being a narrow judge of character. Could they have wanted that reporter dead and gone? Would they have been strong enough to pull it off?"

"Strong enough, maybe," Mason said, "but was there enough time for them to do it?"

"Middle of the night, everyone asleep," Danny said.

"Remember, I heard the dog whining," I said. "There's only one dog in this house—it's Savannah's. Was Saffron whining because she wanted to come outside with Savannah, and Savannah wouldn't let her?"

"All possible. Savannah Evans isn't far down our list of suspects," Mason said.

"Okay, who's next?" Danny asked, pen poised by the easel.

"What about Pepper and Peter Young?" Mason said, and then waited until their names were added. "Peter served as Quinn's bodyguard and then Savannah's."

I added what I knew. "Savannah says that's why Pepper was included in the contest. Pepper spent her time before that first technical challenge checking herself in the mirror and adjusting her makeup. She didn't seem at all concerned about the food she was supposed to prepare."

Lurleen smiled at me. "Some people actually care how they look on screen. That doesn't make her a murderer. In fact, if anything, it suggests she had no idea what was going on behind the scenes. As for Peter, he's a different story. He's got a wandering eye, if you ask me. I don't know if Pepper notices. She may be so sure of her own good looks that she can't imagine Peter wanting to stray."

"What do you mean, Lurleen, about a wandering eye?" Danny asked, and he didn't sound happy.

"Nothing happened, of course. But, Peter said he had time on his hands while his wife was busy, and he'd be happy to show me the estate."

"So, he knew the grounds," I said.

"Like the back of his hand," Lurleen said. "Like the chief, he knew all the secret rooms and he said he'd helped Quinn install the recording devices."

"That means it would have been no trouble for Peter Young to help Bradshaw get a reporter into the house unseen," Mason said, "or to murder him and get his body off the premises."

"Yes, but why?" I asked. "If he was Quinn's bodyguard and then Savannah's, why would he turn on either one of them? They were his source of revenue, weren't they?"

"Peter Young is all about money," Lurleen said, "his wife too. Did you take a good look at the clothes they wear, the shoes, the watches?"

I shook my head.

"I know *you* didn't notice that, Ditie, but what about you two detectives?"

"Enlighten us," Mason said.

"Gladly. For dress, Peter wears Berluti shoes."

We all gave her a blank look.

"Handmade. From Italy. At least two thousand dollars. For his running shoes, it's Dolce & Gabbana Sorrento Sneakers with Rhinestones. Over the top, but that's how he likes it—last time I looked they were more than a thousand dollars. I hope you've checked those shoes for blood stains."

Lurleen smiled sweetly.

"I could go on, but I assume you get my drift. Together Pepper and Peter Young probably spend more money on clothes than most people have in their bank accounts. That's a well-paid bodyguard if you ask me."

"We do get your drift," I said. "Peter might be willing to do anything for enough money."

"Exactly," Lurleen said triumphantly. She turned to Danny. "And you thought I was just a pretty face."

"Never," Danny said. "I always knew what kind of brain buzzed around in that beautiful head of yours."

"How far would Peter go to maintain his lifestyle?" I asked. "Would it include murder? We know Quinn had made some shady connections—perhaps a drug dealer wanted Quinn gone. They'd have the money if Peter Young had the means."

"Peter probably had the means," Danny said. "As a medic in the reserves, he'd know how to start an IV."

"Who's left?" Mason asked. "Who haven't we discussed yet?"

"Granny Flumm and James Bradshaw," I said. "I saw them together at least twice, and one time I heard them talking about their plans to expose Savannah as a fraud."

"We know why Bradshaw hated Savannah, "Mason said. "Anyone know why Gertrude Flumm did?"

Lurleen, Danny, and Mason shook their heads.

"You know anything about her?" Mason asked Matt.

"I do. She's a mainstay in Beaufort. Runs a cafe there and offers the best Southern cooking in South Carolina. Do I think she could be involved with the murders and mischief? No sir, I do not. I can't see what she'd have to gain."

"Why was she included in the show?" I asked. "Savannah chose every person in this contest for a reason."

"Maybe to bring some legitimacy to the contest," Danny said.

"That doesn't explain why she dislikes Savannah as much as she seems to," I said.

No one had anything to add to that, so we moved on.

Mason turned to Danny. "Do we know any more about where Quinn went for his treatments and who took him there?"

Danny shook his head. "It wasn't the service that Anna said he used on occasion. They hadn't taken Quinn anywhere for six months."

"That's what we have to nail down next," Mason said. "Where did Quinn go and with whom? Could it have been Chris Evans? He seems to be a jack of all trades, devoted to Savannah, and he lives close by. What's his story?"

We were interrupted by a tentative knock. Danny turned to the next blank sheet before Mason opened the door.

"Speak of the devil," Lurleen said, as Chris entered the room.

Chapter Twenty-seven

Chris Evans stood before us in what was now a very crowded office. Apparently, he hadn't heard Lurleen's remark, or he chose to ignore it.

"Ah, Detective Garrett," Chris began. "I'm glad I found you here. Savannah wanted me to ask if we might finish the taping first thing tomorrow morning. We only have one more episode to shoot."

"You're just the man we wanted to see," Mason said. "Come in. We have a few questions for you."

"Can this wait twenty-four hours," Chris asked, "until we get the last episode wrapped up? Just one more day, and then I'll be available to answer any questions you might have."

"This can't wait," Mason said. "And yes, possibly, after you've answered our questions, we can let you finish the show. First, tell me how you came to work for Savannah."

"Savannah is my aunt, but I'm sure you know that. When my father died, she took me under her wing, mentored me, sent me to a private school and onto college. I majored in film at UCLA, and I've worked with her since I graduated."

"Is Savannah easy to work with?" Mason asked.

"She has her quirks. We all do. But, yeah, she's easy."

"You're a lucky man, aren't you?" Mason said.

Chris flinched at that. "Was I lucky to lose my dad at age fourteen?"

"What happened?" Mason asked.

Chris took a deep breath. "I don't want to talk about it. It isn't relevant."

"Sorry. There's no telling what's relevant," Mason said.

Chris didn't respond.

"You have a show to wrap up, and I have an investigation to complete."

"My father shot himself, and it doesn't have one thing to do with this investigation."

"Maybe not," Mason said. "Is there anything you can tell me that might have something to do with the investigation?"

"Savannah's good at a lot of things, but knowing who to trust isn't one of them."

"Who are you talking about?" Mason asked. When Chris hesitated, Mason pointed to the clock on the wall.

"Peter Young for one, Anna for another, and maybe Dorian Gray. He's a strange one. He won't even tell you what his real name is. There are a lot of people just hanging on, waiting to take advantage of Savannah's downfall—wanting to help with that downfall."

"Explain that to me," Mason said. "It seems most of the people you named would do better if Savannah were successful. How would Peter Young benefit from the collapse of her empire?"

"Young has nosed into everything around here. He knew about the stolen objects, Olivier, Quinn's financial troubles. If he wanted to blackmail anyone about anything, he had the information to do it."

"And you think he's been doing that?" Mason asked.

"You've seen how he lives? You've seen the car he drives? Yeah, I think he's done it, either with or without the help of Anna. She'd be happy to see Savannah go under. She'd be there to pick up the pieces. She may already be talking to producers."

"And Dorian?" Mason asked. "You know he's Anna's brother?"

Chris looked genuinely surprised. "No, I didn't know that. That explains a lot."

"Like what?" Mason asked.

"Like why those two spend so much time together. I assumed—well, you know what I assumed. Dorian is nothing to look at, but I thought maybe Anna had peculiar taste in men."

"Anything else you want to tell us?" Mason asked.

"Just let me wrap up the show and get out of here before someone else gets killed or hurt."

"You can go for now. I'll get back to you about the final episode," Mason said.

Chris left and closed the door with just enough force to let us know he was annoyed.

Mason made himself another cup of coffee and sat on the couch beside me. "I wish I had some of your oatmeal chocolate cookies right now. I could do some serious thinking with those."

"Funny you should say that," I said. "Rumor has it the last episode allows us to make our signature recipes. I was thinking of my pecan praline short bread, but if you'd rather have the oatmeal chocolate cookies, I could do that."

Mason smiled and then shifted into professional mode. "Maybe we let the show run its course with everyone present and accounted for. If everyone is in the audience, then we can protect Savannah."

"Unless it's Savannah we need to protect everyone else from," I said. "She gets rid of one annoying husband, a pesky reporter, and generates sympathetic publicity about all she's been through."

"Point taken," Mason said. "The sympathy might be enough to rejuvenate her popularity."

"I think that's what Chris is hoping for," I said. "I bet he keeps in the exploding stove top segment."

"Savannah would need someone to help her if she is the murderer," Danny said. "There's no way she could drag a dead body across the estate."

"Peter appears to be willing and able to do whatever Savannah needs," Mason said. "And if they were having an affair as Anna thinks, he'd stand to gain a great deal."

"But, Savannah's told us her secrets," Lurleen said. "How many more can she have?"

Danny had been silent, quietly using his computer. "There might be something more," he said. "I just looked up the death of Chris's father, Savannah's brother. She never mentioned she had a brother who died suddenly, did she?"

We all shook our heads except the deputy chief.

"You knew about this, Matt?" Mason asked.

"I heard about it. I just didn't know how it could be relevant. It was years ago, before my time on the force."

"The coroner's report was that it was a possible suicide," Danny said. "Murder could not be ruled out. No suspect was ever identified in a follow-up investigation. Buddy Lewis was the officer in charge. Want to know something else of interest? The brother, John Evans, was due to inherit almost everything from the recent death of their father, including this house. The will was being challenged by Savannah. And then John mysteriously died. No history of depression. No financial problems. No explanation for the suicide. John's will left money for Chris in a trust and gave Savannah full title to the house. Chris's mother had died of cancer years earlier. The brother named Savannah as the executor of the will and the trust."

"That changes things," Mason said. "If you murder once it's easier to murder again. If it was Savannah, then who helped her get Nick Davis's body off the estate?"

"Peter Young is her bodyguard," I said.

"It also gives Chris a motive of revenge," Danny said.

Mason nodded. "We'll let this last episode play out. In the morning we'll spread some rumors—about the death of John Evans, about people talking more than they should, about blackmail. Let's see what happens offstage. We'll have to make sure no one leaves the area or is unaccounted for. Can you guarantee that, Matt?"

"Yes, sir."

"Are you up for this, Ditie? You'll be on the front line."

"I'm not a target," I said. "I'll stay out of the line of fire." I thought of Lucie and Jason and how close they'd come to losing a second mother the last time I'd said something similar.

"Lurleen, we're going to need your help," Mason said.

Lurleen jumped up. "I thought you'd never ask. Where shall I start spreading my rumors— with Anna?"

Mason shook his head. "Nothing until tomorrow morning, Lurleen. I don't want to give the killer time to carry out a third murder."

He turned to the deputy chief. "You on board, Matt? The chief can't know anything about this."

"Understood. Let's go over the details of where you want men stationed. I'll keep my uncle at my side tonight and tomorrow during the taping."

Mason reviewed what everyone was to say and to whom.

"Places everyone," Lurleen said with a smile. "This may be someone's last performance."

Chapter Twenty-eight

Mason gave one last look at his chart and then at the four of us seated in the room. "If we start the rumors in the morning, that should stir things up without giving the murderer or murderers time to make a decent escape plan. Of course, it may also make them desperate and dangerous. What do you think, Danny?"

"It's what we've got to work with. Makes sense to me."

"And you, Matt?"

"I can't think of a better plan. I'll let my men know what's up for the morning and make sure they're alert for the rest of the night. I'll keep Buddy out of the loop, just in case. The more we can keep our murderer off balance, the better off we'll be."

Lurleen glanced at the time. "Anna usually serves breakfast around 7:30. Should we tell her about the shoot in the morning?"

"I don't want to give anyone a heads up," Mason said. "I'll tell Chris I'm making the decision early tomorrow morning about when and if the last shoot will take place. You tell Anna the same."

We all nodded.

"I'll see you here at 6:30 tomorrow morning," Mason said. "Get some rest."

Lurleen and I went back to her room and found Anna reading in bed.

"It's so late," Lurleen said. "Did you wait up for us?"

"I got a little anxious about both of you, and I wanted to hear what was going on tomorrow."

"Mason said he'd make a decision about a final shoot in the morning," Lurleen said.

"All right then. I'll plan to fix breakfast at the regular time, 7:30." She put her book down. "Is there any more news about—" she stopped for a moment, "—about who might have done all these horrible things?"

Anna sounded nervous.

"Mason is being tight lipped about everything," I said. "He's always like that. Do *you* know anything more?"

"Nothing," Anna said. With that she flipped off her reading light and was asleep or pretended to be in a couple of minutes. Lurleen and I weren't far behind.

* * * *

Anna was stirring by six am. I looked at the clock as she slipped into the bathroom and out again fully dressed minutes later. Lurleen and I were up as soon as she left and in Quinn's office by 6:30.

Mason, Matt, and Danny were already there. We spent fifteen minutes discussing who would spread what gossip to whom. The idea was to make suspects as nervous as possible and to make it clear an arrest was imminent.

Lurleen and I walked downstairs to the dining room, which was empty. We grabbed a cup of coffee and headed for the kitchen.

"I decided on a simple breakfast," Anna said. "Biscuits, scrambled eggs with sausage and gravy, fresh squeezed orange juice. You think that's enough?"

"More than enough," I said.

"Good. That will give me time to work on the snacks. I got the word from Chris that the finale will be shot this morning. Everyone is hungry when we do a show, especially the last episode. Even if they've just had breakfast, they act like they're starving, so I'm fixing something to tide them over."

"Mason seems to think he's figured things out—just needs to nail down a few details," I said. "He expects to make an arrest when the shoot is over."

Anna was cracking eggs into a large bowl. Her hand slipped and the stainless-steel bowl crashed to the floor.

"You seem so jittery, Anna," I said. "I've never seen you like this before. If you know something, you need to tell us now."

"I don't know anything. It's simply too much tension with a murderer wandering around loose. I doubt that anyone will want breakfast when they hear someone is about to be arrested."

"I would think people would be relieved," Lurleen said.

"Perhaps you're right," Anna said, as she cleaned up the mess and rinsed out the bowl. "I hope you're right."

I asked if I could help.

"You could get me the heavy cream from the refrigerator, Ditie. You probably know that's the secret to excellent scrambled eggs."

It seemed Anna had gotten her feet back under her. "Help yourselves if something looks good. We have plenty."

Lurleen ate a macaroon. "*Ooh, la la,*" she said. "As good as one from a French patisserie."

Anna smiled. "I've spent a lot of time in France. I'm flattered."

Danny entered the kitchen, and Lurleen pointed him to the biscuits with ham and cheese. "Really great," he mumbled between mouthfuls.

"Do you have time to talk?" I asked Anna. "We have a few more questions."

"Only a few?" Anna walked to the sink and washed her hands. She gave last-minute directions to the staff and walked out of the kitchen. We followed her into her small office. She closed the door. "What is it you want to know?"

"It seems as if you were expecting us," Danny said.

"Savannah told me last night about her relationship with my brother. He was much more discreet and never mentioned it to me. I assume you're here about that."

"No, not right now," Danny said. "Right now, we want to hear more about Quinn's treatments, where he went and with whom?"

"I gave Ditie a card with information about the driver Quinn often used," Anna said.

"That driving service hadn't picked up Quinn in the last six months. I think you probably knew that," I said.

Anna put her hands on her hips. "I'm sick to death of all these questions. I took him occasionally if you must know. Peter Young was the one who usually took him. Quinn was embarrassed at first. He said it was a New Age clinic, and he didn't want anyone to know. It was near Charleston."

"How did he find this clinic?" Danny asked. "Do you have the name?"

"It was called…something like a new beginning. No, it was 'A New Lease on Life.' That's it. It was a testosterone clinic primarily, but it offered other supplements. I think Quinn found it from Frank or Peter. Those are the only people he trusted enough to confide in. I saw the building. It didn't look sketchy, but there were no signs to indicate it was a clinic of any kind. I guess they were trying to keep the place super private."

"Why didn't you tell us this before?" Lurleen asked.

"I didn't want to humiliate Quinn. Even in death I didn't want that."

We left Anna, and once we were far enough away from the kitchen I told them I didn't believe Anna. "She didn't tell us about the clinic because she knew it would implicate her. She had training as a nurse. She was close to Quinn. He'd trust her."

"She got so nervous when we talked about an arrest," Lurleen said.

"She did," I said, "and every time we try to interview her, she comes up with some new piece of information, which might be the truth—"

"Or another lie," Danny finished for me. "Let's find Frank Moran."

We found him in the main parlor with his wife. Izzy left us saying she needed to freshen up before the final episode. A policeman followed her. When asked, Frank vehemently denied giving Quinn any information about New Age clinics. "You think it's at some clinic Quinn got the drug that killed him?"

"We think it might be," Danny said, "and now that we know the name of the clinic and its location, it won't be hard for us to track down the information we need. I'm surprised Quinn said nothing to you about it. He didn't seem to have many close friends."

"I worked for him. I wasn't his friend," Frank said. "Besides, Quinn was a proud man. He wouldn't tell anyone he was having trouble performing—at least he didn't tell me."

We left.

"That stirred up Frank, don't you think?" Lurleen said. "Now, Quinn wasn't even his friend. Did you notice how glad he was to see us leave?"

"I noticed he picked up his cell as we were leaving," I said.

"We can get hold of that and see who he called," Danny said. "First, let's talk to Young."

"*Bien sûr,*" Lurleen responded. "I know where to find him. Near the bar and the pool table."

An officer stood outside the billiard room.

Questioning Peter Young was like trying to open a locked vault. He finally admitted he'd given Quinn the name of the clinic because he'd heard it was good, reliable, and discreet.

Danny reached the clinic on his iPhone in two minutes. They said Quinn Nelson had a standing appointment every three weeks for a private room. He brought a nurse with him, so all the clinic did was provide space and privacy.

"And the nurse?" I asked.

"They claimed they didn't have a name or a description. The old receptionist had left, and the new one had been there only a few weeks."

We went back to Peter with our information.

"Look," he said. "I never took Quinn there. If you have more questions, you talk to my lawyer."

We left and reported our findings to Mason.

"So," Mason said, "either Young is lying or Anna is."

We heard the bell ring to announce breakfast.

"We'll let people know that we're close to an arrest," Mason said. "We'll act like we're trying to reassure everyone that they are safe, and the murderer will soon be in hand."

"Sounds good to me, boss," Danny said.

Matt Lewis caught up with us. "I've got the officers in place. They're stationed at every exit from the set and down most corridors. Nothing will happen without someone being there to stop it."

"Good. Get everyone in the parlor," Mason said. "I'll let them know they are to go from breakfast directly to the set. Then we'll see what happens."

The gathering in the parlor quieted when Mason entered the room. He explained that everyone was expected to attend the filming of the last episode. No one would be allowed to leave without the express permission of an officer. Mason also announced that new information had come to light that was being investigated. Innocent people would be free to depart, hopefully by the end of the day. If anyone had additional information to share, this was the time to do it.

Savannah, escorted by a policeman, made her entrance into the parlor. She looked drawn. While she tried to reassure her guests and staff that all was well, she didn't look as if she believed it. She searched the audience for Olivier and when she found him, her color returned. She brought him to the front of the room.

"As some of you know, Olivier is the young French pastry chef who has been a sensation in Provence. He'll be joining us for the finale."

Savannah led the way to the dining room and assured everyone they would have a few minutes to freshen up after breakfast.

Mason scowled at her, and she corrected herself.

"Police will escort those of you who need to go to the restrooms before the shoot begins. As you know, no one is to be out of sight of a policeman. This is for your own safety."

Lurleen, Danny, Mason, and I scattered among the other guests. We listened to the concerns of the people nearest us, and as instructed we made sure we said two things— first, that if they had seen anything suspicious, anything at all, they needed to speak to Detective Garrett or Deputy Chief

Matt Lewis immediately. Second, we assured them that the police were likely to make an arrest in the next few hours.

When breakfast ended, we followed Savannah to the kitchen set. She stepped to the center of the stage with Olivier at her side. Granny Flumm, Rose Kirkwood, and I stood at our stations. Everyone else settled on the array of folding chairs.

"Anyone missing?" Mason asked Danny.

"No, sir. Bradshaw is here, and Chief Lewis is sitting with his lawyer. You can bet that's costing him a pretty penny."

Chris signaled to Savannah to start.

Savannah turned her brightest smile to the camera and spoke with apparent joy. "I am happy to announce that Olivier Laurent will help me judge this last episode. He is a renowned pastry chef from southern France. You will be seeing much more of this young man in the US."

She turned to the contestants. "For this final episode I will let each of you prepare your signature dessert. This will be the show-stopper challenge—something in keeping with the holidays ahead. Good luck. You have two hours."

She and Olivier exited the set. As they left, I saw a young officer leave with them.

With another signal from Chris, we three contestants started gathering ingredients. I decided to make both my pecan praline shortbread and my chocolate oatmeal surprise bars. They would look good together on the plate, but they'd look even better as decorations for a gingerbread house that was meant to be eaten. I'd either wow Olivier and Savannah or possibly shock them if the whole thing fell apart. That had happened to me two weeks earlier when Lucie, Jason and I worked on a gingerbread house for the holidays. The whole thing collapsed into a delicious pile of crumbs. Still, it was worth the challenge.

I could make both cookies in my sleep, and I'd fine-tuned the construction of the gingerbread house. Once I got the gingerbread and the cookies in the oven, I had time to look around the room and think.

The front row was reserved for spouses and ex-contestants. I studied the faces. Did any one of them look worried, guilty? The lights made it difficult to see expressions, but from where I stood everyone seemed edgy.

I glanced over at Rose and Granny Flumm.

I tried to imagine Rose as a younger woman with a beautiful body, playing up to the camera. This morning she kept her head down.

Granny Flumm was busy working on an ice cream concoction. It was a perfect choice—she was as cool as the dessert she was preparing.

I watched the monitor and was amazed at what I saw. Granny Flumm looked on camera like a favorite aging aunt—warm and approachable. It was then I wondered if this was an opportunity for her to launch her own show as Savannah had suggested. As the population aged, was it time to look for older chefs as well?

I saw Matt Lewis standing behind his uncle. They both wore the same intense expression—as if they were waiting for something to happen. Mason stood next to James Bradshaw, perhaps to make sure he didn't make a run for it. Bradshaw didn't look to be in any condition to run anywhere. His abdomen was bandaged, and he wore a loose shirt that didn't quite hide the wound. He slumped in his chair.

Mason moved to the side wall of the room. The cameras continued to roll. Unbeknownst to any of the contestants or the audience, one of those cameras made a repeated sweep of the space. I knew about it because Mason had told me the night before how the surveillance would operate.

The camera hung from a beam and moved silently around the room like a giant shark looking for prey. That's what it was, after all, a silent machine taking note of anything out of the ordinary. And the monitor of that machine was Danny, at the back of the set, hidden in a corner, next to a walk-in refrigerator. He could study what the camera saw.

After an hour, Chris announced there would be a fifteen-minute break. He made it sound as if it was because of technical difficulties, but in fact he was doing what Mason ordered him to do. I took my cookies out of the oven and put them on a cooling rack. The gingerbread needed more time, so I stayed close to my station.

Chris said the sound would be off and people could talk among themselves. The cameras would continue to roll, and people were told to ignore them. In reality the mics were still on, and Danny could hear every word said by Chris and the contestants.

At first people said little. Then gradually they loosened up. "Does that mean we can walk around?" someone asked. "Can we get snacks at the snack table?"

"Yes," Chris said.

Normally, Chris would not have allowed milling around in the middle of an episode, but he wasn't in control of this shoot, and he knew it. Individuals gathered for snacks. Anna's staff did their best to keep up with the demand for coffee and food.

Mason worked the room. Matt Lewis kept his eyes on his uncle and the doors.

Once I got the gingerbread out of the oven, I searched for Anna but couldn't find her. An officer stood at the exit that led to the butler's pantry and smaller kitchen. He allowed me through once he'd gotten the okay from Matt Lewis. Anna wasn't there. I poked my head into her office, but that too was empty.

David aka Dorian found me on my way back to the set. I asked him about Anna, and he said she was exhausted. He'd sent her to her room to rest, promising to take over her duties. He'd informed the police about this.

"Should I call you David or Dorian?" I asked.

"David will be fine," he said with a smile. "I'm glad that's a pretense I don't have to keep up any longer."

Before either of us could say more, we heard loud sounds like crashing chairs. Chaos seemed to be breaking out on the set.

Chapter Twenty-nine

The commotion sounded like a free-for-all. I ran back on set to see what was happening. It appeared to be a simple brawl between two men with chairs upended. Bystanders were gathered in a semicircle around the men, leaving enough room to make sure they weren't hit accidentally by a flying fist.

David came up beside me and did a quick inventory. "It looks as if they haven't destroyed any of the equipment. That's a relief."

Chris, Mason, and Matt Lewis ran towards the center of the action.

The brawl was between Peter Young and George Kirkwood. Peter, tall and lanky. George, small, wiry. It wasn't clear who had the upper hand. George was punching to Peter's gut, and Peter aimed for George's face and chin. Both of them fought as if they were used to street brawls. It almost looked staged.

Mason was taking his own sweet time breaking it up, I noticed.

When Mason and Matt each grabbed one of the men, I looked around the room and found Lurleen standing near a door. The officer there had left his position to keep people back from the fight. I watched her disappear into the hallway, but I was too far away to stop her.

Mason told everyone to sit down in the nearest available chair. The cameras had stopped rolling—all but the overhead camera Danny was monitoring. I'd heard Mason tell him before the shoot to stay put unless he signaled for his help.

Mason had his hand on George Kirkwood's shoulder; Matt had Young's arm behind his back. They led both men to the prep area at the back of the set.

Mason called me over to look at the two men. I told him Lurleen had left the room. It was clear he was angry. He grabbed a young officer and told him to find her. That let me focus on the damage done.

George seemed to have gotten the worst of it. I looked at a cut below his eye and checked for an orbital fracture.

"I'm fine," George said, pushing my hand away. "He had thirty years on me, otherwise he'd be the one you'd have to patch up."

"I think you'll be fine, Mr. Kirkwood. I just want to clean up that cut and put a bandage on it."

David brought me the first aid kit, and George didn't fuss as I used disinfectant and put on a bandage.

As it turned out, he'd done more damage to Peter than he knew. Peter was hugging his side. I poked on his ribs, and he squawked. "You could have some broken ribs. At least they're badly bruised. It's likely there isn't much to be done for them, but you should get an X-ray."

"I'm not getting an X-ray."

"You're declining medical treatment?" Mason said.

"Yes," Peter said and then grimaced in pain.

"Fine. I'll interview both of you right here."

Chris and one of the officers made sure everyone else stayed away.

I joined Pepper and Rose who were huddled together. "What happened?" I asked.

Rose started to speak, but Pepper shut her up. "We don't know, and if we *did* know, we wouldn't be talking to you about it. You've caused nothing but trouble. You're dying to lay a murder charge on one of us. We'll speak to the real detectives and police on the case. You need to butt out before you get hurt."

Pepper grabbed Rose's hand and led her to chairs near the front of the set.

I went back to my station waiting for Lurleen to reappear. She didn't. The young officer didn't either. I hoped that meant he'd found her and was keeping her safe.

Mason came from the back of the room and signaled Chris that the taping could proceed. Chris told everyone that the minor argument was now settled.

Mason nodded at me and mouthed the words, "Don't worry."

I hoped that meant he'd found Lurleen, but I wasn't close enough to ask.

As the cameras started rolling, I searched once more for her and then turned my attention to the task at hand. My gingerbread and cookies were now cool enough to use. Granny Flumm already had her ice cream in the ice cream maker. This time no harm was done by the delay, but I knew each of us was wondering what might happen next.

Chris announced we had thirty minutes to finish our show-stopper desserts. Building my gingerbread house took some care and some very strong frosting. The pecan sandies, cut in half, served as tile for the roof made of graham crackers, and the oatmeal surprise bars formed bricks along the lower surface of the house as well as a walkway to the front door. I covered the graham-cracker door with red twisted licorice sticks.

The little house wasn't elegant, but I hoped it had a certain charm, and I knew it would be delicious. I wanted it to look like grandma's house, and not like the witch's hut from Hansel and Gretel. Maybe it would come across as primitive art—delightful if unrefined. I had one more element to add, the homemade lemon ice cream chilling in the freezer. In the last minute I pulled it out and plopped some on the roof and around the house as if there had been a sudden snow fall. It would rapidly melt, but with luck that would make it look all the more natural.

We all finished up seconds before Chris asked us to step away from the table. I suspect we were happy simply to have made it through with ourselves and our desserts intact. Carefully, we placed our presentations on the tasting table. Both mine and Granny's were ensconced in an ice dome that kept our ice cream cold.

Savannah and Olivier entered the room on a signal from Chris and sat at the table. In front of them were each of our creations.

No one was allowed to leave the room this time, so we were instructed to show no emotion as Savannah and Olivier evaluated our efforts. They took their time tasting and conferring.

Savannah began by examining and then cutting two pieces from a five-layer cake decorated with elegant crystallized pieces of fruit tossed like confetti over the cake frosting. Each layer had a different fruit puree filling. This was Rose's creation.

"It's busy," Olivier said, "and I thought it might have too many competing flavors, but in fact it does not. It works. *Magnifique!*"

"It looks and tastes like a New Year's Eve celebration. Excellent," Savannah said.

Olivier and Savannah made a perfect team. Olivier had her same ability to charm an audience.

Granny Flumm's show stopper was next. It was a great pyramid of white ice cream covering a chocolate trunk with green fondant for branches. On the elegant Christmas tree were luminous sugar crystal balls and a fondant angel as the tree topper. It was very impressive and cleverly maintained under its chilled dome. As Olivier and Savannah tried to figure out how to taste it, I heard Mason behind me.

He was still interviewing George in a spot not far from my station. I think Mason was determined to stay close to the action.

He tried to keep his voice down.

"George, you still haven't told me what started this."

"It was a crack Young made about my wife. No one makes a crack about my wife."

I glanced back at them. George Kirkwood looked ready to continue the fight.

"What crack?" Mason asked.

"He said he couldn't imagine any man wanting to watch my wife undress in a movie."

"You knew what he was referring to?" Mason asked.

"You mean that Rose was a porn star before she met me? Yeah, I knew. We never discussed it. That was history. We all done things in our past we're not proud of."

"You too?" Mason asked.

"Sure."

"Like what?"

"Like none-of-your-business stuff."

"Everything's my business," Mason said.

"Like maybe I beat a few people up for someone when they wouldn't pay their bills on time."

"Did you ever threaten Quinn Nelson?"

"How could you know about that?"

Mason didn't respond.

"Yeah, maybe I did. Maybe he offered me a better deal and I didn't have to beat him up. Maybe he promised to give me the money for my pig farm if I'd help get his debtors off him."

"But, you've had the farm for years," Mason said.

"And Quinn's had money problems longer than that. Always trying to make like he was wealthy, but he never was. You know how folks live from paycheck to paycheck? He lived from one bad deal to the next."

"How'd you help him out?"

George was quiet.

"We'll find out whatever it is you think you can hide. It'll be better to hear it from you," Mason said.

"I'm not admitting anything," he said, "but maybe I helped him get rid of some jewelry— from Savannah's family jewels. Stuff she never wore but kept in the safe deposit box at the bank. Enough to pay off his creditors. I never stole anything. Quinn gave it to me, and I found a buyer."

"You fenced Savannah's missing necklace from the party?" Mason said.

"My work for Quinn ended years ago."

"Why was your wife included in the contest?" Mason asked.

"I heard about it, and there was an e-mail address where you could apply online. Rose started talking about how much fun she'd have on a show like that and how it would take place near her home town. She's the best cook in Albany, Georgia, so I called Quinn—figured he owed me a favor and might like me to keep my mouth shut. He talked to Savannah and she agreed to include her. I had no idea Rosie would be putting her life at risk."

"Rose didn't know what work you'd done for Quinn?"

"No. Rose thought I'd never forgive her for what she did in her twenties, but I knew she'd never forgive me for what *I'd* done."

"If someone threatened to tell her about your work with Quinn, that might be a motive for murder," Mason said. He ignored George's sputtering protest and sent him to sit in the audience. On a signal from Mason, an officer brought over Peter.

"You were Quinn's bodyguard and now you serve the same function for Savannah. What else do you do for her?"

"What are you talking about?"

"A bodyguard's salary wouldn't let you live the way you do," Mason said.

"I get paid well for what I do."

"And what is that exactly?"

"I do whatever people want me to do, within the law, of course." Peter said. "I'm done talking to you without my lawyer. You want to arrest me for some stupid fight, go ahead." At that moment, Peter clutched his side. "Look," he said, "can I lie down somewhere? My wife will look after me. My side's killing me."

Mason motioned to a police officer to escort Peter and Pepper outside. "Don't go far and don't let them out of your sight."

That was the end of the conversation. I turned my attention back to Olivier and Savannah who were continuing their critiques.

"That tree was an elegant treat," Savannah said. "It looks as if we've covered two of our three upcoming holidays—Christmas and New Year's. Now, we turn to Thanksgiving."

I have to admit I blushed slightly at the sight of my little cottage next to the two polished works of edible art.

Olivier smiled and turned the house around on its rotating plate. "Charming," he said.

"Olivier doesn't celebrate Thanksgiving, of course," Savannah said, "but he knows about the tradition. I would say this is grandmother's house complete with surrounding woods."

The trees were Lucie's idea. She thought up a forest of pretzel sticks that looked stark in the winter outside the cabin. Jason came up with pumpkin-shaped candy corn, most of which went in his mouth when I wasn't looking. I managed to save enough for a small pumpkin patch.

"It's lovely," Savannah said, as she moved the plate around to take a complete look.

I breathed a sigh of relief. It certainly wasn't going to win the grand prize, but if it didn't look out of place with the other two entries, I was happy. Savannah and Olivier nibbled on a cookie and a piece of gingerbread.

"This tastes even better than it looks," Savannah said. "What's novel about this little house is that it is composed of delicious layered gingerbread cake with lemon curd between layers. With the lemon ice cream, it's perfect. This works."

Savannah and Olivier put their heads together, and for thirty seconds they whispered.

I looked around the room. Mason stood a few feet behind me. Buddy Lewis and his nephew Matt stood near the front entrance to the kitchen and stage set. Three uniformed officers had their backs to the wall along the side of the set, and one more officer was stationed at the back door. The roving camera continued to swing on its overhead beam around the room.

George Kirkwood sat near Mason, looking straight ahead and saying nothing. I watched as an officer escorted Peter and Pepper Young out the door. Izzy and Frank sat in the front row next to James Bradshaw. I searched the audience and still couldn't find Lurleen.

Chris called Granny Flumm, Rose, and me to the tasting table. It appeared that Savannah was about to announce the winner.

"This has been an outstanding finale," she gushed. "The gingerbread house was a delight to look at and taste. It took me back to my childhood, Southern but with a new twist. The five-layered cake was perfection, but it was the mint ice cream over the delectable chocolate Christmas tree that stole the show. A perfect ending to a lovely holiday meal."

"Enough to rival the traditional *Bûche de Noël*," Olivier added.

Savannah opened the card with the names of the contestants and what we had prepared. "The winner is Gertrude or 'Granny' as she prefers to be called. Congratulations!"

Before Granny Flumm could respond, we heard a loud bang—like a single firework exploding. Was it a gunshot? Some people scrambled to find an exit. Others dropped to the floor and covered their heads. Mason stood, gun out of his holster, searching the room for a shooter or the victim.

Chapter Thirty

"Stay down," Mason yelled when a few people started to stand or crawl. "Keep still and quiet. If you're hurt, shout out."

He, Buddy, and Matt canvassed the room for a victim or perpetrator. I followed behind. Mason motioned me to stay down.

"I'm a doctor," I reminded him.

"And I want you to remain alive. Do you have any idea where the shot came from?" This was a question for Buddy and Matt Lewis.

"No," they both said.

"But it wasn't loud enough to be from inside the room," Buddy said. "There's no smell of gunpowder."

Danny joined Mason and Buddy, gun in hand. "I was watching the monitor. I heard the gunshot, but I didn't see anything. I think the shot came from somewhere outside the set."

That made me panic. "Where is Lurleen? I have to find her."

"You're not going anywhere. You go, Danny. We'll make sure these people stay put. Call me if you need backup."

"Right," Danny said, heading out the main entrance to the hall.

I had to know if Lurleen was all right. Mason had his hands full at the front of the set. I managed to slip through the back exit while his back was turned, and the officer near me was struggling to keep two crew members in their seats.

I caught up with Danny in the central hall and motioned him to follow me. "I think I know where Lurleen is."

I bolted down the hallway that led to the billiard room. Danny ran beside me, gun out.

"That's far enough," someone yelled. "I'll take that."

Just inside the door to the billiard room stood Peter Young with a Glock 19 pointed in our direction. I recognized it because it was the same gun Mason carried.

When Danny hesitated to give up his revolver, Peter nodded towards me. "You want to see her hurt?"

Danny handed over his gun. "How did you get away from the officer?" he asked.

"Where is Lurleen?" I yelled.

"One question at a time."

This voice came from the man standing behind Peter. It was David Hayes. "Where are your manners? Let these people in," he said.

"I thought it must be you," I said to David. "What have you done with Lurleen?"

Peter shoved the two of us into the billiard room. Lurleen sat on the window seat, hands tied behind her back, a gag in her mouth. The officer who'd been sent to find her was seated beside her, also gagged and tied. On the floor, another officer lay unconscious. It must have been the policeman sent to guard Peter and Pepper when they left the set.

Lurleen rolled her eyes to the left, to the shadows at the back of the room. There I saw Pepper Young, face contorted.

"How could you have done this to me, Peter?" she screamed. "Why did you get me involved in this?"

"Shut up," Peter yelled back, "and come here." He handed her Danny's gun. "Do what I tell you, and we'll get out of this all right."

I ran toward the unconscious man as Peter made a grab for me.

"Let her go," David said.

I checked the officer's pulse—it was strong and steady.

"Now, move away from him," David said. "He'll wake up with a headache, nothing more."

David stood next to the open gun cabinet, a rifle in his hands.

"Where is Anna?" I asked.

"She's not involved with this."

"This isn't a family affair?" I asked.

"What are you talking about?" David said. "Anna knows nothing about this. She's too trusting for her own good. I had to take matters into my own hands when I saw what Savannah was doing to her."

David didn't look well. I'd noted that in the past, but I'd never had a chance to see him in the light. His face was ashen and his body wasted.

"You're ill," I said. "You told me you were coughing from allergies. But, Lurleen saw you with an inhaler and you told her it was childhood asthma. You looked worse every time I saw you, wearing a coat that no longer fit. You're wasting away from cancer, aren't you, David?"

"Don't play doctor with me. It's too late for that."

I sat beside Lurleen. "May I take the gag out of her mouth? She's having trouble breathing." At that moment, Lurleen put on a dramatic display of gasping for air.

"You can take the gag out," David said, "but if you make one sound, Lurleen—one sound—it goes back in. Understood?"

Lurleen nodded her head and tried to look obedient.

I untied the gag. "And her hands?" I asked.

"Her hands stay just the way they are," David said. He nodded at Peter. Peter put down his gun, gathered more rope and trussed me up like a turkey. Danny was next. Finally, four of us were seated on the window seat, hands secured behind us.

"None of you will get hurt," David said, "if you follow directions. It's not you I'm after. If Lurleen hadn't interfered, Savannah and Olivier would be dying right now."

"Why Olivier?" I asked. "He's as much an innocent as Anna."

"He would inherit all of this. I couldn't allow that," David said.

"You would have shot them both and expected to get away with it?" I asked incredulous.

"Not shot them. They would have been poisoned in a congratulatory curaçao cocktail—a drink with a little antifreeze in it to give it that lovely blue color and sweet taste. I made it with orange juice, Savannah's favorite beverage. Easy enough to do and hard to trace. Only those two would have received the special cocktail. I'm not a cold-blooded murderer. I only kill when necessary."

"Anna would be the obvious suspect," I said.

"Of course—that's why I sent a death threat to her. That's also why I gave her a sedative this morning in her juice—so she couldn't be accused of poisoning anyone. It's Gertrude Flumm who was meant to take the blame. Copies of the threatening notes are already on her computer."

"What about the gunshot?" I asked.

"A big mistake. Your clever friend here reached for the rifle and it went off. Pure luck none of us was hurt."

"Why are you doing this?" I asked. "Savannah was going to give Anna a culinary school. Is this about Savannah breaking off an affair with you?"

"You're as naive as Anna. Savannah was never going to build a culinary school for Anna. She made promises to Anna about a spin-off show of her own. She was never going to do any of it, and Anna kept making excuses for her." David stopped to catch his breath. "I know what it's like to give up your dreams."

It was a long speech, and David sat down hard on a bar stool to regain his strength.

Peter kept his eyes and his gun aimed at Danny. He told Pepper to keep Danny's gun aimed at me and Lurleen. Pepper looked as if she'd never held a gun before.

If I could keep David talking, maybe help would get to us in time.

"You orchestrated both murders?" I said.

"I had to act. I'm a dying man. When I heard Savannah talking about her son Olivier, I had no choice. She would try to rebuild her empire with her son, not Anna. I thought if Quinn was gone, and Savannah and I had a relationship, we could make things work for Anna. I could show her what a team they could be, and then I discovered she had a son and heir apparent."

David started wheezing, and it took several seconds before he could continue.

"Bradshaw got that poor dumb reporter involved. I couldn't have him sniffing around. I was going to kick him out, but when I saw him there asleep, his gun beside him, there was a simpler solution. Peter and I got him off the property. I didn't know Savannah's dog would almost give us away."

Peter shouted at David. "We don't have time for this. They'll be looking for these guys, and you know they heard the shot. Stand up," he said to Lurleen, me, and Danny. "Over here."

Peter swept back the rug and opened the trap door. There lay the famous tunnel leading to the river, and I could see steep steps leading downward.

"The boat's waiting for us," Peter said. "Is everything on board?"

"Yes," David said. "Don't harm these people unless you have to. Leave them in the tunnel."

David nudged Danny with the rifle in his hand. "You first, after Peter."

He handed Peter a flashlight.

Peter edged down the stairs. It was obvious he was in pain from his fight with George, and I could see the stairs were more like a stone ladder than steps. "I'm down," he called. "Got the gun and flashlight on Devalle."

Danny started down the steps.

"You're next, Dr. Brown."

I stood, and Lurleen and I shared a look of pure understanding. I stumbled forward into Pepper. We both went down. It was a gamble, but not a big one. Pepper hadn't taken the safety off the gun. She dropped it, and I shoved it out of the way with my foot.

When David tried to intervene, Lurleen jumped up and kicked him in the groin. As he writhed in pain, she kicked him again and he fell, curled up in a fetal position.

She moved in my direction, but I didn't need her help. I lay on top of Pepper. She was slight from years of dieting, and my body, more pillow-like than svelte, covered most of hers. I could hear her struggling to breathe.

What happened next was a circus.

Buddy Lewis kicked in the door of the billiard room. "Didn't know I still had it in me," he said as he burst through the broken wood. Danny clumped up the stairs, dragging a moaning Peter Young with him.

Mason ran in behind the chief with Matt Lewis at his side. A cadre of police officers followed, guns drawn. Matt went to the side of the unconscious officer. "He's alive," he shouted back to Mason.

"This all of them?" Mason asked.

"Isn't this enough?" Lurleen asked. "How many did you want us to tackle?"

"Where is Anna?" Mason asked.

"Anna isn't involved," I said. "This is all David's doing with help from the Youngs."

"Nice work," Mason said to the three of us as he untied Lurleen's hands, mine, and the officer's.

"David had plans to poison Savannah and Olivier," I said. "We need to make sure they're safe."

"I'll find them," Buddy said.

Mason didn't try to stop him. "How'd you get free?" he asked Danny.

"Old party trick," Danny said. "I'll show you sometime."

Anna opened the door from the passageway and elevator that led to Savannah's office.

"What are you doing here?" I asked. "David said you were sedated and asleep upstairs."

Anna didn't respond to me, and for a moment I wondered if I had the story wrong.

She entered the room with an officer behind her. "I've been hunting for you everywhere, David," she said.

David raised his head, and Anna rushed to his side.

"Oh my god, David, what's going on?"

"I tried to do what should have been done years ago," he said.

Matt Lewis spoke, sounding far older than his twenty-something years. "I'm sorry, Anna, but I'm about to arrest your brother and his accomplices on two counts of murder."

"No," Anna said. "You're joking. David is the gentlest man I know."

"I'm sorry, Anna," her brother said. "I wanted to give you everything you deserved, but I've made a mess of it."

"You're sick. You're delirious. You don't know what you're saying." She stroked his face and tried to get him to look at her. "I begged you not to stop treatment, and you promised you wouldn't. I told you to stay away from Peter, that I didn't trust him."

She looked at Pepper. "You're involved as well?"

Pepper shook her head vehemently. "No! No! Peter dragged me into this."

"The medicine wasn't helping me, Anna," David said. "I wasn't going to get better. I promised I'd always take care of you, and I had to keep that promise. I made Savannah provide money for a culinary institute in her will. Then all I had to do was make sure she died."

"You were taking doxorubicin?" I said.

David nodded. "At a local cancer clinic."

"How did you get it out of there?" I asked. "That's expensive medicine. It's carefully monitored."

"It wasn't that difficult." David gave a dry laugh that ended in a cough. "I brought Peter on board as my personal nurse. As a medic he had most of the qualifications he needed, and those he didn't have he manufactured. The clinic was overcrowded, so they used him on a temporary basis. He pretended to give me the doxorubicin and used a red liquid substitute. No one questioned him, and the inventory never showed a deficit. Then he took the drug and administered it to Quinn."

"Why that drug?" I asked. "There are far easier ways to kill a man."

"I wanted him to suffer," David said, "as my Anna had suffered, as I had suffered. And it all worked like clockwork. Why couldn't you have left things alone? Let the bad people die and the good ones live?"

Anna started to cry as David finished speaking. "Our parents died in a car crash when David was twenty and I was just a kid," she said. "David gave up his dreams of becoming a famous actor and dropped out of school to take care of me. He had so much talent, it was crushing for him, I know."

"I had to take care of you," David said. "Then, when I saw how Savannah was keeping you down, I couldn't bear to let your dreams be destroyed."

"I've never needed to be famous," Anna said. "That was your dream, not mine. All I ever wanted was you at my side."

"You can see," David said to the rest of us, "I made her too soft. She didn't know how to fight for herself."

Anna was sobbing.

"You never let her grow up," Lurleen said. "You never taught her how to make her own decisions. You assumed she wanted what you did, and that's the tragedy."

Savannah walked into the room, climbing over the broken door. The chief was beside her.

"I sent Olivier to my suite. He doesn't need to see this. Buddy told me what happened."

She went to Anna and hugged her. Then she turned to David. "I think I understand why you did this. I might have done the same for Olivier."

She looked at and spoke only to David.

"You were right about me, David. I could see what a natural Anna was on screen and I knew what a wonderful chef she was. I needed her, but I could never let her replace me."

We were silent.

David took Anna's hand. "I'm sorry. My plan was to keep you out of all of this—to sedate you just enough, so you couldn't be blamed for any of what happened next."

"I didn't drink the juice you gave me," Anna said. "Something about the way you said goodbye made me worry about you."

"You said you didn't harm innocent people," I said, "but you were willing to set Granny Flumm up for murder. What had she ever done to you or Anna?"

"I can answer that," Savannah said. "Granny Flumm was the person who created my entire empire. I paid her for recipes, and she agreed to remain anonymous. I said they were my grandmother's, and for a while that worked. Then as my empire grew, Flumm wanted more money to keep her mouth shut. Finally, she wanted a spot on my show with the chance to have one of her own."

"Once again my Anna would be pushed aside," David said, "so someone else could be famous."

"Where do the Youngs come in?" Mason asked.

David took a moment to catch his breath. "You can tell by the look of them Peter will do anything for money," he said. "He didn't shoot Nick Davis, but he was happy enough to help me get rid of the body."

"What made you come to the billiard room, Lurleen?" I asked.

"It's where all the action seemed to be. And you, Ditie? How did you know where to find me?"

"I'd seen you here earlier. Things started to fall in place. If David had cancer, as I suspected, the treatment might have included doxorubicin. He'd be the one to have access to that drug. David is a very good actor.

He always had the ability to be whatever people wanted him to be. When I learned he was Anna's brother and not her lover, I couldn't imagine he would choose Savannah's welfare over Anna's.

"What I didn't know for sure was whether or not Anna was involved. I remembered your statement about how I liked to put people in boxes—all good or all bad. I didn't know if I could trust my instincts about her after all her lies. When I couldn't find her in either kitchen, I worried. I remembered the billiard room was the place people could get into and out of with no one knowing."

I turned to Anna. "I'm sorry I suspected you, and I hope you can forgive me."

"There's nothing to forgive. I lied to you to protect David. You had every reason to doubt me. I told you I suspected Dorian Gray wrote that letter because that's what David wanted me to say. I could see he was doing things that didn't make sense, but I didn't want to know what was really going on."

"Your turn, Lurleen," Mason said. "Let's hear what happened this morning."

Lurleen sat down on the window seat as if to savor every moment of the story she had to tell. "I actually got here before anyone else. I just assumed if there was mischief to be done or a great escape to be made, this would be the place. I hid in the secret doorway before David came. He entered with a police officer beside him. Apparently, you sent someone to look for me."

Mason nodded.

"David explained I didn't seem to be there, and the officer was about to leave when the Youngs came in. Peter was dragging a poor police officer with him. Peter struck him once on the head and he was out.

"David didn't seem too happy about that, but he grabbed a rifle from the gun rack at the back of the room and ordered the other officer to sit on the window seat. He had Peter gag him and tie him up.

"David said the drinks were ready for Savannah and Olivier. 'You two will be long gone before they die,' he told Peter. Pepper looked as if she was about to faint, and Peter put a hand on her arm. He ordered her to get herself together.

"David said he'd testify that Gertrude Flumm insisted on making the drinks, and that Savannah not only stole her recipes but then refused to let her be a star with her own show. He thought they might be able to pin Quinn's death on Flumm as well since she'd had a bout with cancer and was treated with doxorubicin."

Lurleen paused for dramatic effect, I think, and then sighed. "I must have moved in the passageway. These long legs in such cramped quarters. Anyway, David noticed the door was cracked open. He ordered me out and pointed the rifle in my direction. I lunged at him. That's when the gun went off."

"You could have been killed, Lurleen," Danny said, hugging her tight.

"Could have been but wasn't." She smiled brightly. "I knocked the gun away, just like my old boyfriend Jake taught me to do if I was ever in a close-range gun fight."

"Close-range gun fight?" I asked.

"Jake was a stunt man," Lurleen said.

"He doesn't sound French," I said.

"He was," Lurleen smiled sweetly. "He changed his name from Jacques to Jake, so he'd make it in Hollywood."

I smiled. I would never catch Lurleen in a lie.

Danny did not look happy. "When was Jake?" he asked.

Lurleen counted on her fingers. "I think he was after Pierre and before Michel. He was always doing things to impress me, jumping out of windows, leaping over cars—I got tired of it. It's you, sweetheart, that I want to be with. You offer me all the excitement I need."

Chapter Thirty-one

It took several hours to sort through the details of what had happened.

Over his protests, David was taken to the local hospital to be checked out. Anna and a police officer went with him. Buddy and Matt Lewis escorted the Youngs to the local jail to await arraignment.

I couldn't understand the role of Peter and Pepper. Mason explained that to me.

"When David suggested activities that would make Peter a wealthier man, he was all in. Pepper got dragged along. All she wanted was social standing in Atlanta and a nice lifestyle. By the time she knew what was happening it was too late to back out.

"Peter planned to escape with enough money and jewels to take them to a new life and new identities somewhere in South America. You can bet Pepper wasn't happy about that. She's ready to provide all the information she has about Peter if it means she can stay out of jail and in the US."

"And what about David?" I asked.

"David always planned to stay behind and make sure Anna was not suspected of wrongdoing." Mason sat back on the sofa in the parlor. "I never realized this before, but there's a lot to be said for being in a place in which I have no jurisdiction."

"You still have to settle up the case in Atlanta," I said.

"I've called my captain, and it can keep until Buddy and Matt finish up their paperwork here. I'll help with some of the details."

"You seem to have a lot of faith in them now," I said.

"I do. My first wife's brother is a lot like Buddy, happy to get up to no good but fundamentally honest and smart. That's how I see Buddy. And his nephew never once asked for special favors for either one of them."

"Your first wife?" I asked.

"That's right. You'll be my second wife someday, and then I'll stop counting." Mason leaned over and gave me a tender kiss.

Most of the other participants were long gone. Savannah had seen them off and assured them they'd feel better once they viewed the show when it aired.

Granny Flumm remained behind. She was naturally appalled by what David had planned to do. I was in the room when Mason and Savannah spoke with her.

"I just can't believe it," she said. "Even if they couldn't make the murder charge stick, I could never stay in Beaufort."

"And I, of course, could never leave," Savannah said, "being dead and all."

Granny patted Savannah on her knee. "Yes, I suppose it would have been bad for you too."

As soon as we were done with Granny Flumm, I called home. The kids were in school, but Tommy was working from the house and happy to hear from me.

"Wrapped up another one, did you?" he said.

"More like Lurleen, Mason, Danny, and I did, along with half a dozen local police."

"You're going to be as famous as I am," Tommy said.

"Fame is not all it's cracked up to be," I said. "Even *you* know that."

"I know, I know. Josh tells me that every day. I concede. Just don't quote me that Emily Dickinson poem."

"You mean the one that goes, 'Fame is a fickle food upon a shifting plate—' "

"Yeah, that one. Have mercy."

"Okay, I'll stop." Actually, I had to stop because I couldn't remember the other lines. "It would do you good to memorize that poem, Tommy."

Tommy laughed and then suggested that he and Josh could drive up with the kids for the weekend. Eddie had volunteered to look after Hermione and Majestic.

"Great. I'll find a place for us to stay in Beaufort," I said.

Lurleen overheard me, and after I hung up, she seemed in a rush to speak to me.

"Beaufort?" she said. "You want to stay in Beaufort?"

"I've heard it's a lovely town, and we haven't seen anything of it. Won't it be fun to enjoy a little time with the kids in a brand new environment?"

"I don't know. I might have to get back to Atlanta. I have things to do."

"What things, Lurleen?" I asked. "From the first moment you found out the contest would take place near Beaufort, you've acted like you were scared to death of something. I've never seen you frightened like that, except when you thought a friend was in danger."

Lurleen sighed. "Ditie, I just don't think I can face it."

Before she could say more, Savannah joined us in the parlor.

Savannah looked upset. "I feel so bad about Anna—what she must be going through. Her brother is dying, and she has to face what he did. I always felt Dorian—David—was on my side, but it was all pretense. It's horrible what he did, but he did it to protect Anna, to get her what she deserved. And so much of what he suspected about me was true."

" 'Fame, men eat of it and die.' " I remembered the last line of Dickinson's poem and said it without thinking.

"I know that poem," Savannah said, "and I know what you mean, but I'm a changed woman. I'll give Anna everything she wants."

"So, she'll come before Olivier," Lurleen said.

"No, of course not. Olivier is my son, and we'll make a wonderful team."

"She'll get a show before Granny Flumm?" Lurleen pushed again.

"You know as well as I do, Granny Flumm is a force to be reckoned with. I can see us together—the old and the young, the sweet and the . . . not so sweet."

Savannah grew quiet. "I hear what you're saying, Lurleen. I will get Anna her culinary institute. At least I'll do that."

"And for Anna that will probably be enough," I said.

I did secretly wonder, however, if Anna would continue to fly under the radar. Wouldn't someone else recognize her talent and her beauty? Maybe she'd end up competing with Savannah for best Southern television chef.

"I want you all to come to my chateau in southern France," Savannah said, "the prize I offered. I'll include everyone in the contest. It will be a grand celebration."

"You have the money for that?" I asked.

"I will after this show airs," Savannah said. "I'll be the chef who survived against all odds. Peter and Pepper's trial will keep my name on the front pages for months. I hope David won't have to stand trial. I think that would break Anna's heart.

"But, for me, the future looks bright. Think of the endorsements. They'll want to make a miniseries about me. I think Reese Witherspoon should play me. What do you think, Lurleen?"

Lurleen didn't say a word.

Fame, I thought. The allure hadn't lessened for Savannah.

Savannah left us with a wave of her hand. "Think on the trip. Right now, I have to spend time in the kitchen with Granny Flumm. She's going to teach me how to cook—how to actually cook! I brought her on the show to keep her quiet, but I've looked at the outtakes. The camera loves her. We could be a highly successful duo, and I think we can work something out— a grandmother in the kitchen, perhaps."

Lurleen and I stood.

"We'll be packing up," I said.

"Please don't rush off. I owe you my life. Stay for lunch at least. Granny will prepare it."

I didn't want to rush off anywhere. "We'll happily stay for lunch. My brother is coming with my children for the weekend. Do you know a good bed and breakfast in Beaufort?"

"No need," Savannah said. "You'll stay here. Your children will love it here with all our secret rooms."

"Maybe too much," I said, thinking of the places Jason could hide.

"We'll look out for them. Olivier may do a cooking show for kids. Perhaps your children will enjoy testing some of his recipes over the weekend. Granny Flumm might want to participate as well."

"Lucie will love it," I said. "Jason will prefer running around the yard and exploring the secret passageways."

Granny Flumm made us a wonderful lunch of country-fried steak with peach cobbler for dessert.

Lurleen and I spent the afternoon walking through the gardens.

Danny, Mason, Lurleen, and I had a light supper on the back porch upstairs—something Savannah insisted on and Olivier prepared.

I still had a few questions.

Who sent the video of Izzy and released it to the press? Did Anna honestly not know what her brother was up to? Was Frank as innocent as he proclaimed? Who was fencing the latest stolen items? And finally, what about the ghost Savannah claimed roamed the house and disappeared into a wall?

"Phew," Danny said. "Let's see if I can get your questions straight. Pepper sent out the video from her cellphone to a friend in Atlanta before we confiscated all the phones. She hoped it would go viral and she'd become a prized member of Atlanta society—full of juicy gossip about the famous Savannah Evans. Instead her friend sent it to a TV reporter."

"As to what Anna knew," Lurleen said, "you remember how you felt about Tommy and the Sandler's case."

"I do remember. It was horrible to doubt him. Horrible."

"That's how Anna explained it to me," Lurleen said. "She saw things that didn't seem right, but she couldn't bear to think her brother might be involved."

"As far as we can tell," Mason said," Frank is a straight shooter. Quinn had a separate set of books for his corrupt activities. The latest stolen items were fenced by Peter, who took a big commission. He's a jack-of-all trades. Quinn gave him the necklace at the party and forgot to close the safe. He was a very sick man at that point. Peter's greatest coup was the centerpiece, the epergne, and getting someone to make an exact copy of it."

"Now, to the ghost issue," Danny said. "It turns out that wall hid another secret door that led back to Savannah's office. She showed me the trigger to open it, next to a picture of some long-dead relative. You remember, Ditie, she was fully dressed when we saw her and claimed she'd gone nowhere? She'd actually been to see David. He begged her to put something in writing to ensure Anna got money for a culinary institute should anything happen to Savannah. Savannah saw how agitated and unwell David was, so she had Frank Moran add a codicil to her will the next day. She signed her own death warrant at that point. Luckily, things didn't work out as planned."

"That all makes sense," I said. "I'm satisfied, except..." Something wasn't quite right.

"Wait. When we saw Savannah she was dressed in a maroon skirt and sweater, wasn't she? You told me, Danny, that the person you saw was dressed in a flowing white gown."

"I did." Danny gave me a crooked grin. "Savannah's ghost?"

"Maybe," I said, "but I'm too tired to worry about it."

I spent the night in Mason's room. He had a lot of work to do and didn't join me until after midnight. I didn't mind his waking me up. It had been a long time since we'd had some privacy, and we enjoyed every minute of it.

Breakfast was at nine, and I wasn't about to miss that. Savannah had a hen house on the property and promised us fresh eggs for breakfast. Olivier made an exquisite French omelette, served with croissants right out of the oven. I was in heaven.

Mason told me after breakfast that Savannah had dropped all charges against Buddy. She didn't feel she could have Olivier's father on trial for what was essentially mischief.

Buddy found me alone later that morning and told me he'd confessed to his wife the night before. She accepted it as a youthful indiscretion. There wouldn't be a divorce, and as long as Olivier was making no financial demands on the chief, his wife felt she could live with that. She was young

once, she'd told Buddy. That apparently made Buddy a little nervous, but
he was in no position to explore that further.

I talked to Lurleen over lunch. "What do you think of Savannah's offer?
We could all travel to France together."

Lurleen shook her head. "I would love to go to France. I mean really
go to France, not just in my head, but we don't need Savannah to take us.
I have a house in Provence."

When I gave her a quizzical look, she smiled. "A lot of what I've told
you is true, Ditie. My aunt really did leave me a house near Beaufort and
another in France. I made a vow that before I could go to either house I'd
have to settle up with my past."

"And?" I asked.

"I think I'm ready to do that."

Tommy called in the mid-afternoon to say he, Josh, and the kids would
get an early start Saturday morning.

I found Lurleen in her room alone. "We're free for the rest of the day,"
I said. "The kids are coming tomorrow morning. They have a week off
school, so we don't have to hurry back. I've called Vic at the clinic to let her
know about the situation. She told me to take the whole week if I wanted it."

"You have a great boss," Lurleen said. "If I'd tried that at Sandler's I
would have been out on my ear."

"Do you miss working?"

"Ditie, I'm still working."

"I didn't mean to insult you. I couldn't manage my life without you."

"And I love taking care of the kids, but I do other things while they're
in school."

Now, I felt foolish. I assumed Lurleen spent her days exercising, watching
morning TV and eating bon bons. "You've never told me how you spent
your days, and when I've asked, you've brushed aside the question."

"Do you really want to know what I do when I'm not with you or the
kids during the day?"

I nodded.

"Mondays, I spend two hours as a volunteer at a methadone clinic. On
Tuesdays, I work in an agency that provides daycare for children in foster
care. Wednesdays, I do art at a center for children and adults with disabilities,
and on Thursdays, I take Dorothy out to the movies or maybe help her
with homework. That's why I don't stay for dinner most Thursday nights."

"Dorothy?"

"I'm in the Big Brother, Big Sisters program. And on Fridays, I eat bon bons and watch daytime TV." Lurleen looked at me and laughed. "You can close your mouth now."

"I had no idea. Do you want to drive to Beaufort today?"

Lurleen looked at me. "I think I need to go," she said, "and if you'll go with me, I think I can."

I took her hand. "I'll never leave your side."

"It won't be pretty, Ditie, what I have to tell you, what I have to show you."

"I know, Lurleen. I've always known that."

We didn't say much to Mason and Danny beyond the fact we were going to have a girls' afternoon. The chief and Danny had already made plans to go fishing. Mason and Matt Lewis were finishing up paperwork.

We drove to Beaufort in Danny's Honda. Lurleen stared out the window.

"It's the way I remember it," she said when we entered the town.

She told me to drive down a side street and stop beside an ice cream store. "It's still here," she said.

"Do you want to go in?" I asked.

"No. That store and the library are my two happy memories of Beaufort. When my mother was in a good mood, she'd buy me an ice cream cone. I just wanted to know if it was still here."

"How long did you live here?" I asked.

"Off and on from the time I was born until I was twelve."

"Off and on?"

"My mother couldn't care for me. She got into drugs soon after I was born. She blamed it on my father. I never knew him. He was sent to prison and died there when I was still a baby. My mother went to pieces. Drugs were the only thing in her life—using, buying, selling. I knew the social workers better than I knew her. They'd pick me up when things got bad and then deliver me back home when she was better."

"Oh, Lurleen."

"Please, Ditie, I can't bear your pity. I'd make up stories about where my mother was, so they wouldn't take me away from her. Somehow they always knew when I was lying. They'd put me in one foster home or another. Some were okay, but all I wanted to do was get back to her. I needed her and she needed me."

I stayed silent.

"Mom had a lot of boyfriends. They were all into drugs. I learned to get away from them when my mom was out of it. I became an escape artist, and when I ran off it was always to the library. Books saved my life, Ditie. Could we see if the library is still here? It's on Scott Street."

We turned down Scott and there it was, Beaufort County Library, a sprawling brick building.

"Oh," she sighed. "I was so afraid it might be gone. It's bigger than when I was a girl, but it's still here."

We parked and went inside. Lurleen wandered through the children's section. She asked about the children's librarian.

"Anita Jennings?" the current librarian asked. "She retired years ago, but she still reads to the children once a week. Your timing is perfect." She glanced at her watch. "She should be in any minute now."

We waited five minutes as Lurleen looked over the shelves. She smiled at me, and it seemed as if the weight of the world had lifted from her shoulders.

"Ditie," she said, "it's just the same, my safe haven."

Then she saw Anita Jennings.

She rushed up to her.

"Miss Jennings, you won't remember me, but—"

Miss Jennings held both of Lurleen's hands. "Not remember you? My dear girl, I'm old, but not *that* old. We all remember you, all us old-timers. I've wondered what became of you. I knew you from the time you were six and could read and ride a bike. You always flew in here as if the devil were chasing you, and then once you got inside, you became a different child."

Lurleen was in tears, and so was I.

"It's so good to see you, child, and look what's become of you. I knew once Theresa Goodman got her hands on you, everything would be all right. It is, isn't it?"

"Yes, Miss Jennings, now everything is all right."

"I'm so glad, Lurleen. You were the smartest, most determined girl I ever met. I'm glad to see that hasn't changed. Now, I must get my books to read."

A small gathering of six- and seven-year-olds settled on a colorful rug in the children's section. Their parents sat on child-sized chairs nearby.

Lurleen looked at me.

"Of course, we can stay, if it's okay with Miss Jennings."

Lurleen hadn't yet introduced me. She blushed. "This is my best friend, Ditie Brown. She's a pediatrician."

Miss Jennings shook my hand warmly. "Another lover of children."

Then she sat down on a small chair on the edge of the rug and began reading. The first book was *The Day the Crayons Quit*, a favorite in our house. Lucie read it almost nightly to Jason. The second was one I didn't know yet, *A Dog by Any Other Name is Not the Same*.

For half an hour, Lurleen and I were transported to our childhoods, and neither one of us wanted to leave.

It was Lurleen who stood first. "Thank you," she said to Miss Jennings. "You are one of the people who helped me survive."

Miss Jennings smiled. "You survived, dear, because that's the person you are."

We went outside and ran to our car, ducking storm clouds that were about to open up.

"Is your house still here?" I asked when we were safely in Danny's car.

Lurleen shook her head. "I don't think I can bear to find out."

"You don't have to."

"Maybe I do. It's the end of the story, Ditie. The end of the bad part, and I think I have to face it. 142 Weldon Street, that's where we lived. My mother was born in that house, and that's the house she died in."

I drove slowly to the address. It was now a small apartment complex, nicely kept up.

"They've erased every trace," Lurleen said. "I'm glad. I can tell you the rest now. You know the scar on my back—the scar you've never asked me about?"

I nodded.

"Mom had a boyfriend Nixon who was into meth before most people even knew what it was. He saw it as a way to make money, so he built a meth lab—in the back of the house. Mom never let me go anywhere near it. The explosion happened as I was coming home from school one afternoon. I ran inside calling for her. A neighbor dragged me out, but not before I got scorched on the back from a flying piece of burning metal. I tried to go back in, but my dog—the dog I told you about—barred the door, growling, ready to keep me out no matter what the cost."

I took Lurleen's hand. Her eyes were closed, and it was the only way to let her know I was there with her.

"Mom didn't get out. Nixon didn't either. It was lucky the whole neighborhood didn't burn, and that was the end of my childhood."

I have no idea how long we sat in silence. Lurleen didn't cry. I didn't either. Sometimes, things are too horrible for tears.

"I've said it now, Ditie. You are my witness. I don't have to be afraid anymore. And the rest of the story is a fairy tale, a good one. A woman in a big house just outside Beaufort took me in. She'd donated money to an agency that helped children of drug-addicted parents. I didn't realize until years later that she'd lost her own daughter to heroin before it became the epidemic it is today. She took me in, and I'll never know why. She said there was just something about me—something worth saving."

This time Lurleen did cry.

"She didn't put it that way. She said I had a spirit about me that said I was a warrior—I would save myself no matter what. I don't know if she was right or not, but she made all the difference. She showed me I could depend on someone after all."

"Thank God," I said. "There really was an Aunt Thérèse—the woman Miss Jennings mentioned."

"Theresa Goodman. A perfect name don't you think? She loved to travel, and when I wasn't in school, she took me everywhere, but her favorite place was Provence. Before I knew she was ill, she bought a farmhouse near Aix-en-Provence. We stayed there only once. She died a few months later as peacefully and gracefully as she'd lived.

"So, you see, Ditie I have been so lucky. First, she found me, and then I found you and the kids and Danny. I have been blessed, and I don't take anything for granted."

"You are a wonder, Lurleen," I said and hugged her as hard as I've hugged anyone in my life.

We spent the next half hour driving around town. The school had been renovated, and Lurleen said she hardly recognized it. I asked if she was hungry, and we decided to eat in Granny Flumm's Cafe.

"She really is a marvelous cook," Lurleen said. "The best I've seen— next to you of course."

"She's the best Southern cook I know," I said, "including me and Mason's mother."

The cafe was small and crowded. We had to wait half an hour to get a seat. As we ate Brunswick stew and fried okra, Buddy Lewis came up to us.

"Hi, Chief," I said.

"Just left Danny at the house with our catch."

We offered him a seat at our table.

"No, thanks. Mary wants me home for dinner. I don't want to interrupt your meal," he said to both of us, "but I wonder if I might have a minute with Lurleen."

I jumped up to go the restroom, but Lurleen motioned me to sit back down. "I don't have any secrets from Ditie," she said, "not anymore."

Buddy nodded. "I thought I recognized you, Lurleen, as soon as I saw you at Savannah's, but I couldn't place how I knew you. Then it came to me. You look like your mother, and I was a young cop on the police force when it all happened. I knew your mama. We all did. She was a good woman, just ran with the wrong crowd. I've never seen anything so awful as that fire and you just a kid and all."

"You never said a word," Lurleen said.

"It was clear you didn't want to talk about it, and you'd been through enough, too much. I knew Miss Theresa, and when she took you in, I knew you'd be okay. I didn't need to stir up anything."

"Thank you, Buddy," Lurleen said.

Lurleen and I enjoyed the rest of our meal. We got home around eight, and I asked her if she wanted to be alone that night.

"I'd like you to stay with me," she said.

We talked until the middle of the night. She had a lot of stories to tell me, all of them true, and not all of them sad. One was about her work with a vet, and the lab he let her adopt. She had to keep it outside her home because Nixon wouldn't let it inside the house.

"That's why the dog survived and saved me as well. Aunt Theresa didn't ask me to give her up. 'You come as a package,' she said. 'I wouldn't have it any other way.' "

Tommy, Josh, and the kids arrived at 10:30 on Saturday. After everyone had been properly kissed and hugged, I asked what time they'd set out.

"The children woke us up at 5:00 am, I kid you not," Tommy said. "We were on the road by 5:30. There isn't a lot of traffic at that hour."

"I'm on the hungry side," Josh said, after he kissed me. "Any chance we can get a late breakfast?" he asked. "Here or in town?"

Savannah heard his request. "We can manage that with three cooks on the premises. What's your pleasure?"

Josh rattled off all his Southern favorites and then backtracked. "Anything will do, honestly." He was a good Southern boy at heart.

"We'll get you all settled and then give you a wholesome brunch," Savannah said.

I hadn't realized how much I missed the kids. Lurleen seemed to feel the same way. We fussed over them all day until they'd finally had enough. Lucie went off to read her latest book, and Jason begged Danny and Mason to take him fishing. Mason still had paperwork, but Danny was free.

The next day we explored Beaufort and the coastline surrounding it.

"You lived here?" Lucie asked Lurleen. "You lived near the ocean? And you could bike to the library? Any time you wanted?"

"I could," Lurleen said.

"Do you miss it?" Lucie asked. "I know I'd miss it. I'd love to live by the ocean, and maybe I will when I grow up."

"I miss some of it," Lurleen said. "I was a little older than you when *my* mom died, so that made it sad for me."

"Oh," Lucie said.

"I've meant to tell you that for a long time, Lucie. Like you, I found someone—my Aunt Theresa—who loved me the way Aunt Ditie loves you. I feel very lucky about that. We can come here again. We can even stay in my aunt's house—she left it to me when she passed. I turned it into a bed and breakfast, but there will always be room for us when we want to stay here."

Lucie smiled. "I'd like that."

"And, when you and Jason are a little older, we'll go to Provence in France. My aunt left me a house there as well."

Lucie sighed as if she'd died and gone to heaven. "*Ooh la la*, Lurleen, that would be *très, très bon*."

For a moment, I panicked at the thought of two Lurleens in my life. Then I caught myself. Lurleen brought me such comfort and joy. If Lucie had some of her spirit, that could only be a good thing.

Southern Comfort Recipes

Flourless Chocolate Cake

I don't think this recipe is actually Southern,
but it is definitely comfort food for those of us who love chocolate.
Another interesting fact, to me at least,
is that I found the recipe on the King Arthur Flour website.
You will note it uses no flour.

Servings: 8-12 servings
Difficulty: Easy

Cake Ingredients:

1 cup semisweet or bittersweet chocolate chips
1/2 cup (1 stick) unsalted butter
3/4 cup granulated sugar
1/4 teaspoon salt
1 to 2 teaspoons espresso powder (optional) There seems to
be a lot of debate about what espresso powder really is. One
baker ordered it from Amazon. I used coffee beans, ground up
extra-fine.
1 teaspoon vanilla extract (optional)
3 large eggs
1/2 cup unsweetened cocoa powder, Dutch process

Glaze Ingredients:

1 cup semisweet or bittersweet chocolate chips
1/2 cup heavy cream

Instructions:

Preheat the oven to 375 degrees F. Lightly grease a metal 8 inch round
pan. Cut a piece of parchment to fit, grease it, and lay it in the bottom of
the pan, greased side up.

To make the cake: Put the chocolate and butter in a microwave-safe bowl
and heat until the butter is melted and the chips are soft. Stir until the chips

melt, reheating briefly if necessary. You can also do this over a burner set at very low heat. Transfer the melted chocolate/butter to a mixing bowl.

Stir in the sugar, salt, espresso powder, and vanilla. (Espresso enhances the chocolate flavor much as vanilla does. Using one teaspoon will simply enhance the flavor, while 2 teaspoons will lend a hint of mocha to the cake.)

Add the eggs, beating briefly until smooth. Add the cocoa powder, and mix just to combine.

Spoon the batter into the prepared pan.

Bake the cake for 25 minutes. The top will have formed a thin crust, and it should register at least 200 degrees F on an instant-read thermometer inserted into its center. (While overcooking the cake doesn't do much harm, undercooking it will leave you with soupy glop in the middle—you do need a thermometer check.)

Remove it from the oven and cool it in the pan for 5 minutes.

Loosen the edges of the pan with a table knife or nylon spreader and turn it out onto a serving plate. The top will now be on the bottom. That's fine. Also, the edges will crumble a bit, which is also fine. Allow the cake to cool completely before glazing.

To make the glaze: Combine the chocolate and cream in a microwave-safe bowl and heat until the cream is very hot but not simmering. Remove from the microwave and stir until the chocolate melts and the mixture is completely smooth.

Spoon the glaze over the cake, spreading it to drip over the sides a bit. Allow the glaze to set for several hours before serving the cake.

Momma's Banana Pudding

This recipe is from Jeanne Lee and it's an old one.
One true Southerner has proclaimed this the best banana pudding he's ever tasted.

Servings: 6-8
Difficulty: Moderate (getting the custard just right takes a little practice)

Ingredients:

> 1 box vanilla wafers
> 6 large ripe bananas
> 3 eggs (separated) - yolks for custard, whites for meringue
> 1 large can evaporated milk
> 1 cup water
> 3/4 cup sugar + 6 Tbsp for meringue
> 2 Tbsp. butter
> dash of salt for meringue

Instructions:

Cover bottom of a small rectangular glass baking dish with layer of wafers, then a layer of bananas until you have three layers of each.

For the custard: Combine all ingredients and mix until egg yolks are well beaten with the rest of the ingredients. Cook over low-medium heat, stirring constantly, until the consistency of a medium sauce. This will take patience and care—up to twenty minutes to get the custard the right consistency. If the heat is too high the custard will curdle. Pour over bananas and wafers.

For the meringue: Beat egg whites with a dash of salt until stiff. Add 6 Tbsp. sugar. Mix well. Cover pudding with meringue and brown in 425 degree F oven.

Favorite Buttermilk Biscuit

This is from *Southern Living* magazine online, and it claims it's a no-fail biscuit recipe. Believe me, making the perfect Southern biscuit is the sign of a true Southern cook.
Follow these directions precisely and then stand back and feel proud! Eat them warm with honey, and you'll be in heaven.

When the recipe says stir the dough 15 times, believe it! Don't press down too hard when rolling out the dough and don't overwork it.

Servings: 12
Difficulty: Moderate

Ingredients:

1/2 cup butter (1 stick) frozen
2 1/2 cups self-rising flour (It recommends White Lily self-rising flour, which is lower in protein than King Arthur, my go-to flour. In this case you want the lower protein)
1 cup chilled buttermilk
Parchment paper
2 tablespoons butter, melted

Instructions:

Preheat oven to 475 degrees F.
Grate frozen butter using large holes of a box grater
Toss together grated butter and flour in a medium bowl and chill 10 minutes.
Make a well in center of mixture. Add buttermilk, and stir 15 times. Dough will be sticky.
Turn dough out onto a lightly floured surface. Lightly sprinkle flour over top of dough.
Using a lightly floured rolling pin, roll dough into a 3/4 inch thick rectangle (about 9 by 5 inches).
Fold dough in half so short ends meet. Repeat rolling and folding process 4 more times.

Roll dough to 1/2 inch thickness and cut with a 2 1/2 inch floured round cutter, reshaping scraps and flouring as needed. (If you don't have a round cutter, use the top edge of a glass).

Place dough rounds on a parchment paper lined jelly-roll pan.

Bake at 475 degrees F for 15 minutes or until lightly browned. Brush with melted butter.

Oven-fried Chicken

This is a prize recipe from *Cooking Light,* a wonderful magazine that has now been subsumed by *Eating Well.*
This takes some time, but it is worth every minute. After frying, the chicken is baked in the oven and can be served at room temperature, which gives you time for clean-up and whatever else you might want to do before you serve it.

Servings: 4-6. (I usually double or triple the amount of chicken. I can get by with doubling the rest of the recipe. You will want to eat this for more than one meal, I promise you.)
Difficulty: Moderate

Ingredients:

 2 tablespoons hot sauce
 1 cup buttermilk
 1 (4 pound) chicken cut in eight pieces. (You can use boneless chicken breasts but bone-in chicken is much juicier.)
 2 cups all-purpose flour
 2 tablespoons salt, plus more to taste
 2 tablespoons chopped fresh parsley. (I often leave this out, and the taste doesn't suffer much in my opinion.)
 1½ tablespoons freshly ground pepper, plus more to taste
 1 tablespoon paprika
 1 cup canola oil

Instructions:

Whisk together hot sauce and buttermilk in a shallow bowl. Place chicken into mixture, turn to coat, and chill 30 minutes or up to 1 hour. (I've left mine in the refrigerator for longer with no bad effects.)
Preheat oven to 425 degrees F. Combine flour and next 4 ingredients in a bowl. Heat oil over medium-high heat in a large, deep skillet until sizzling hot (about 350 degrees F).

Remove chicken from buttermilk mixture, 1 piece at a time, shaking off excess. Dredge in flour mixture and place in hot skillet. Cook in batches, 3-4 minutes per side or until golden brown.

Place fried chicken on a wire rack in a baking sheet and bake 40-45 minutes or until cooked through. Remove from oven and place on paper towels to drain. Season with additional salt and pepper, if desired. Serve hot or at room temperature.

Gingerbread (Molasses Cake) and Lemon Ice Cream

The gingerbread is an old recipe provided by the Falmouth Historical Society. My goal was to find the densest, moistest gingerbread I could find. This might be it.
The lemon ice cream is a bit of my own creation. If you want to be even more decadent, drizzle warm caramel sauce on top.

Servings: 6
Difficulty: Moderate

Ingredients for Molasses Cake:

4 tablespoons shortening
1/2 cup sugar
3/4 cup molasses
2 cups rye, oat or barley flour (I ended up using a blender to make oat flour from oat bran and liked that taste best.)
4 teaspoons baking powder
1 tablespoon ground ginger
1 teaspoon allspice
1/4 teaspoon salt
3/4 cup milk

Instructions:

Preheat oven to 350 degrees F.
Cream shortening.
Add sugar and molasses, beating well.
Add half the flour, which has been sifted with baking powder, spices and salt.
Mix in half the milk. Then add the remainder of the flour and remainder of milk.
Mix well.
Bake in greased 9 inch square pan for 20-30 minutes.

Ingredients for Lemon Ice Cream:

Use any recipe you like for basic vanilla ice cream. Here's one I like:

    2 eggs
    2/3 cup sugar
    1 3/4 cups milk
    2 cups cream
    2 teaspoons vanilla
    2 jars (8-10 oz.) lemon curd

Instructions:

Beat eggs and sugar with an electric mixer until thick and cream-colored. Add milk, cream and vanilla. Mix well.

Divide mixture in half. (My ice cream maker will accommodate only half the mixture if I want to add the lemon curd at the end of the process.)

Churn for 20 minutes. Add one jar of lemon curd and let it mix another 10 minutes.

Repeat the process with the remaining mixture the following day—that's how long it takes my ice cream cylinder to refreeze. (I keep my cylinder in the freezer covered with plastic wrap, so I can make ice cream anytime I feel the urge or have company coming.)

Crockpot Low Country Boil

This is a traditional dish in the low country of South Carolina and Georgia—
easy, forgiving. Add what you like and take out what you don't.

Servings: 10-12
Difficulty: Easy

Ingredients:

1.5 lbs small red potatoes cut in half
5 cups of water
1 bottle (12 oz) beer (you can sub in broth)
1/4 cup Old Bay seasoning
2 stalks celery, cut into 1-inch pieces
1 onion, cut into quarters
3-4 garlic cloves, minced
2 lemons cut in half
1 lb cooked kielbasa sausage cut into 1-inch pieces
4 fresh cobs of corn, cut into 3-inch chunks
2 lbs fresh uncooked large shrimp in shells
Optional : cocktail sauce, fresh lemon slices, Cajun seasoning

Instructions:

Start by spraying a 6- or 7- quart slow cooker with cooking spray. Add in water, beer, Old Bay seasoning, and garlic. Stir until well combined.

Place potatoes, onion and celery in slow cooker and squeeze lemons over mixture in crockpot.

Place lemon halves in crockpot.

Cover the crockpot and cook on low heat setting 4-5 hours.

Add sausage and corn, cover, and cook 2 hours longer.

Increase heat setting to HIGH and add in shrimp. Your crockpot will be very full, so do your best to stir a little and squeeze in your shrimp. Cover and cook 30-40 minutes or until shrimp are pink.

Drain the ingredients using a large strainer. Serve this meal on a newspaper covered table for easy clean-up. We enjoyed ours with cocktail sauce, fresh lemon and some Cajun seasoning.

Photo by VagabondView Photography

Sarah Osborne is the pen name of a native Californian who lived in Atlanta for many years and now practices psychiatry on Cape Cod. She writes cozy mysteries for the same reason she reads them—to find comfort in a sometimes difficult world. TOO MANY CROOKS SPOIL THE PLOT is the first novel in her Ditie Brown Mystery series. The second book in the series is INTO THE FRYING PAN. You have just finished the third book: MURDER MOST SOUTHERN. She loves to hear from readers and can be reached at doctorosborne.com or on her Facebook Fan Page: Sarah Osborne, Mystery Author. You may also e-mail her at sarah@doctorosborne.com

Printed in the United States
by Baker & Taylor Publisher Services